Praise for Detective Emilia Cruz

CLIFF DIVER

"From the moment I started the first one, I couldn't put it down. . . Her work touches on important issues affecting Mexico in a real, human way and is exciting, fast paced and utterly gripping." – *Mexico Retold*

HAT DANCE

[Emilia] is a force to be reckoned with." – *Mystery Sequels*

DIABLO NIGHTS

"Amato brings her characters to life with her vivid writing style and sets them on the streets of a Mexico steeped in Catholicism and corruption." – *OnlineBookClub.org*

KING PESO

"Danger and betrayal never more than a few pages away." – *Kirkus Reviews*

PACIFIC REAPER

"Carmen Amato . . . out does many of the best crime authors out there." – *Artisan Book Reviews*

43 MISSING

"A fast-paced procedural . . . a real page-turner . . . a very original plot." – *The BookLife Prize*

Also by Carmen Amato

DETECTIVE EMILIA CRUZ SERIES
CLIFF DIVER: Detective Emilia Cruz Book 1
HAT DANCE: Detective Emilia Cruz Book 2
DIABLO NIGHTS: Detective Emilia Cruz Book 3
KING PESO: Detective Emilia Cruz Book 4
PACIFIC REAPER: Detective Emilia Cruz Book 5
43 MISSING: Detective Emilia Cruz Book 6
RUSSIAN MOJITO: Detective Emilia Cruz Book 7
NARCO NOIR: Detective Emilia Cruz Book 8
MADE IN ACAPULCO: The Emilia Cruz Stories
THE ARTIST/EL ARTISTA: A Bilingual Short Story
FELIZ NAVIDAD FROM ACAPULCO: A Detective Emilia
Cruz Novella
THE LISTMAKER OF ACAPULCO: A Detective Emilia Cruz
Novella

GALLIANO CLUB SERIES
ROAD TO THE GALLIANO CLUB: Prequel
MURDER AT THE GALLIANO CLUB: Book 1
BLACKMAIL AT THE GALLIANO CLUB: Book 2
REVENGE AT THE GALLIANO CLUB: Book 3

THRILLERS
AWAKENING MACBETH
THE HIDDEN LIGHT OF MEXICO CITY

NARCO NOIR

A Detective Emilia Cruz Novel

Carmen Amato

Published 2023 by Laurel & Croton (second edition)
Trade Paperback Edition

Identifiers: ISBN: 979-8-9885363-8-3 (print)
ISBN: 978-0-9997122-5-2 (ebook)

Regarding names and monetary conversion

Regarding Mexican names: It is the custom in Mexico to use two surnames. The first is from the father's family and is always used. The second surname is the name of the mother's father. The second is sometimes dropped in conversation and/or to shorten the name in keeping with American and European naming conventions.

Conversion rate: For the purposes of this novel, \$US1.00 = 10 Mexican pesos.

Spanish words: A glossary of Spanish words and terms commonly used in the Detective Emilia Cruz series is included.

> **"At the end of the day, we can endure much more than we think we can."**
>
> *Frida Kahlo*

CHAPTER 1

Emilia Cruz Encinos leaned forward in her seat, mesmerized by the climax unfolding on the big screen.

Glamorous jewel thief Laura stood on a rocky beach, facing handsome Clive and his gun. The sky behind her was streaked with angry indigo storm clouds. Jet black hair fluttered in the wind, contrasting with the white silk scarf at her throat. A jagged bolt of lightning momentarily sharpened her famous features.

"Don't do this, Clive," Laura said, her accented English husky with emotion. The camera zoomed in. A tiny tear glistened in the corner of her eye. Her trademark pout trembled with emotion. "I love you."

Te amo. Spanish subtitles ran across the bottom of the screen but Emilia didn't need them.

"Give me the diamonds," ordered Clive. In Laura's bed 15 minutes ago in a scene that made Emilia's cheeks grow warm, but now Clive was all business as he motioned to his lover with the black handgun.

Laura's hands went to the leather crossbody bag that contained a treasure in diamonds. She lifted the strap over her head and held out the bag to Clive.

Still keeping the gun trained on Laura, Clive used his free hand to fling the bag into the seat of a sleek red convertible parked just beyond the rocks. He produced a pair of handcuffs. "Turn around," he ordered.

"Don't humiliate me," Laura said. "If you ever loved me, Clive, you'll do it in front, not in back." She held out her hands, wrists together.

Clive hesitated.

"Please," Laura begged. "I love you, Clive. I know you love me."

Bolts of lightning flashed across the screen while thunder roiled through the theater. The tempest was upon them all.

"I do," Clive vowed as rain pelted down. "I swear I love you. But I love diamonds more."

He shoved the gun in his belt, grabbed her wrist, and snapped on one of the steel bracelets.

Before he could fasten the other, Laura slammed her head into his chin. Clive stumbled backwards, arms windmilling for balance. Hair and scarf flying behind her like a matador's cape, Laura whirled into a slow motion roundhouse kick. Clive took it on the jaw and fell to the ground, unconscious.

Next to Emilia, Kurt Rucker gave a snort of derision. Emilia dug her elbow into his side.

"I knew who you were all along," Laura declared to the prone figure. "But as God as my witness, I still love you."

She scooped up the gun, handcuffed Clive, jumped into the red convertible, and sped off. A helicopter view tracked the car as it zoomed through hairpin turns above a surging ocean. Laura's white scarf unraveled as she drove and billowed into the storm.

Back at the beach, Clive massaged his jaw, muscular chest on display under a shirt rendered transparent by the downpour. Borne by the wind, the white scarf settled onto the rocks next to him. Clive reached for it.

Laura had cuffed his hands in front.

"This isn't over," he said and pressed the scarf to his lips.

The action cut to Laura again, handling the convertible like a Formula One racer. She yanked the wheel and the car skidded sideways through the gates of a small airport. Carrying the leather crossbody bag and surprisingly dry, Laura ran to a waiting helicopter.

Music swelled over the thwap-thwap-thwap of the churning rotors. Laura's voice crooned *Adios, mi amor, adios* as the helicopter rose, tilted, and turned to reveal a large logo painted on the side. A globe surrounded by a laurel wreath was sandwiched between a sword hilt and the scales of justice. INTERPOL, the acronym for the International Criminal Police Organization, filled the screen in stark white letters.

Adios, mi amor, adios, adios.

The credits for *Diamond Run* starring Alejandra Messi as Laura and Ben Barrett as Clive rolled as the helicopter got smaller and smaller and finally disappeared.

The lights in the cinema came up. Emilia slumped in her seat, as breathless as if she'd raced through Europe with the two superstars, not to mention getting blindsided by the plot twist at the end.

"What did you think?" Kurt asked. His ocean-colored eyes danced with fun.

"Did you know Alejandra Messi was the Interpol agent

from the beginning?" Emilia asked.

Kurt stood and offered Emilia his hand. "I suspected. Did you?"

"No, and it's my job to know stuff like that." Emilia let him pull her upright.

"You're only a detective in real life, Em," Kurt said. "Not at the movies."

They walked out of the Cinépolis to find that the sun had set while they watched the Hollywood blockbuster, although Acapulco's swankiest commercial district was never dark. The city's best stores, restaurants, nightclubs, and hotels fanned out from the intersection of Avenida Farallón del Obispo and Costera Miguel Alemán where the famous monument to Diana the Huntress presided over a perpetually chaotic traffic circle. Beyond the circle, Acapulco's beaches kept up the pretense that the deadliest city in Mexico was still a glamorous tourist attraction.

Emilia tucked her hand into the crook of Kurt's elbow as they jostled with the crowds along Avenida Farallón del Obispo. Under a hazy indigo sky studded with stars, Saturday night felt like a carnival. Palm trees edged the sidewalk, trunks outlined with white paint. Restaurants offered open-air seating and the inviting sounds of music, laughter, and the click of flatware against china. A strolling guitarist moved from table to table, strumming romantic tunes, and collecting pesos. A woman with a basket over her arm sold roses in his wake. Business was good.

"I really thought Laura and Clive were going to end up

together," Emilia said.

"Jewel thief and Interpol agent." Kurt grinned as they skirted a gaggle of pre-teens heading into the multiplex. "Doomed, if you ask me."

Emilia thought of the love scene. "But they had chemistry."

"True. I'd see a sequel."

"For Alejandra Messi," Emilia teased.

Undisputed superstar Alejandra Messi was originally from Mexico City but had conquered Hollywood with her famous pout and charming accent. She sang two of the songs on the movie soundtrack, including *Adios, mi amor*, which was on every radio station in Mexico both day and night, helping to make Diamond Run a worldwide phenomenon.

"Only because she reminds me of you," Kurt said and pulled Emilia closer. "You have the same shaped face. Same nose. Of course you're hotter. And smarter."

Emilia rolled her eyes. "Flattery, Señor Rucker."

"Have I ever lied to you?"

"Let me think."

Kurt laughed. She was the one with the loose concept of honesty and they both knew it.

On the opposite side of wide boulevard Avenida Farallón del Obispo, families enjoyed the offerings of Parque Bellavista. It wasn't a proper park, like the enormous Parque Papagayo to the west, but a skinny triangle of green shoehorned into the urban landscape. A playground with a carousel anchored the space, which often hosted family entertainment like musical groups or puppet shows. Toy and balloon vendors were always there, along with food stands and old men hawking ice cream from wheeled carts.

Through the trees, Emilia could see kids bopping helium-filled balloons and running around pulling toys with sparkly streamers. It had been a long time since she enjoyed the city like this, rather than rushing by on her way to another homicide.

"We've got a couple of minutes before our dinner reservation," Kurt said. "I want to show you something across the street."

"In the park?"

"Next to it."

The blocky Santander Bank presided over the 3-way intersection where Avenida Bellavista emptied into Avenida Farallón del Obispo. Café Coco, the new French restaurant Kurt wanted to try, stood on the opposite corner. Paris had come to Acapulco with flamboyant iron filigree and a striped awning over an entrance that faced the wider street. Emilia figured the restaurant had opened near a bank because most patrons would have to take out a loan to pay the dinner bill.

As they walked, Emilia savored the touch of Kurt's lean body against hers. He was in much better shape than the actor who played Clive. Whatshisname was also a gringo from El Norte, but he probably didn't have Kurt's military background or addiction to endurance sports.

The traffic light turned red. Cars stopped on Avenida Farallón del Obispo. Kurt tugged her hand and they ran across the broad avenue before the traffic from Avenida Bellavista streamed into the intersection. Emilia's new wedge espadrilles and the shoulder holster under her black moto jacket made her feel slow and flatfooted but she kept up with Kurt's athletic strides.

He guided Emilia to a cluster of upscale stores on Universidad hugging the southern tip of Parque Bellavista and stopped in front of a shop with tall windows. Curving gold lettering proclaimed Joyas Alameda. Rolex. Cartier. Philippe Patek.

"See anything you like?" Kurt asked.

"Who wouldn't." Emilia gave a laugh and bumped her head against Kurt's shoulder. Thick bulletproof glass distorted displays of Swiss watches and glittering jewelry. "This is probably the most expensive store in Acapulco."

Tourists who floated to Acapulco aboard private yachts shopped in stores like Joyas Alameda, not chica police detectives whose entire annual salary wouldn't cover the cost of walking in. On the other hand, Kurt had money to spare. He was the general manager of the Palacio Réal, inarguably Acapulco's most luxurious hotel, but never seemed to notice the huge financial and social gap between them. Emilia noticed, however, and at times like this it pricked her pride.

Kurt tapped the center window. "I saw this the other day," he said. "Made me think of us."

Three white boxes, mounted on folds of turquoise satin, held rings created from twists of gold and silver. Each box held two braided bands, one a little larger than the other. The plaited designs varied, making each set unique. A spotlight created a prism effect, casting soft color on the white boxes, as if the two metals vibrated at different frequencies.

More turquoise satin looped around the base of an easel that held a placard. A tagline accompanied a sepia photo of a jeweler sitting at a workbench with a loupe in his eye.

Mexican silver and American gold. Bound together in timeless love.

Emilia caught her breath.

"I asked you once before," Kurt said. He touched her cheek. "You said you weren't ready. But a lot has changed since then and I'm hoping your feelings have, too."

This was it. The moment Emilia both longed for and dreaded. "Are you--."

Screeching rubber engulfed her words. Both turned from the window toward the intersection in time to see a minivan hurtle across the lanes of traffic, totally out of control as it barreled directly at them. Kurt threw his arm across Emilia's shoulders and plastered their bodies to the store building. The minivan whipped by them, close enough for Emilia to feel the heat of the exhaust, before smashing headlong into a palm tree rising from the sidewalk just a few yards away.

Kurt's arm released her. Noise erupted all along the street, punctuated by the cannonade of multiple collisions and ceaseless honking horns. Calliope music from the carousel in the park filtered through the cacophony.

The front end of the minivan was a crumpled mess but

Kurt managed to lever open the driver's door. A deflated airbag draped over the steering wheel. The driver, an older man, was badly shaken.

"An encapuchado," he said hoarsely as Kurt settled him on the ground. "He had a gun. Ran out in front of me. With a gun."

"Where?" Emilia bent to hear him better. The term encapuchado, meaning a person whose face was hidden by a hood, never had a good connotation. "Where was he?"

The driver raised a trembling hand and pointed to the intersection. "By the taxis."

"Call it in," Emilia said to Kurt. "Officer in pursuit."

She didn't wait for his answer but ran toward the intersection with Avenida Bellavista, where they'd passed a line of taxis waiting for fares. The clump of her wedge heels against the sidewalk was drowned out by frustrated shouting and blasting car horns. Engines rumbled as people tried to drive past the pileup.

A woman screamed like a siren, the note high and piecing. Emilia instinctively dropped into a squat, sheltered by the night shadow of some rosebushes. Heart hammering and eyes swiveling to find the source, she saw a scrum of people rushing away from Café Coco.

Across Avenida Bellavista from the stately Café Coco, white and yellow taxis were hemmed in by the mess in the intersection. A slight figure in jeans and a hoodie leaned against the driver's door of the first taxi, his back to the chaos.

From the width of the shoulders and the cut of the jeans, Emilia knew it was a man. Before she could register more than that, the figure took a step back, revealing a large handgun. He fired point blank into the taxi through the open window.

Twice.

CHAPTER 2

The shooter jinked around the tangle of cars in the intersection and ran into Parque Bellavista a mere 20 strides from where Emilia crouched by the rosebushes. She sprang up and pushed herself into a dead run, cursing the leaden weight of the awkward wedge heels.

He swerved around a crowd of parents frantically grabbing their children and gained the sidewalk on the Universidad side of the park before launching himself across the street, holding out a hand as he dodged cars and leapt over the curb. Emilia did the same, nearly getting clipped by a fender. She ignored the irate driver and stretched out her stride. Her footsteps were loud enough to announce her coming.

The shooter pounded down the street, only to veer left and plunge into a break between buildings. Emilia threw herself after him.

She found herself in a narrow service road in back of a hotel with an outdoor restaurant that was closed. Tables and chairs were chained up for the night. Emilia got a glimpse of the back of his hood and shoulders as he vaulted a wrought iron table, caught the top of the wall enclosing the restaurant and leaped over. Emilia scrambled onto the table after him, heaved herself over the wall, and dropped onto the roof of a parked car on the other side.

Her heel caught the door handle and the car alarm pulsed

like a klaxon. Headlights flashed. The noise turned adrenaline into wings and Emilia raced through another alley behind commercial buildings. The shooter was half a block ahead.

Head down and feet flying, he didn't look over his shoulder or shoot again. Emilia didn't waste her breath shouting at him to a stop. No plainclothes cop readily identified themselves as such on Acapulco's streets. Only an *idiota* would risk coming to the attention of random gangbangers and cartel *sicarios* for whom kidnapping, torturing, and killing civil authorities was a highly competitive game.

Emilia heard the slap of his cross trainers on the pavement as the *encapuchado* fled down dark streets, leading her further and further away from the relative safety of the lively entertainment district. As she ran, she unzipped her jacket, but she wasn't nearly close enough to confront him with her weapon.

He veered to the right and disappeared. Emilia followed without hesitation, sprinting through a dogleg of a skinny pitch-black alley. Two and three storey buildings huddled on either side, sharing strings of overhead electrical wires and the city noises of people who lived packed together. Candy wrappers rustled in the gutter. Urine and tamarindo sugar perfumed the darkness in equal measure.

Familiar music flowed from an open doorway, interrupted by drunk women screaming epithets at each other.

Adios, mi amor.

Emilia's lungs burned. The streetlights here were broken stalks, but random patches of light from curtainless windows showed her a path between potholes and broken tarmac.

The opaque figure ahead of her turned at the end of the street and disappeared again. Sounds of rushing traffic grew louder and moving lights flickered on the edge of a building. Emilia kept going, trying to figure out where she was, and came upon a fast-moving thoroughfare before she realized it. There was no curb to warn her, no wide sidewalk.

Tire squealed. A horn blared. A chrome-plated beast scooped her up. Emilia cartwheeled aloft like an ungainly bird flapping out of the nest.

The pavement rose up to meet her. In the split second before everything faded to black, Emilia was sure the movie wasn't supposed to end this way.

Adios, mi amor.

CHAPTER 3

Emilia spent Sunday sulking on the sofa, nursing a bruised hip. Kurt rallied around with her favorite risotto from the Palacio Réal's flagship restaurant. Neither revisited the conversation outside the jewelry store. To Emilia, the shooting felt like the hand of fate.

If Kurt had finished the proposal, what would she have said?

She got a sporadic round of applause when she limped into the detectives squadroom on Monday morning. Emilia greeted it with a couple of comic bows and headed for her desk.

"The mayor called," Castro crowed from the murder board where he was pinning up pictures of the weekend's homicides. "Carlota wants you to carry the flag when she hosts the Olympics."

Ignoring him, Emilia unlocked her desk and stowed her bag, before picking up her favorite Maná coffee mug. Souvenir of a concert, it now sported three crude interlocking circles drawn in permanent marker. Guitarist Sergio Vallín's face was all but obliterated.

"Olympic flag has five circles," Emilia announced and held up the mug. To a man, the other detectives were suddenly entranced by their computer screens. "Five circles, *pendejos*, not three."

Someone had also left a copy of *El Sol de Acapulco* on

her desk. The headline below the red masthead was impossible to miss. *Taxista Executed!*

A black and white close-up of the dead driver, still sitting behind the wheel but slumped to the side, splashed across the newspaper page. His face was hidden by the center console, but his white shirt was badly stained and the interior of the taxi smeared with blood.

It was a fairly tame photograph, given the lurid choices the newspapers had on any given day.

Emilia sat and skimmed the article. A lone gunman had carried out the execution-style killing of Pablo Arrocha Puente, 32, then disappeared into the Saturday crowds in Parque Bellavista. There was no mention of an *estupida* police detective running after him.

In a message left on the body, the Los Mozos gang claimed responsibility. A second photo showed a scrap of paper covered in hand printed letters.

Who will be the next to die because you are the first in line? You men of the taxi syndicate must pay your full dues! More will die if you don't. Signed LOS MOZOS. Take care of your women or you will fear us.

The rest of the article was a mashup of homicide statistics and the latest talking points on crime from Carlota Montoya Perez, Acapulco's popular mayor. There was nothing more about the Los Mozos gang. Emilia had never heard the name before.

Gomez drummed on the top of the page, causing the newspaper to rattle noisily. His detective badge dangled from a lanyard against a tee as threadbare as his goatee. "Cruz," he drawled. "Bet if you'd showed more tit the guy wudda slowed down to take a look."

"Move along, *pendejo*," Emilia replied. "I don't want to have to beat your ass this early in the morning." She threw the newspaper down and headed for the coffeemaker.

Gomez stuck a match in his mouth as he crowded behind her. "You need help catching your perps, you know my number." He made a kissing noise around the sliver of wood and sauntered off.

Fortified with a swallow of tar masquerading as coffee, Emilia logged in to the police network, opened her email and nearly had a stroke. The first message in her inbox was an alert that fugitive human trafficker Rafael Gamboa Escobar, also known as El Acólito, had been spotted five days ago in the city of Veracruz on Mexico's Atlantic coast.

A man resembling Gamboa had purchased a digital movie camera, an iPad, two burner phones, and a fistful of memory cards at a place that sold refurbished electronics. The store only took cash, the norm in poorer neighborhoods, and the large purchase was unusual.

The store did not have a security camera system and there was no footage of the transaction. But when the owner went to the police in Veracruz to ask about the reward for El Acólito, he positively identified his customer from an old photograph from the days when the fugitive was an up-and-coming *telenovela* star using the name Rafa Gamboa.

Her sore hip was completely forgotten as Emilia printed the alert and ran over to the lieutenant's closed office door. She pounded twice on the nameplate reading "Lieutenant Franco Silvio" and charged in.

"*Rayos*!" Silvio swore, spilling coffee down the front of his white shirt.

"Yeah, I'm fine, thanks for asking." Emilia kicked the door closed and slammed the printout on his desk. "Have you seen this?"

"For fuck's sake, Cruz." Silvio hauled a wad of creased paper napkins out of a desk drawer and scrubbed at the spreading coffee stain. He jerked his chin at a file folder on the corner of his desk. "There's the prelim report on your taxi shooting victim. Name of Pablo Arrocha Puente. Autopsy later this morning. Prade said he'd wait for you."

"Sure," Emilia said. "Victim is already identified. Some gang took responsibility. Easiest case ever."

She flung herself into one of the chairs facing the desk and was momentarily taken aback by a framed photograph of Silvio and Mercedes Sandoval on top of the file cabinet. Mercedes, a former ballroom dance champion, was Emilia's best friend. Under pressure from Silvio, Emilia had played matchmaker, but she didn't realize the relationship was serious enough to merit a framed picture.

Silvio never had pictures in the office before, not even one of his wife Isabel before she was murdered last year. But not only was this a framed photograph, it had been taken in a studio, which carried a host of worrying implications. Silvio stood ramrod straight in white shirt and dark pants, with his usual granite-faced expression. Mercedes fairly glowed next to him in a long pink dress with dark hair cascading over one shoulder.

"Off you go," Silvio growled.

Emilia blinked away from the picture and rapped the untouched printout. "El Acólito. He's in Veracruz."

"So I heard."

"Did you actually read this?"

Silvio crumpled the damp napkins into a ball, pitched it into the trash can by the door, and took a maddeningly slow slurp of coffee.

Instead of screaming at him, Emilia snapped her fingers. "Well? Did you?"

Silvio pushed the printout away. "Give it to Macias. He and Sandor are liaison to the *federales*."

"Macias and Sandor?" They were solid detectives and Emilia had worked with both before, but this was different. "What are they going to do about it? This is my case. I need to be in Veracruz, like, yesterday."

"You're not going to Veracruz," Silvio said.

"Watch me." Emilia jumped up. "This is my case. You owe me."

"I don't owe you shit," Silvio said. "We both know why you want to take the case and we both know why it isn't going to happen."

Emilia looked away, refusing to admit Silvio could be

right. She was never going to say the word.

Brother. Because he's my brother.

While undercover as a Santa Muerte folk saint worshipper at one of El Acólito's rallies, she'd discovered that his act concealed a human trafficking operation. Emilia became one of his victims, kidnapped, chained, and raped by El Acólito himself.

DNA proved that the human trafficker and former actor was Emilia's sibling, exposing a family secret kept for nearly 30 years. As a toddler, Rafa Gamboa was taken from Emilia's mother. He was raised in a mansion high in the hills overlooking Acapulco, becoming a monster willing to rape and murder at will.

"You ever been to Veracruz before?" Silvio demanded.

"No. Doesn't matter."

"That's right, Cruz. It doesn't." Silvio leaned back in his chair and folded his arms, like a *pendejo* who thought he was in charge. "The *federales* have jurisdiction. If the Veracruz cops need our help, they'll ask for it. I'll bet the place is swarming with undercover *federale* types who don't need some *chica* detective from Acapulco telling them how to do their job in fucking Veracruz."

"The *federales* are a bunch of stooges," Emilia replied hotly. "And you know it."

"You run down there and fuck stuff up and they'll be saying that about us," Silvio said. "Besides, have you read more than the subject line? Could have been him or a thousand other men. Didn't say anything about a Santa

Muerte tattoo."

"Listen." Emilia forced herself to simmer down and inject a little honey into her voice. "Say I fly out this afternoon. Meet with the point of contact in Veracruz. Do a little information trading. They let me talk to the witness and I'll give them what we know about Gamboa. His upbringing here in Acapulco. Diego Barrielos Luna's possible interest in him. Emphasize the Santa Muerte connection, how both are believers."

The hunt for El Acólito once led Emilia to cartel kingpin Diego Barrielos Luna, now the most wanted man in Mexico. After meeting him in prison, Emilia was part of a convoy extraditing him to prison in the United States. When Barrielos Luna's *sicarios* rescued him, Emilia was the only member of the extradition team left alive, with the narco's promise to find her again ringing in her ears.

Known as the Barrel Bomber for his penchant for dissolving his enemies in vats of acid, the fugitive druglord kept his promise. He orchestrated the kidnapping of Emilia's stepfather, Ernesto, with a clever ransom delivery ruse meant to snare Emilia. Both Emilia and Ernesto survived, thanks to both Kurt and Silvio, but it was a terrifyingly close call.

"No," Silvio said.

"One day," Emilia insisted. "That's all, just one day."

"You're not going to Veracruz," Silvio repeated. "It isn't your case."

Emilia glared but Silvio was never one to back down from a staring contest. "I need two days off," she finally said.

"No."

Before Emilia could draw breath for a counterattack, someone knocked on the door.

"I'm in," Silvio bellowed.

It was Macias, the best looking detective in the squadroom, wearing a lime green *guayabera* shirt that made Emilia wince.

"*Mi jefe*," he said to Silvio. "You've got that meeting with the database people."

"*Rayos*," Silvio growled. He held his thumb and forefinger an inch apart, giving Macias the traditional gesture for *Give me a couple of minutes*. When Macias disappeared, the forgotten folder on the taxi shooting victim was thrust under Emilia's nose.

"Get out, Cruz," Silvio said.

As soon as Emilia was buzzed into the morgue, her eyes watered. The smell was a mixture of cloying sweetness and industrial antiseptic. The cleaning crew of older women, who seemed immune to the death around them, continuously mopped the floor. But nothing in their buckets ever affected the air quality.

Demand for morgue services continued to outstrip capacity. The weekend's collection of homicides was on display in black body bags stacked on double decker gurneys. Last week's unidentified bodies were oversized sardines in the big freezer vaults.

Emilia walked by, trying to ignore a drip plinking to the floor under one of the gurneys. The hallway overflow was the all-too-tangible evidence that Acapulco was losing the fight.

One of the assistants directed Emilia into the morgue's newest extension and closed the door behind her with the soft *thwip* of a spaceship airlock. Emilia wore a jean jacket but still shivered as she looked around. Rough cinderblock, meat locker cold, and 60 steel body drawers. Overhead fluorescent lighting gave off a greenish glow and a noticeable buzz.

"Ah, Detective Cruz." Antonio Prade, coroner and in charge of the Acapulco city morgue, peered at Emilia over tortoise shell reading glasses. He was in his mid-fifties, with short brown hair and a stained lab coat over faded jeans and ancient running shoes.

"I'm here for the taxi driver who was murdered Saturday night near Parque Bellavista," Emilia said.

"You just missed his wife." Prade adjusted his glasses and consulted a clipboard, running his finger down a list.

Emilia perched on a stool next to Prade's stainless steel worktable. "She waited until today to identify the body?"

"Apparently she's been ill," Prade said. "A miscarriage."

"*Madre de Dios*," Emilia murmured.

"She was very stoic," Prade said absently and tossed the clipboard on the table before plucking a pair of latex gloves out of a cardboard box. "I assume you want to see the body?"

"Yes."

Prade found her a disposable surgical mask and tugged open a numbered drawer.

"Cause of death was two shots at point blank range," Prade said. "One in the chest and the other in the head."

With the surgical mask clapped against her mouth, Emilia fought a gag reflex. Half of Arrocha's face was gone. The top of his skull was an empty cavity. White bone rimmed with dark hair held thin strings of pinkish-brown goo.

"The round in the chest penetrated the left ventricle," Prade went on as if he didn't notice Emilia's backwards stumble. "Death was immediate."

Emilia forced herself to look again. Arrocha's body was pristine, almost chiseled, with broad shoulders, sculpted arms, long, powerful legs, and visible abdominal muscles.

"He was in good shape for a taxi driver," she remarked.

"Exceptionally fit." Prade nodded. "Excellent lung capacity."

Emilia took a few obligatory pictures of the dead man with her cell phone. "Is that it?" she asked. "Two shots. No surprises?"

"Unless you want his clothes." Prade pulled a plastic carrier bag out of the drawer where it was lodged next to the body. "His wife didn't."

He closed the drawer and Emilia found that she could breathe again. Wearing a pair of blue latex exam gloves from the box on the Prade's worktable, she opened the bag to find the basic uniform for a driver of an upscale *sitio* taxi. Black pants, short-sleeved shirt, skinny black tie, black socks, sporty black shoes. The tie crackled with dried blood as did the front of the still sharply creased white cotton shirt.

The door gave a hydraulic hiss and a man in a magenta polo shirt strode in carrying a black briefcase. He smiled cautiously as he scanned the sterile room, trendy eyeglasses catching the overhead. "I'm looking for Doctoro Prade," he announced.

"I'm Doctoro Prade." Prade stripped off his own latex gloves to extend a hand. "Who are you?"

"Lieutenant Vicente Campos of the Financial Crimes unit."

The two men shook hands. Campos appeared fascinated with the rows of stainless steel drawers but saw Emilia perched on the stool by the worktable.

"This is Detective Cruz," Prade said. "How can we help you?"

"Your assistant said you had the body of man named Pablo Arrocha Puente in here," Campos said.

"That's my case." Emilia came forward. "How can I help you?"

"*Disculpe*, Detective," Campos said. "We've obviously had a miscommunication. Financial Crimes is handling this."

Emilia frowned. "Arrocha is a homicide, *teniente*."

"I'm aware." Campos turned to Prade. "Do you have the autopsy report?"

Prade nodded. "I'll have my assistant send you a copy."

Emilia wanted to laugh. If Campos was the head of Financial Crimes, he was an accountant suffering some sort of delusion. Financial Crimes had been in existence for no more than six months; a handful of number crunchers stashed in some office building on the outskirts of Acapulco to compile data and fret over fraud claims that would never be prosecuted. Chief of Police Salazar announced the unit on a Friday afternoon. By Monday it was all but forgotten, blotted out by another weekend wave of homicides.

"The case has already been assigned to me as the lead detective, *teniente*," Emilia said, striving for politeness while making the point that she wasn't backing down. "Arrocha was murdered at point blank range. A homicide. If you have information pertinent to the case, I'd like to discuss it. In the detectives unit or your office."

The lieutenant pressed a forefinger to the temple of his trendy glasses. They were teal. "Detective," he said with an unmistakable hint of humor in his voice. "While your resolve is admirable, this case belongs to Financial Crimes. I suggest you don't spend any time on it until I've spoken with your superior officer."

"That would be Lieutenant Franco Silvio," Emilia said with as much ice in her voice as she could muster.

What right did this fashionista of a *teniente* have to say he was taking over her case? He hadn't seen the murder. He hadn't tried to run down the suspect through dark streets.

He wasn't in her chain of command.

"I'll be contacting him later today," Campos said.

"I'll let him know."

"Doctoro. Detective." Campos left. The door closed behind him, sealing itself with an automatic kiss of compressed air.

"*Pendejo*," Emilia muttered.

"This is why I prefer working with the dead," Prade said. "Never any confusion about who's in charge."

CHAPTER 4

As soon as Emilia walked into the lobby of the Palacio Réal, she knew something was wrong. She often got a you-don't-belong-here niggle when she was in workout clothes, but this wasn't it.

Yet the enormous vaulted lobby was the same as when she left for work that morning. A row of royal palms, soaring out of blue and white *talavera* pots as tall as her shoulder marched down the center of the cathedral-like space. The trunks were wrapped in thousands of fairy lights, creating a romantic atmosphere as twilight descended. Guests lounged, drinks in hand, on the sofas and chairs dotted around the periphery for those who wanted a more private cocktail experience than the hotel's famous open-air Pasodoble Bar.

The long check-in desk was staffed by hotel employees wearing the Palacio Réal's signature blue floral shirts.

A few sniffed back tears, others wore stoic expressions.

Emilia crossed the lobby to the desk where head concierge Christine Boudreau was typing, her bloodless lips pursed in concentration. The woman wore the hotel's signature floral as well, which set off her milky skin, blue eyes, and wispy frame. The tag pinned to her dress gave her hometown as Geneva, Switzerland.

"Hey, Christine," Emilia said. "What's going on?"

The concierge's face tightened at the sight of Emilia's sweaty tee, cropped leggings, and cross trainers. "Emilia," she said primly. "No one has to guess where you've been."

"I hope not." Emilia cut her eyes to the employees moping behind the check-in desk. "Has something happened?"

"Hasn't Kurt told you?" Christine asked with a show of false innocence.

"Told me what?"

"Oh, I'm sure he'll want to tell you himself."

"Is he in his office?" Emilia thumped the bulky sports bag onto the desk. Christine recoiled in distaste and Emilia decided that even small triumphs counted when it came to her rival. Christine never hid her dismay when it came to Kurt's taste in women and never lost an opportunity to try and kick Emilia out of the hotel.

"No," Christine sniffed. "He went upstairs."

Puta. Emilia swung her bag off the desk. "Thanks, Christine," she said, falsely sweet. "You've been so helpful."

"Any time, Emilia," Christine said, in a voice to match

Emilia rode the elevator up to the penthouse level and let herself into the apartment. She heard Kurt's voice coming from the room they used as an office.

He was seated at the desk, the house phone tucked between his ear and his shoulder, while he texted on his cell phone at the same time. Emilia pantomimed that she was going to take a shower and he gave her a swift thumbs up.

Curiosity gnawed at Emilia while she showered and donned shorts and a clean tee. Meanwhile, ice cubes clinked from the dining room.

"Do you want a drink?" Kurt asked. He held up a bottle of Scotch.

"Not right now." Emilia leaned against the doorframe as he poured the amber liquid over a couple of ice cubes. "What's going on? Everybody downstairs looked like they were headed to a funeral."

"Ironic choice of words." Kurt drank down half the Scotch in a long swallow.

Emilia waited.

"Our hotel in Hong Kong got overrun by protesters," he finally said. "They drove a truck into the lobby and the police came after them with tear gas."

"*Madre de Dios*," Emilia exclaimed.

Kurt swirled the remaining Scotch around the glass. The ice rattled. "As the whole thing was going down, our manager had a heart attack. Died before they could get him to the hospital."

"I'm so sorry," Emilia said. "Did you know him?"

"Adam Ramsey." Kurt drained the glass. "Good guy. The best. He was the manager here before me. Hired most of the staff we have now."

"Oh." No wonder the lobby was in mourning. "Is there anything I can do?"

Kurt shook his head. "The hotel in Hong Kong is wrecked and the staff is traumatized. We need to assess and see what can be salvaged."

"We?" Emilia picked out the word with the greatest meaning. "Are you telling me you're going to Hong Kong?"

"Corporate asked me to lead the recovery effort." Kurt put his empty glass on the sideboard next to the bottles of expensive liquor. "I'll take stock, see what it's going to take to get the hotel operational again, or if it makes more sense to close for good."

Emilia gaped at him. "While the protests are still going on?"

"It's only slightly less safe than here."

"With crazy people driving cars into hotels?" Emilia pressed. "In Mexico we only shoot each other."

The house phone in the living room rang. The extension trilled from the office.

"It's for me," Kurt said, stating the obvious. He gave Emilia a swift peck on the cheek and loped down the hall.

Three hours later, Emilia and Kurt stood on the balcony outside their bedroom and leaned over the wall to watch the restless churn of the ocean far below.

Their nightly ritual of a glass of brandy on the balcony was one of her favorite things about living in the penthouse at the Palacio Réal, the architectural marvel offering seven stories of luxurious hospitality on the southeastern spit of Acapulco Bay called Puerto Marques. The balcony continued around the corner of the building and was accessible from every room. Teak chaise lounges and a matching dining set were accompanied by big pots of geraniums and trailing greenery that someone else cultivated and cared for.

On this side of the penthouse, the balcony overlooked the hotel's marina and private beach, as well as the famous two-level Pasodoble Bar. A dozen ceramic lanterns, each as big as a barrel, created a dramatic screen of flames and color between the edge of the Pasodoble's lower terrace and the shore. Red pindots gently rose and fell against the horizon, evidence of the reflectors on the hotel's swimming dock. Puerto Marques, the bay-within-a-bay, made for peaceful waters and expensive seclusion. Music filtered up from the Pasodoble, but even that was soothing tonight.

Sometimes it was hard to believe she lived here, with this yellow haired *gringo* who thought nothing of jetting off across the world to solve problems that were far beyond her experience. On more than one occasion Kurt had introduced her to diplomats, rock stars, and global business tycoons who braved Acapulco's rising crime rates for the world's finest in food, accommodations, and relaxation.

Kurt leaned over the wall with his elbows on the ledge. "How was your day?"

Emilia took a sip of brandy. The tile floor was cool under her bare feet. She decided not to tell Kurt about the store owner identifying El Acólito in Veracruz. Kurt had enough to deal with as it was.

"Better than yours," she said at length. "I got assigned to the murder of that taxi driver. His name was Pablo Arrocha Puente. Two shots at close range. Head and chest."

"Any suspects?"

"A gang called Los Mozos," Emilia said. "Left a note. It was in the newspaper today. Very clearly wanted everybody to know he was killed because the *sitio* wasn't paying enough protection money."

They finished their brandy and climbed into bed, both too distracted and tired for more than a swift embrace. Drawn over the French doors, linen curtains suffused the bedroom with milky moonlight.

"Em?" On his side facing her, Kurt propped his head on his hand.

"What?" Emilia pulled up the matelassé coverlet.

"Let's not talk about anything serious until I get back from Hong Kong." Kurt hesitated. "You know what I mean?"

Serious like Saturday night's half-finished proposal?

"Sure," Emilia said.

"Think about what you want me to bring you back from Hong Kong."

"Just you." Emilia slid her thumb over the angle of his jaw.

Kurt rolled away from her. In a few minutes Emilia heard his breathing grow deep and even. Her hip ached; she should not have tried to work out again so soon.

Tired thoughts tumbled through her head. A store in Veracruz. An athlete with half a face. Braided wedding bands in a fancy jewelry store.

Was she ready to make a life-changing commitment? Life

together in the Palacio Réal right now was good. She and Kurt had separated, reconnected, and passed through the fire of Ernesto's kidnapping and ransom delivery together.

Kurt had proposed once before, long before she was ready. As far as Emilia knew, his grandmother's engagement ring was still in a dresser drawer.

Would marriage to a rich *gringo* end her police career? Emilia's position as the only female police detective was precarious enough. The higher-ups could use it as an excuse to boot her out with the claim that she was now too vulnerable to kidnapping.

She'd have to sacrifice her police career, such as it was, if Kurt's job led somewhere else. What if he wanted to move to Hong Kong? The other manager did. So could Kurt.

All that paled before the huge dark hole that was the assault she couldn't remember. El Acólito dosed her with a date rape drug, making her pliant and unable to resist. She had no memory of it and what she didn't know taunted her. Closure was impossible.

No matter how much time passed, Emilia feared she'd always be hostage to what happened, wearing it like invisible chains. How could she bring this cancer into a marriage?

She turned on her side, her back against Kurt's. His trip to Hong Kong was a temporary reprieve, giving her more time to consider their future together.

It was also an opportunity for Kurt to change his mind.

Neither thought was comforting.

CHAPTER 5

"Once more, exactly why are we here?" Emilia asked.

"Play nice, Cruz," Silvio growled.

The ground level of the office building that housed the Financial Crimes unit was eerily silent. Emilia saw closed doors with business logos, but it was clear no one worked there anymore.

Their footsteps scraped on the stairway winding up to the second floor.

"*Rayos*," Silvio paused halfway to the top, looking at the dim lobby below. "Somebody could film a horror flick here."

"Talking about movies," Emilia said. "Have you given any more thought to a quick trip to Veracruz?"

"I don't want to go to Veracruz."

"Very funny," Emilia said, resisting the urge to stick out a foot and trip him. "One day. I could go in the morning. Be back before midnight."

Silvio grunted and began climbing again. "Mercedes wants to see *Diamond Run*. Have you seen it?"

"She'll love it," Emilia said brightly. "Big twist ending. Alejandra Messi turns out to be an Interpol agent. Never saw it coming."

"Fuck, Cruz." Silvio glowered.

Emilia continued up the stairs.

Financial Crimes took up the entire second floor. The

nerve center was an atrium with a circular skylight. An older woman who identified herself as Señora Mendez escorted them down a corridor to a large conference room.

Lieutenant Campos was there waiting for them in another *norteamericano* college student outfit; green polo shirt, trendy glasses, shock of chestnut hair. He seemed younger than when Emilia saw him the day before, but then again, the stomach curdling atmosphere of the morgue made everyone appear older before their time.

He seemed genuinely happy to meet Silvio and whipped out a few statistics about the boxing career that predated Silvio's years as a police officer. Emilia waited as Silvio succumbed to flattery and even threw a couple of shadow boxing moves before they took seats around the conference table.

Two other Financial Crimes officers were introduced. Emilia caught the names Jorge and Bruno. They seemed happy enough to be overshadowed by the extroverted Lieutenant Campos.

Just like in the detectives squadroom, Emilia was the only woman in the room.

"We have video from the night that taxi driver Pablo Arrocha Puente was murdered," Campos said. "I know there's some confusion about who will move forward with the case and I thought it would help if we watched it before having that discussion."

A television mounted on the wall winked and a video player filled the display.

"As I explained to the champ on the phone," Campos began with a nod to Silvio. "This video is from the security camera from the ATM machine on the side of Santander Bank facing Avenida Bellavista. The camera was angled incorrectly. Luckily for us, it recorded the street rather than the machine's transaction. When the Santander security team saw the footage, they immediately turned it over to us."

The television screen filled with a silent black and white video. The time stamp in the bottom corner showed last Saturday's date.

Emilia immediately recognized the line of taxis waiting for fares at the corner of Avenida Bellavista and Avenida Farallón del Obispo. She and Kurt had crossed right at that intersection.

The cars shone brightly in the murky footage, parked nose to tail along the curb. The passenger side of each taxi was to the camera, showing off the Taxis Coco logo. Palm trees obscured slender slices of the second and third taxis in line.

The view on the screen represented a quintessential part of urban life. *Sitio* stands were usually found near large intersections. *Sitio* taxis were a much safer alternative to crowded buses and the scores of unlicensed taxis that roamed the city vying for clueless tourists to fleece. A ride in a licensed *sitio* was more expensive, but always cleaner and more reliable. *Sitio* drivers wore ties.

For several minutes, the video was nothing more than the chronicle of a busy night in the Acapulco entertainment district. Traffic flowed up and down Avenida Bellavista ferrying night owls from the smaller restaurants and clubs on one end to Café Coco and the Cinépolis on the other. The intersection with Avenida Farallón del Obispo was partially in the frame, showing its wider lanes and streams of cars and minibuses. Couples ran across Avenida Bellavista to Café Coco.

Two men in white shirts and dark ties, obviously drivers, lounged against the third taxi in line.

As they talked, one smoked and the other held a cell phone. Their faces were striped by the shadows of palm fronds stretching into the sky out of view. More pedestrians walked by. No one appeared to be in a hurry.

"Here we go," Campos murmured.

A dark shape popped into view at the top of the video frame where the northbound lanes of Avenida Farallón del Obispo were visible. As the figure drew closer to the line of taxis, Emilia recognized the *encapuchado* who had outrun her.

A minivan swerved into the intersection and passed out of the frame.

At the same time, a woman carrying a plump shopping bag approached the *sitio* stand. One of the standing drivers noticed and appeared to call out to her but she continued past him and got into the back seat of the first taxi in line. There was nothing remarkable in that; everyone knew to take the taxi waiting at the head of the line.

Before the taxi could drive off, the hooded man opened the door behind the driver. His face was lost from view as he leaned inside, but a second later, the woman scrambled out of the taxi from the opposite side, in full view of the camera. Still clutching her heavy tote, she took a few steps backwards before opening her mouth in a silent scream.

The *encapuchado* went to the driver's window. His shoulder lifted although his hands were hidden from view. Recoil jerked him once, twice. He walked past the front fender, then broke into a run that took him out of the frame.

As the video counter ticked off the seconds, nothing happened. The other two drivers were frozen in shock or confusion, but neither appeared to be staring at the first taxi in line. Without sound, the scene was almost comical.

Eventually, the taller man opened the passenger door. He quickly backpedaled, sat on the sidewalk, and put his head in his hands. The door stayed open. The camera angle only captured the driver's torso, still upright behind the wheel. The other *sitio* driver came to gape at the dead man. Two female pedestrians opened their mouths and gestured wildly before running away.

"We spoke to the *sitio* license owner last night," Campos said as the video ended. "A man named Francisco Donoso Garay. He's been paying protection money to the Los Mozos gang. When they threatened to kill the first driver in line, he upped the payment."

"I saw the note," Emilia offered. "Los Mozos wasn't shy about claiming responsibility."

Campos gave her an approving nod. "Exactly, Detective. Of course, there were no prints."

"Okay," Silvio broke in, putting the brakes on the other lieutenant's friendly manner. "We'll need the interview transcript and a copy of that footage, too."

Campos pushed on the temple of his designer glasses with a forefinger. "Extortion is a financial crime, champ."

"Homicide trumps extortion." Silvio gave Campos a hard smile. "You can get back to your number crunching."

Campos crossed his knees in a relaxed manner. His socks matched his shirt. "Chief Salazar said that you would lend assistance."

"We will," Silvio agreed. "We'll open a homicide investigation."

"We'll expand our extortion investigation."

"Financial's got no jurisdiction over a homicide case," Silvio pointed out.

Campos steepled his fingers. "Chief Salazar has agreed that Financial Crimes will investigate the murder."

Emilia stifled a gasp. Financial Crimes was three accountants, a calculator, and an empty building.

"Exactly how would Financial Crimes catch the killer?" Silvio asked, his voice larded with a warning to Campos that flattery wasn't having the desired effect. "Hypothetically. Also, keep in mind you need to protect the other drivers at the same time."

"Los Mozos has a soft spot for women," Campos said. "The killer let that woman out of the taxi and the note left behind called for citizens to protect women and children."

Silvio scowled. "So?"

Campos nodded. "We plan on using a female undercover officer."

Madre de Dios. Emilia hunched in her chair, trying to make herself invisible.

"Replace the dead driver with a female driver?" Silvio asked. "There are no female *sitio* drivers."

"There will be," Campos said. "We have Chief Salazar's permission to borrow Detective Cruz."

CHAPTER 6

Standing on the other side of the marble-topped island, Emilia's mother, Sophia Encinos, rinsed a shucked tomatillo and handed it to her daughter. "When was the last time you made *salsa verde*?"

"I don't know." Emilia cut the green globe in half and placed the pieces on a baking sheet. "I haven't cooked anything in months. The hotel chef keeps the refrigerator full or we eat out."

"You shouldn't forget how to cook," Sophia said.

Emilia's mother was slim and attractive, with long dark hair roped into a braid down her back. She wore plastic flip-flops and a flowered apron over a dress with an equally cheerful print. Most people assumed Sophia was Emilia's older sister rather than her mother.

"I should do more," Emilia agreed. Considering Lieutenant Campos's plans to stash her in a safe house during the undercover assignment nobody bothered to ask if she wanted, cooking was a distinct possibility. "I'm going to be on an assignment for work, Mama. I wanted you to know because I might not be able to answer the phone. Do you remember how to leave me a voice message?"

Sophia blinked in concern and wiped her hands.

"If I don't answer, call Tío Raul or Alvaro," Emilia said hastily, naming her uncle and cousin. Her mother's new house was still close to other family members. "When the assignment's over, I want you and Ernesto to come out to the hotel for a day and sit by the pool."

Sophia blinked again, still processing the shift in topic. Eventually the frown smoothed over and she nodded. "He'd like that."

Relieved and surprised at her mother's casual reaction, Emilia sprinkled the baking sheet of tomatillos with oil.

Sophia's response to unexpected change was usually more dramatic. Her endless nervous breakdown began when her husband died and her eldest child was taken away by her own sister. Emilia had been a toddler then and grew up with a mother who retreated into a closed world of rosy serenity whenever things got too hard or too complicated. If that didn't work, Sophia burst into tears of confusion until Emilia invented some lie that made the problem go away.

But moving to the new house had blown a breeze through the cobwebs in Sophia's mind.

This house was bigger and much more modern than the tiny house in central Acapulco where Emilia and her mother had lived for nearly a dozen years. When Emilia moved into the Palacio Réal, Sophia married Ernesto Cruz, an itinerant knife grinder who bore the same name as Emilia's late father. He was kidnapped in broad daylight from that house by *sicarios* answering to fugitive druglord Diego Barrielos Luna. After his rescue, Emilia and Silvio used money confiscated from a crooked Russian diplomat to move Sophia and Ernesto to a safer place.

In addition to the house, the Russian's millions bought

fake ownership records so Barrielos Luna couldn't trace the Cruz family. The ruse bought Emilia time, but unless the hapless *federales* found the fugitive cartel boss soon, she knew he'd find new and inventive ways to get at her.

"There's a whole book about the oven." Sophia's eyes sparkled as she produced a booklet with the drawing of an electric range on the front. "I had to study it to know how to turn it on."

"Mama, do you think I should get married?" Emilia asked, buoyed by her mother's new-found wellbeing. "Would you like that?"

"Yes, of course." Sophia stopped pushing buttons but didn't put down the appliance manual. "When you find a good provider like Ernesto."

"What about Carlos?" Emilia casually threw out her mother's name for Kurt. "He's a good provider."

"Carlos?" Sophia's eyebrows drew together in vague concern. "But he's not Mexican."

"Doesn't matter."

"I'm sure it would be against the law." Sophia shook her head. "Carlos is very charming and his hotel is nice, but anything could happen with a man like that."

Whatever Emilia expected her mother to say, it wasn't this. "He's a *gringo*, Mama, not some criminal."

Sophia tentatively poked at the digital panel again. An electronic tone sounded and her face lit with excitement. "Look, Emilia. I turned on the oven!"

"That's great, Mama." Emilia slumped on the kitchen

stool.

"We have to wait now," Sophia informed her daughter. "When it gets hot, the bell rings again. After that we put the pan in."

"Shall I make some coffee for Ernesto while we wait?"

Sophia kissed Emilia's cheek. "That's nice, *niña*. It's still too hard for him to move around."

As Sophia gazed rapturously through the oven window at the roasting tomatillos, Emilia poured fresh coffee into a mug and took it through to the living room, chiding herself for raising the notion of marrying Kurt. The decision was Emilia's.

She could hardly kick it to someone else.

Ernesto was on the sofa, a blanket over his legs, watching *fútbol* on the widescreen television. Like the oven, the television came with the house, along with motion detection exterior lights, three palatial bathrooms, and a formal *comedor* with a crystal chandelier that Sophia was afraid to turn on.

"Emilia." Ernesto gave her a half smile as he accepted the mug. The kidnappers had kept him in a coffin, stashed in an abandoned hotel. To pressure the family into coming up with an absurdly high ransom, they'd shot him in the leg and streamed the act on live video. Ernesto was left with sunken cheeks, strands of gray in his hair, and a shuffling gait.

"Your mother likes the new kitchen, no?" he asked and blew across the hot surface of the coffee.

"I do, too." Emilia settled in the armchair.

Not yet 50 years old, Ernesto looked twice his age. Emilia got a frisson of guilt every time she saw him. His terrible ordeal and wrecked health were her fault, a direct result of her first ill-conceived encounter with Diego Barrielos Luna.

"Do you want to watch something else?" Ernesto asked.

"No," Emilia reassured him. "I'll read Mama's magazines."

"Your mother just finished that one," Ernesto said.

Alejandra Messi gazed languidly at an adoring world over sunglasses perched on her perfect nose next to bold letters: *Go inside her world!* Alejandra's famous pout was candy red. A matching string bikini top barely contained her equally famous breasts.

Emilia surrendered to Hollywood fever and rifled through stories about cat-fighting on the set, starlets sleeping with directors, makeup tips worthy of high class hookers, and crazy Hollywood diet plans until she found the glitzy spread about the star's pink-infused home in Beverly Hills.

It was a nightmare swathed in pink velvet, the sort of place that would have Kurt calling the hotel decorator in less than a second. Pink kitchen, pink velvet sofa, pink chandelier over a white sideboard inlaid with pink crystals. The superstar floated through the garish rooms holding a poodle with a pink collar.

"You could be her," Ernesto said.

"I think she's mostly made of plastic," Emilia replied, unable to avoid a little comparison shopping. Alejandra Messi had a body too perfectly sculpted to be natural. The woman would be no help in a bar fight.

"She sings good," Ernesto said.

Emilia agreed and picked up another magazine. She was halfway through an article on what Antonio Banderas ate for breakfast when Ernesto spoke again.

"I know about him, you know."

"Antonio Banderas?"

"No." Ernesto tilted his chin at the doorway that led through the dining room to the kitchen. "Him. Her boy."

The new house was clearing away more cobwebs than anticipated if Sophia had finally told Ernesto about her lost son, Ernesto Cruz Encinos, Junior, who grew up to become El Acólito. Santa Muerte priest. Human trafficker. Murderer.

Rapist.

"There's no reason you shouldn't," Emilia replied carefully.

Ernesto held his mug in both hands. "She . . . Sophia wonders about him."

"Wonders? What do you mean?"

"What happened to me," Ernesto said. "It was bad for Sophia."

"It was bad for all of us," Emilia acknowledged. "We're glad to have you back."

"Sophia got scared," Ernesto said sadly. "She talks about losing him now. How that Karina woman took him. I think maybe now Sophia wants him back."

Antonio Banderas's breakfast slid off her lap as Emilia leaned forward and put her hand on the blanket covering

Ernesto's legs.

"Ernesto, listen to me," she said urgently. "Mama's son grew up to be a bad man. A very, very bad man."

Ernesto patted her hand. "Maybe."

"He's like those kidnappers." Emilia hoped the analogy would resonate. "He's done terrible things."

"A man without a mother is like that," Ernesto said uncertainly.

A shiver of apprehension traced down Emilia's spine. "Mama can't go looking for him. He'll destroy all of us."

"He's just one man." Ernesto was clearly discomfited by her intensity. "I think it would be good for Sophia to see him after all these years. Maybe." He trailed off.

"No," Emilia kept her voice low but packed as much authority into the word as she could. "Promise me, Ernesto, that you won't let Mama search for him. Ever."

Ernesto looked down. "All right."

"After all, Mama's getting better," Emilia said. "We wouldn't want anything to send her backwards."

CHAPTER 7

The transfer to Financial Crimes would last a week or two at most. The only thing Emilia bothered with taking from her desk in the squadroom was the binder of Missing Persons reports she referred to as *Las Perdidas*.

Upon arrival in the echoing building, Señora Mendez handed Emilia a box of office supplies and led her to an inner office.

Emilia slung the strap of her shoulder bag over the back of the chair and dumped the box next to the files. Besides a desk and chair, the room was empty. No computer. No window. No dial tone when Emilia picked up the phone.

The box yielded the bare necessities including pens, a pad of paper, a stapler, a package of colored sticky notes, and a clean white mug.

"Welcome to Financial Crimes, Detective." Campos stood in the doorway, resplendent in his teal spectacles and a pink polo. "Do you have a minute?"

"Of course."

"Let me introduce you around before handing over the case files," Campos said.

He guided Emilia down the hall, stopping at office doors to re-introduce her to Jorge and Bruno. Both welcomed her with perfunctory nods, more intent on the spreadsheets plastered across their computer screens. Emilia didn't ask what they were working on and neither volunteered.

Campos's office was closest to the secretary's desk in the atrium. He had another double decker computer set-up, an industrial printer, and a safe twice the size of the one in Silvio's office. A homemade nameplate proclaimed Vicente Campos in a child's block print. Photographs of Campos with a smiling woman and boy were pinned to a strip of cork mounted to the wall.

Two armchairs fronted his desk, which was piled with file folders. He invited Emilia to sit and took the chair opposite.

"You have a lovely family, *teniente*," Emilia said.

Campos grinned. "My boy takes after my wife. He's 16 years old and wants to be a doctor."

"That's wonderful."

The tall boy in the snapshots was the spitting image of his father, with hipster glasses and the same shock of hair falling over a tall forehead. Campos wasn't what Emilia would consider a handsome man, but he had an appealing vitality. It shone on the son's face as well.

"We really appreciate you joining the team, even temporarily." Campos nodded. "I've seen your file. Very impressive."

His genuine warmth was a nice change from Silvio's habitual growls. "Thank you."

"Here are the files on the Pablo Arrocha shooting and what we have so far on Los Mozos." Campos took a short stack of file folders off the desk and handed them to Emilia. "I want you to go through it all. In the meantime, Señora Mendez is working on your new identity. You'll have to apply for a chauffeur's license, deal with car repairs, and so on."

"Of course."

"Once you get to the *sitio*, your goal is reconnaissance," Campos went on. "We need everything you can get on Los Mozos. Names, of course, but no arrest, no heroics. I'm not expecting Superwoman."

Emilia nodded. Campos's friendly manner was a nice change from the squadroom, where backstabbing, cutthroat competition, and psychological warfare were all business as usual.

"Now, I have to say something a bit delicate here." Campos coughed and adjusted the temple of his glasses.

"What is it, *teniente*?"

"Could you be a little more, er, plain when you have new identification pictures taken?"

"Plain?"

"And dull." Campos looked abashed. "The first female *sitio* driver shouldn't be attractive enough to be noticed. The more layers of pretense, the more layers of protection."

It was a nicely delivered compliment, neither flirtatious nor patronizing. Emilia dipped her head in appreciation, feeling herself warm to the lieutenant even more. "How soon before the paperwork is ready, *teniente*?"

"We're on a fast track," Campos said. "I want you in that taxi by next week."

"Well." Emilia stood up with the folders in her hands. "I'd better get to work."

"Before you go, Detective." Campos gave an embarrassed chuckle as he walked her to the door. "Did I overplay my hand with Lieutenant Silvio the other day?"

"Overplay?"

"You know, calling him 'Champ.' Trying to get on his good side." Campos mimed a couple of short jabs and chuckled again.

"I don't think he minded, but Lieutenant Silvio doesn't have a good side."

"Just my luck." Campos mimed punching himself in the jaw. "You were his partner, weren't you? Tough man to work with, I hear."

"And he's dating my best friend," Emilia said.

Campos shook his head at the grave injustice. "*Por Dios.* I admire your resiliency, Detective."

Their eyes met in a moment of solidarity against Lieutenant Franco Silvio, sinner and evildoer.

Emilia edged closer to the door. "Basically, don't step on his toes and he won't step on yours."

"Good advice," Campos said. "Thank you, Detective."

Emilia fled to her cubby hole of an office with the files, torn between excitement and guilt. She didn't know why she'd blabbed about Silvio dating Mercedes, except that Lieutenant Campos had an open, easy manner that invited familiarity and created rapport. He absorbed everything she said as if it held great significance.

She was going to like working for him.

The first file contained all of the interviews conducted by uniformed cops who were first on the scene after Arrocha was shot. In terms of a murder investigation, Emilia gleaned more from what wasn't written down, than from what was.

None of the Café Coco patrons saw the shooting. A few mentioned the car accident. The rest were too busy eating.

No one in Parque Bellavista saw the shooting.

No one on the sidewalk in front of Santander Bank saw the shooting or even someone run by.

The woman who scrambled out of the taxi and screamed on the sidewalk did not stay to give a statement. No attempt was made to find her.

Emilia wasn't surprised. Everyone wanted criminals to be caught and the flood of homicides to stop, but mostly everyone was terrified of becoming the next target. Seeing a murder and talking about it to the police was a death sentence for both the witness and their families.

Even the driver whose taxi was parked along the curb immediately behind Arrocha saw nothing. Ricardo Heredia was the first to approach the first taxi and see the dead driver. No, he had not seen the killer's face. Extremely distraught, Heredia nonetheless volunteered to break the news to Arrocha's family and was not interviewed again. Like Heredia, the second driver at the scene, Juan Miguel Lagos saw nothing but was distraught over the murder of his fellow taxi driver.

Francisco Donoso Garay, owner of the *sitio* and the dispatcher, didn't see the murder, either. He was inside the dispatcher's booth and claimed that Arrocha's vehicle blocked his view of the killer. He was also distracted by the accident in the intersection.

Emilia took her feet off the desk and flipped through all the statements again to make sure she hadn't missed anything. Neither Kurt nor the driver of the minivan made a statement.

Outside her office, the corridor was completely silent. No footsteps, no casual conversations, no tapping on computer keyboards. She missed the clamor and camaraderie of the detectives squadroom, even if the jokes were sick and Gomez kept photocopying his dick and leaving the images on her desk.

She found the little kitchen on the other side of the atrium, filled the clean mug with artificial foam and flavor from a capsule coffeemaker, and decided to meet her victim.

By the time she was halfway through, Pablo Arrocha Puente was a real person instead of a dead body with half a head.

Emilia knew dozens of men just like Pablo Arrocha.

Went to school with them. Worked as a beat cop with them. Even dated her fair share of men just like Pablo before meeting Kurt.

For the most part, they were fun, decent guys who would mature in about 10 years. Their jobs required some training, but not enough to earn real money, so they had a side hustle. Every Pablo had a friend who rubbed elbows with a gang or was killed in the latest round of street violence. They got married, had kids, grew tomatoes in a pot next to a grill made from half a barrel.

Loved sports, cheap tequila, fresh tortillas, and their mothers.

The dead *taxista* was 32. The picture from his *cédula* national identity card showed a strapping man with a square jaw and hard eyes.

Originally from Iguala to the north, Arrocha graduated from the Escuela Secundaria Federal Jaime Torres Bodet, a military school where he excelled in basketball. He moved to Acapulco shortly after graduation and trained as a mechanic before buying a *sitio* permit and driving for Taxis Coco. His wife was a teacher and together they owned a house and the taxi, a 4 year old Ford sedan. The annual vehicle inspections were up to date. No outstanding taxes or traffic tickets. They had a daughter, age 5.

Tucked into the back of the file was an article taken from the website of FIBA, the Mexican national basketball federation. Arrocha was cited as an up and coming player in 3x3 basketball competitions.

Señora Mendez appeared at the door, startling Emilia out of her reverie.

"We have lunch catered daily," the secretary announced.

"Would you like to see the menu?"

Kurt gave Emilia a distracted kiss and flew off to Hong Kong.

Emelia had plain pictures taken for her new identity documents, bought Arrocha's taxi using Lieutenant Campo's money, and applied for a chauffeur's license using her cover name. Señora Mendez handled most of the paperwork and was obviously familiar with managing this sort of thing. While she waited for the transactions to be finalized, Emilia drove around the Parque Bellavista commercial district to get a feel for the *sitio's* comings and goings, nicely hidden behind wraparound sunglasses and the tinted windows of her Suburban.

After a few passes down Avenida Bellavista, it was clear to Emilia that the *sitio* catered to well-dressed tourists and wealthy Acapulco residents.

The corner of Avenida Farallón del Obispo and Avenida Bellavista was prime real estate, with a constant flow of foot traffic heading to shops, restaurants, and the cinema, as well as Parque Bellavista. Santander Bank provided another stream of pedestrians, thanks to the ATM machine. A few meters from the money machine, the dispatcher's booth acted as the *sitio's* headquarters. The booth resembled a plexiglass and wood frame bus shelter, outfitted with a bench for drivers and customers, and a plywood podium.

Back in her windowless office, Emilia pored over the scanty Financial Crimes files.

The interview with *sitio* owner and dispatcher Francisco Donoso Garay was the critical piece of information. Six months ago, two men who claimed to be from the Los Mozos gang visited his home. It was late, almost midnight, and he had just returned from closing down the *sitio* for the day. The men demanded that the *sitio* pay protection money to the gang and provided Donoso Garay with the number of an account at Banamex Bank. He was to deposit a certain amount of cash every week.

The two gangbangers identified his wife and children by name. They knew where the children went to school and what time they came and went every day. They knew his wife's route to the market, what grocery store she frequented, what car she drove, and where her mother lived.

The men slapped Donoso Garay around, right in front of his house, so that he understood they were serious. When they disappeared into the night, he was left with a bloody nose, the bank deposit information, and a deadline. He had two days to save his family.

Donoso Garay immediately told the ten *sitio* drivers about the visit by the Los Mozos thugs. All agreed to pay up. Donoso Garay made the first deposit the same day and continued every week like clockwork. Los Mozos stayed away from his doorstep.

But two months ago, the men reappeared at the *sitio* owner's home and demanded 25 percent more. He protested, knowing what a huge chunk of his drivers' income that represented. In response, they beat him badly and left him in the street with the warning that the first driver in line at the *sitio* would be killed until the deposits increased.

Once again, the drivers agreed to the gang's demand. Now in the wake of Arrocha's murder, Donoso Garay was frantic. He had no way of contacting the gang. He had no way of knowing if they would strike again.

Meanwhile, the remaining nine drivers agreed to pay an additional 10 percent in hopes of placating the gang.

Emilia had seen the technique before. Imported from Colombia, the gangs called it *gota a gota* because they bled their victims dry, drop by drop.

Gota a gota.

Protection money was paid in ever-increasing increments. Interest rates on informal loans ballooned until all the blood was squeezed from the stone.

As far as the file went, there was no indication that Donoso Garay looked at mug shots of suspected gang members or sat with a sketch artist.

An official request had been sent to the headquarters of Banamex Bank to access the account Donoso Garay was paying into. The request was still pending.

On her last day in Financial Crimes, Emilia sat down with Lieutenant Campos and Señora Mendez for a final briefing.

She was ready to drive.

Her new *cédula* bore the name Ester Ruiz Garcia with a plain and dull photograph, along with an address in the Costa Azul neighborhood. Ester was the proud owner of a taxi chauffeur's license, *sitio* permit, and a newly repaired Ford sedan taxi. She also had a credit card, a grocery store loyalty card, a big box store membership card, and a death certificate for a man named Daniel Llosa Vega backed up by paperwork from an insurance company.

Ester was a widow.

"Here's the key to the house," Campos said and produced a brass key on a simple steel ring.

"It's a spring break rental but it has all the basics," Señora Mendez said apologetically. "Sheets, towels. Dishes. Everything is clean."

The three of them were in his office, going over the final details before Emilia pretended to be Ester Ruiz Garcia for two weeks or so to figure out what the Los Mozos gang was really up to.

"We got Ester the latest technology, too." Campos handed her a silver BlackBerry. The square device was no bigger than Emilia's palm, with a tiny keyboard and a screen the size of a postage stamp.

When she was in high school a BlackBerry was an inconceivable luxury, something only movie stars and the president could afford. Now it was prehistoric technology.

"It's got location tracking so we always know where you are, even if it seems to be powered off," Campos went on.

"See the key with the letter scratched off? Press it three times and it sends an emergency signal to Dispatch. Both Lieutenant Silvio and I will also get an alert."

"I've written down some additional questions for Señor Donoso Garay," Emilia said as they wrapped up. "He should look at mug shots of known gang members to see if he can identify the Los Mozos thugs who came to his house. Los Mozos could be a splinter group or an old gang with a new name."

"Excellent work, Detective." Campos passed Emilia's short action list to Señora Mendez. "Could you have Enrique work on this, please?"

"Of course, *teniente*." Señora Mendez left the office, paper in hand.

"Should I speak to Enrique?" Emilia hadn't encountered anyone named Enrique during her stint in Financial Crimes.

"We don't have the time." Campos adjusted the temple of his glasses. "I have to ask you to turn in your service weapon now. It'll stay in my safe for the duration."

Emilia slowly unbuckled her shoulder holster and laid both leather and weapon on his desk. Guns were illegal. Ester Ruiz Garcia, widow and taxi driver, would not have a handgun.

"You're there to gather information, not to make an arrest," Campos reminded her. "No unnecessary risks. Anything scares you, send the alert."

"Understood, *teniente*."

"I've got your back, Detective." Campos offered his hand

to seal the bargain.

    Emilia believed him.

CHAPTER 8

Emilia parked along Avenida Bellavista, remembered to shift into neutral, and let the engine idle. Arrocha's taxi, complete with new seat but the same number 17 stenciled on the rear bumper, gave off a morgue-worthy stench of purple Fabuloso liquid cleaner.

Three Taxis Coco taxis were parked in a line ahead of her.

Emilia was ready, in character as Ester Ruiz Garcia in a short-sleeved white shirt and skinny black tie, her face scrubbed clean and free of makeup. Her hair was pulled back in a flat braid. She knew the landscape, thanks to her reconnaissance missions. She was ready to meet the other drivers, especially the two who were at the *sitio* when Arrocha was murdered: Ricardo Heredia and Juan Miguel Lagos.

She was ready, too, for the reception she was likely to get as Acapulco's first female *sitio* driver. It would be exactly like her first day as the city's first female police detective. First, she'd be an object of curiosity for the rank-and-file. Donoso Garay would bray that she was only there out of the goodness of his heart and expect a display of gratitude to the region below his belt. Next, when Donoso Garay and the drivers found out she wasn't a doormat, there would be outright hostility and a slew of dirty tricks designed to force her out.

The only thing that caught her by surprise as she prepped

for the undercover assignment was the taxi's manual transmission. She'd stalled it at least six times between the safe house and the *sitio*.

"Now or never, *chica*," Emilia muttered to herself and swung out of the vehicle. Documentation in hand, she headed for the dispatch booth.

Two drivers sat on the bench in front of the podium. Both wore the requisite *sitio* uniform of white shirt, black tie, and black pants. Eyes widened in recognition of her clothing.

"*Buenos dias*," Emilia murmured in greeting.

The men got up and walked away.

Francisco Donoso Garay studied a notebook spread open on the plywood podium. Over his shoulder, the operating license for the *sitio* was encased in plastic and taped to the Plexiglas surround.

The *sitio* owner and dispatcher had a pompadour haircut and a thick moustache with a distinctive part in the middle, like two hairy caterpillars reaching for a kiss. If it wasn't for the white shirt and tie embroidered with the *sitio* logo, he could be a stand-in for Tin Tan, the legendary comic actor who entertained Mexican audiences for decades.

"Good morning, señor," Emilia said. "I'm your new driver."

The Tin Tan moustache twitched as Donoso Garay regarded her balefully. "Good morning."

Emilia placed her brand new documents in their shiny plastic sleeves on the top of the podium and in the process got a peek at Donoso Garay's notebook. It was the kind she remembered from a long-ago geometry class. Rows of figures marched across graph paper.

"Ester Ruiz Garcia." Donoso Garay pronounced her name as if he was a mourner at a funeral. "We've never had a woman driver before."

"Really?" Emilia tried for an expression that said this was news to her.

Donoso Garay carefully copied down the information from her documents. "It is very costly to buy a permit," he said, keeping his eyes on the page. "This is why only men can afford them."

"My husband is dead," Emilia said, bolstering the lie with a sad sigh. "He left me some money. I could open a restaurant or buy a *sitio* permit."

Her reward was a stern look. "Women don't belong in a taxi except to go to the beauty salon," Donoso Garay said.

Emilia shook her head. "I can't cook, señor. Or fix hair."

He glared at her but the expression didn't suit him. Emilia decided he was fairly good natured, even if his views about women were 20 years out of date.

"Ordinarily, I would not have allowed you to buy in but no one else would buy a dead man's taxi, God rest his soul. I had to take your offer." Donoso Garay shook his head at the tragedy. "But business is business. May the Virgin protect us."

The first taxi nosed into traffic and headed for the intersection. The next two vehicles rolled forward, leaving a gap along the sidewalk in front of Emilia's taxi.

Donoso Garay gave her back the documents. "You will display the permit at all times in your vehicle," he admonished her. "You will follow the rules and not cause problems. You take instructions from me only."

"*Si*, señor."

"This *sitio* is in a prime location and we are known for cleanliness and safety." He pointed his pencil at her. "Clean hands. Always clean hands. No smoking in the car. No pictures or rosaries hanging from the rearview mirror. You take your passengers where you are told to go. When you are done, you come back here. No personal trips. This is a very busy *sitio*. There are no lazy drivers. You understand?"

"*Si*, señor."

"When you are driving, only the fare is allowed in the taxi. Nobody who does not belong." Donoso Garay paused. "No boyfriends."

"Of course," Emilia replied.

Sitio taxis had a good reputation because they were safe. Unlicensed taxis often slowed long enough for an accomplice to hop in and rob the passenger.

"Now this is very important," Donoso Garay said. "As long as you drive for Taxis Coco, never get into a Viva Taxis car. They steal our business, just for spite."

"Is that *sitio* near here?" Emilia asked.

The moustache quivered. "Viva Taxis is next to a restaurant with a big blue fish on it. Their cars smell like fish, too. So you never get in their cars. Understand?"

"Absolutely, señor.

"Good." He nodded, evidently pleased with his new driver's attitude, if not her sex. "Now, the *banderazo* is 70 pesos, you understand?"

The *banderazo* was the base charge on the meter at the start of a fare. Most *sitios* set it at 40 pesos. Only the prime location explained how Taxis Coco got away with 70 pesos.

"Your salary is calculated by the meter." Donoso Garay produced a small canvas bank deposit bag. The key was in the lock. "This is for your fares and tips. You turn in all cash at the end of every shift. All the drivers are paid in cash on Fridays." He paused. "You get 30 percent."

"Does the rest go to Los Mozos?" Emilia asked.

"What do you know of Los Mozos?" he asked sharply.

"They killed Pablo Arrocha," Emilia said simply. "I am taking his place."

"Thirty percent means no more trouble," Donoso Garay said. "We will not speak of it again."

"I understand, señor," Emilia murmured, mentally kicking herself for having moved too fast.

Donoso Garay held out a dozen business cards. "Write down your phone number for your best customers," he said. "You want the ones who will hire your taxi for a whole day."

Emilia took the cards, which were blank except for a raised Taxis Coco palm frond logo. They were a touch of luxury befitting an outfit that charged a 70-peso *banderazo.*

"These are very nice," Emilia said.

"You may address me as Don Cisco," he added.

"Thank you for your help, Don Cisco," Emilia said.

He gave her a regal nod and focused on his notebook again.

Emilia crossed the sidewalk to her vehicle, slotted her permit in a plastic display envelope that had once held Arrocha's documents, and eased forward until she was tucked behind the next taxi. At 9:00 am, the traffic through the intersection was relatively light but on the other side of Avenida Bellavista, people were walking out of Café Coco with cups and bags, fueled on caffeine and pastries. Cars streamed up and down Avenida Farallón del Obispo.

The driver ahead got out of his taxi and sauntered over. Emilia got out.

"Ricardo." He introduced himself, tall and lean, with a pair of expensive sunglasses clipped to the pocket of his white shirt.

"*Mucho gusto*. I'm Ester. Ester Ruiz Garcia."

Instead of shaking her hand, he tapped a cigarette out of a package of Boots. "You smoke?"

"No."

Ricardo lit his cigarette with a cheap plastic lighter. "You know you bought a dead man's permit, don't you?"

"Yes." This was the man who sat on the ground and put his head in his hands when he saw Arrocha's dead body. He had obviously recovered. Emilia wondered how much trouble Ricardo Heredia was going to make for poor, dull Ester.

"He died in that car." Ricardo inhaled deeply and flicked ash toward her taxi. "His ghost is still in it."

Did the *pendejo* really think ghost stories would scare her away? He needed to take a lesson from Castro and Gomez in the detectives squadroom.

"I'll let you know if I see him," Emilia said.

"You won't." Ricardo blew a stream of smoke at her. "Pablo knew how to keep his secrets."

Another vehicle pulled in behind Emilia and a gray-haired driver bustled over.

"I am Juan Miguel Lagos." He reminded Emilia of her uncle, Tío Raul. Older and jollier, but with the same wiry bantamweight build of a man who worked all day and helped his neighbors at night. He pumped her hand with enthusiasm. "No *sitio* ever had a woman *taxista* before. Taxis Coco will be famous."

Ricardo gave a harsh laugh and stalked away.

"I don't want to be famous," Emilia said. "Or end up like Pablo Arrocha."

"Ah." Juan Miguel nodded sympathetically. "These are bad times."

"Los Mozos," Emilia said. "Are they out there?"

"Pay attention when you are first in line," Juan Miguel said seriously. "No listening to the radio or talking on your phone. If we help each other, everyone stays safe."

Two more taxis pulled in, making a queue of five cars along the sidewalk. Juan Miguel introduced Lobo and Felipe, both wiry men in their late 20's. Lobo's nickname clearly came from an oversized canine tooth, while Felipe had the bedroom eyes of a successful womanizer. Obviously deferring to Juan Miguel, both gave Emilia's hand a perfunctory shake. Neither spoke much.

Ricardo perched on the front fender of his taxi and smoked in sullen silence while scanning the intersection.

CHAPTER 9

Silvio met her at 10:00 pm at the safe house, packing beer, pizza, and a sack of apples.

"First day of your new career," he said, looking at her dubiously as Emilia met him in the courtyard. "You look like shit."

"Yeah, well," Emilia bristled. "You try sitting in a tin can for twelve hours while people scream into their cell phones."

She led Silvio into the house.

"Nice place you got here," Silvio stopped to blink at the green ping-pong table in the center of the living room. Two mismatched sofas, an end table, and a floor lamp huddled against the walls.

"*Norteamericano* spring break décor," Emilia said wryly and led him into the kitchen.

Silvio dumped his load on the table, taking in the cement countertop, rusty window frame, and the portable two burner gas cooktop that passed for a stove. "Kind of a change for you."

"I'll manage," Emilia said. She handed him a beer, forestalling some snide truth about how living in the Palacio Réal made her soft.

"Did Los Mozos show up to introduce themselves to the new driver?" Silvio whacked the top of the beer bottle against the edge of the table and the cap flew off.

"No." Emilia found a bottle opener in a drawer for her

own beer. "But the dispatcher, who styles himself Don Cisco, admitted that they're paying protection money to the gang. But nothing more than that."

Emilia's butt hurt and she had a thundering headache. Pepperoni and hot peppers smelled like heaven compared to sweaty vinyl and manufactured lavender. The muscles of her right leg kept cramping from the day-long dance between brake and accelerator in busy Acapulco traffic while she fought the manual transmission. She ripped off the narrow black tie and grabbed a slice of pizza.

"What about the other drivers?" Silvio prompted, before chomping half a slice in one bite. "Get anything out of them?"

"Nothing, besides some *pendejo* claiming my taxi is haunted." Emilia grinned around another bite.

Silvio nearly choked on a mouthful of beer. "Is it?"

"Sure. Arrocha navigated while I drove."

Silvio reached for another slice of pizza. "What do they talk about? Los Mozos?"

"It's a pretty busy outfit," Emilia observed. "There wasn't a lot of down time. When I was there, the other drivers mostly ignored me."

"So how much did you make?"

"Thirty percent of the meter and tips," Emilia said. "And I have to pay for my own gas. At that rate, the drivers must be starving to death."

Silvio waved his beer bottle at her. "This Don Cisco character probably pays his regulars 50 percent. He'll put you down as 50 percent, too, and pocket the difference."

"Doesn't matter," Emilia said, nettled that Silvio thought she was clueless. "It's not like I get to keep any of it. I have to turn it all over to Financial."

Silvio snorted. "Counting money. Campos's specialty."

"So what brings you all the way over here?" Emilia changed the subject before her loyalties were completely confused. "Mercedes busy tonight?"

"Remember that sighting of El Acólito in Veracruz?"

Emilia dropped her half-eaten slice of pizza. "He's been arrested, *Madre de Dios*—."

"The store owner retracted his statement," Silvio said. "Said it wasn't El Acólito at all."

"He was bought off," Emilia exclaimed.

"Or maybe it wasn't him."

Emilia poked at the remains of her pizza, too disappointed to finish it. "Veracruz police is probably riddled with informants."

"Same as here," Silvio said. "And everywhere else."

"The *federales* are never going to find him," Emilia said. "They've been paid off, too."

"Don't buy trouble, Cruz." Silvio stuffed the rest of her slice into his mouth, took a tiny velvet pouch out of the pocket of his jeans, and slid it across the table to Emilia. "Supposedly you just lost your husband. You should wear this. Widow in mourning and all that shit."

Emilia scrubbed her hands with a napkin from the takeout place before loosening the tiny drawstring threads. She shook out a thin gold band, misshapen and scratched from years spent on a hand that did hard work. "Was this Isabel's wedding band?" she asked, already knowing the answer.

"Yeah."

"I can't wear her ring." Emilia's fingers were clumsy with emotion as she juggled the ring back in the pouch.

Silvio's wife Isabel was murdered in a home invasion and the aftermath was as horrible as her death. Accused of the crime, Silvio ended up in jail. Emilia uncovered the truth, which didn't reflect well on Isabel, and connected the crime to a vast money laundering conspiracy run out of a casino. Silvio got back on his feet, as evidenced by his new relationship with Mercedes, but only Emilia knew what it had cost him to crawl back from the brink of devastation.

"Put it on, Cruz," Silvio said roughly. "Don't get stupid on me."

"It wouldn't be right. It's your memento of Isabel."

"You're out there alone, no backup." Silvio stood up abruptly, brandishing the empty pizza box as if to ward off any sentimentality. "The ring's a little bit of added protection. Campos says Los Mozos won't hurt a woman but we both know everybody and his brother on the street is going to lick their chops over you. If they see a ring, maybe the wolves will think twice."

Emilia gaped at him. Silvio was menacing, exasperating, emotionless, and obtuse. Yet at the most surprising moments, he was there for her in ways that mattered.

He shoved the pizza box in the trash can and left. The

velvet pouch and its painful memories stayed on the table.

Emilia found another beer and poked around the little bungalow. She was tired but not yet ready to face a second night in a strange bed, despite the many choices. Like many rental properties that catered to beach-loving students from *El Norte*, the place was jammed with beds. The upstairs rooms each held two narrow beds. Downstairs, the dining room had been converted into yet another bedroom. She'd slept there last night, under the chandelier with an ancient buffet as a bedside table.

She wandered outside and stood on the porch with the light off. The real charm of the old bungalow was its seclusion. It was on a cul-de-sac, with a thick stucco wall guarding it from the street, braced by solid corrugated gates. Metal spikes ran across the top of the entire enclosure. Some were bent by rust and vandalism but most were the daggers of old warriors pointed at the sky. The inner courtyard had a drive that could accommodate three cars parked end-to-end, which meant that the house itself was well away from the street.

Hot pink bougainvillea and ruddy flame vines created another layer of seclusion with masses of foliage blooming above the spikes. Bird of paradise and Mexican ginger bordered the drive. The ginger's red cone-like blooms nodded sleepily in the night air.

The back yard was mostly just a patio made from slabs of crushed coral aggregate. More plants crowded between the perimeter wall and the patio, arching over the edges to make a natural privacy screen. Crushed beer cans twinkled amidst the greenery. The place was ready for the next party with a stack of white plastic lawn chairs, a rough wooden table, and a grill made from half a barrel on an iron frame.

She wrote her cell phone number on the embossed Taxis Coco cards, then climbed into bed in the dining room wearing one of Kurt's old tee shirts. Night sounded different here. No comforting male breathing, no rhythmic sigh of the ocean. Instead, she heard city traffic and the monotonous hum of insects. Moonlight created a wedge of swirling dust motes that bounced off the brass chandelier above Emilia's feet.

The little pouch containing Isabel de Silvio's wedding band was on the buffet, within arm's reach. It went over her knuckle with ease. Emilia held up her hand. The worn gold band shone dully in the semi-darkness, a tangible symbol of commitment and fidelity.

It felt uncomfortably tight.

CHAPTER 10

By her third day, word was out that Taxis Coco had a female driver. Gawkers from other *sitios* crept along Avenida Bellavista, braking hard to pelt Taxis Coco drivers with ribald comments. Emilia heard 100 varieties of "*Oye! Is that the puta?*" as she waited by her taxi, gleefully noticed but wholly ignored.

Passengers had a similar reaction. Some got in the taxi, realized that the driver was female, and scrambled out in alarm. Others exclaimed loudly that the *sitio* was pulling a stunt.

But the novelty of a female driver also brought in more business. Don Cisco's double caterpillar moustache rippled in satisfaction as his pencil flew across his notebook.

Emilia eavesdropped on conversations about children, schools, wives, recipes for flan, garden fertilizer, muffler problems, shortcuts, basketball, and mothers-in-law. Ricardo once mentioned Arrocha's widow, Maria. Apparently, she was too ill to work. On a happier note, Lobo's wife was pregnant. A discussion about what color to paint the baby's bedroom went on for 20 minutes in front of the dispatch booth. None of the drivers, including Lobo, wondered if his wife had an opinion.

No one talked about the shooting, the late Pablo Arrocha, or Los Mozos.

More importantly, Emilia identified two kinds of Taxis

Coco drivers. It was all about what happened when they were at the head of the line, like Pablo Arrocha on the night he was killed. All the drivers got out of their taxis; clearly no one was going to be a sitting duck again.

The first type of driver stood still on the sidewalk, scanning the intersection for danger like a military guard. Richard Heredia led this category, although he occasionally perched on his fender and smoked in studied silence.

The second type of driver paced nervously as they watched the intersection. The younger drivers were all in this category.

Whoever wasn't first in line loitered around the dispatch booth, talking and laughing like good-natured brothers. Don Cisco was aloof as he presided over his podium, but occasionally joined in.

Whether stock still or pacing, the first driver in line never indulged in conversation but scanned the intersection until a passenger got into the taxi. The taxi always pulled away from the curb as quickly as possible, leaving the danger zone to the next in line.

The fear was contagious. Emilia caught it right away.

Emilia was the fifth in line, giving her time to grab a latte at Café Coco's takeaway counter. She came back to see her taxi sagging on its hindquarters like an injured dog.

Once upon a time the taxi had four tires. Now a rubber

ribbon with treads was draped around the rear passenger side wheel.

Traffic flowed past the crippled taxi. A couple hovered over the ATM machine under the bank sign. Don Cisco was at his podium, absorbed in his columns of figures. Nobody gossiped on the bench in front. Four other drivers sat in their vehicles.

Even the first *taxista* in line.

And so it begins.

Her cooling latte was relegated to a cup holder in front. Emilia opened the trunk and lifted out the heavy cross-shaped tire iron. Thankfully, the spare was a match for the tires on the vehicle, not some anemic temporary only good for a trip to the closest *llanteria*.

Felipe and Lobe got out of their vehicles to watch the show.

Ignoring them, Emilia lay on the sidewalk to shove the jack in place and crank up the taxi's sagging back end. It was hot, heavy work. Sweat soaked through her blouse.

The tire iron spun through slippery hands as she worked the lugs loose. The tire was a complete loss with the sidewall deliberately slashed beyond repair. A new tire would cost her at least 500 pesos. That would be a big bite out of 30 percent if she didn't have the good sense to pocket a portion of her tips like she knew all the other drivers did.

Somebody gave a shout. Felipe and Lobo trotted off. The taxis ahead of Emilia rolled forward, leaving hers beached like a whale against the curb.

She lowered the jack and Taxi Number 17 settled onto all four tires again.

When Emilia popped the trunk and stowed the ruined tire in the well, Don Cisco scurried across the sidewalk and shook his pencil at her. "Go home, Ester," he said. The moustache drooped like two sad caterpillars. "You're too dirty to stay on shift."

"Someone owes me for a new tire," Emilia said, picking up her tools.

"Don't lock your tire iron in the trunk," Don Cisco said quietly. "Put it on the floor of your front seat. If Los Mozos comes again, you need to protect yourself."

Emilia hefted the heavy crossbar in her hand. Each end of the tire iron's four ends had a flanged opening that fit the hexagonal lugs. The tool made a clumsy weapon.

"All the drivers have put their tire irons in the front seat." Don Cisco opened the taxi's passenger door. "It is good to be prepared."

It occurred to Emilia that he was caught in a hard place. Don Cisco knew who destroyed her tire but was bound by codes of driver loyalty and male solidarity. Moreover, his position as owner of the *sitio* meant that he didn't fix cars or change tires. If he wanted to preserve the balance of power, this advice was the best he could do.

Emilia laid the tire iron on the floor of the front seat.

CHAPTER 11

Emilia bought a new tire at a *llanteria*, then showered at the safe house and took an unlicensed taxi to the south end of Parque Bellavista. She resisted the urge to pause by the window of Joyas Alameda and strolled to the western side of the park along Universidad.

The day was warm, the sky was a brilliant blue, and it was a relief to escape the confines of Arrocha's taxi. She passed teens in school uniforms headed to Vips for a sandwich or Cinépolis to see a matinee. Tourists were easily identified by sunburned noses, socks with sandals, and sudden stops to consult an actual paper guidebook. Playground rides twirled to calliope music but the real crowds would come later.

Emilia picked out a gap-toothed woman who presided over an ingenious stand made up of a wheeled cart, two coolers of fruit, and a chopping board.

"Did you hear what happened at the *sitio* on Avenida Bellavista?" Emilia asked casually after asking for pineapple and producing ten pesos.

"I heard they got a lady driver." The woman shook her head. "*Oye.* Crazy."

"I meant the shooting. A driver named Pablo Arrocha was killed." Emilia watched the knife flash in a swift ballet as the woman skinned the pineapple to expose juicy yellow fruit. Four downward strokes and the pineapple fell into slabs and was quickly diced into chunks. The woman used the flat of the knife to scoop half the fruit into a plastic cup.

"Ah, the *pobrecito*." The woman stuck a plastic fork into the fruit like a feather in a cap and presented it to Emilia. "I didn't know him so good."

"They say a gang killed him." Emilia dropped her voice. "The *sitio* paid them, but a gang called Los Mozos killed him. It was in the newspaper."

The woman gave a sorrowful shrug and filled another cup with a deft flip of her knife. "Everybody pays somebody."

Emilia edged closer to the stand. "Do you pay Los Mozos, too?"

A second pineapple arrived on the chopping board with a thud. "I don't know this Los Mozos," the woman said. "Maybe they just bother the taxis."

A young couple with two excited toddlers moved in and Emilia edged away. The fruit exploded in her mouth like a cool, sweet bomb. She ate the pineapple slowly, savoring the natural sugar rush as she assessed the other vendors. Which of them was an easy a target for an extortion gang?

She tossed the empty plastic cup into a barrel emblazoned with the face of the mayor, Carlota Montoya Perez. The barrels were sprinkled around the bay, but those outside tourist areas had quickly disappeared. Coincidentally, dozens of *parrilla* restaurants had new charcoal grills.

A toy vendor, whose cart had so many balloons attached to the handle it was in danger of lifting off, was more than willing to chat. "Los Mozos?" the vendor echoed as Emilia examined his offerings. "Sounds like a new band."

"No, Los Mozos isn't a band." Emilia picked out a rubber ball tethered to an elastic string on one end and shiny streamers on the other.

"I know." The vendor was a stooped old man with a striped apron and hands knotted with arthritis. "But that would be nice, eh?"

Emilia picked out a set of jacks. She'd give the toys to her cousin Alvaro's children. "Things are hard in Acapulco now. Even around here."

"Los Mozos isn't in the park," the vendor said with a shrug. "Not yet."

"Has someone said they're coming?" Emilia dropped coins into a hand curled into a permanent cup.

The money disappeared into a homemade belt pouch. "There's talk. I watch."

"You know what they look like?"

"The drivers said two men threatened Don Cisco himself." The vendor shook his head. "Enforcers, I think. Men who would threaten a respectable man like Don Cisco will have evil written all over their faces."

Emilia gathered up her purchases and made a show of looking around. "The *sitio* is so close. Aren't you afraid?"

"Ignacio keeps us safe," the vendor revealed.

"Do you pay him?"

"Of course. Every Friday." His cupped fingers poked over her shoulder at the street. "Look, there he is now."

Emilia jerked her head around so fast she nearly lost her balance. A police cruiser waited at the light. The toy vendor waved, as did the woman at the fruit stand.

From behind the wheel of the cruiser, a uniformed cop waved back.

Emilia recognized the *pendejo*. His name wasn't Ignacio.

CHAPTER 12

Emilia quickly established the dispatcher's routine. Don Cisco arrived at the *sitio* before 9:00 am, stayed until 2:00 pm when he left to go home for a meal, and came back two hours later, remaining in his booth until closing time at 11:00 pm. His only day off was Sunday, which meant that he deposited the protection money payments to Los Mozos via the account at Banamex Bank every day during his break.

She didn't know if that detail was significant or not, as she sat alone on the bench in front of the dispatch booth, hoping to overhear one of Don Cisco's many cell phone conversations.

Ricardo was first in line. He stood by his taxi, scanning the intersection.

A young girl walked up, one shoulder sagging under the weight of the strap of a heavy sportsbag.

"Ester!" Don Cisco pointed to Emilia. "You take this fare."

"Me?" Emilia shoved her sunglasses into her hair and squinted at the dispatcher. Jumping the line was a serious breach of etiquette. "Ricardo is ahead of me. I'll tell him."

"No. Not this time." Don Cisco's gaze narrowed. He scribbled on a scrap of paper and held it out. "Here's the address."

The teen followed Emilia to the car. She wore a revealing crop top and a denim skirt that barely covered her ass.

Racoon circles around dark eyes were the product of exhaustion, not makeup. Blue polish flaked off her fingernails. Greasy hair fell long and loose and was patchy at the hairline, a sure sign of poor nutrition. Her legs were those of a high school runner, however, and she wore a decent pair of cross trainers.

A young girl taking a *sitio* in the middle of the afternoon wasn't a rarity, especially if she was in a school uniform. Music practice, ballet lessons, coding classes. This girl wasn't going to any of those places.

Emilia ignored Ricardo's glower as she pulled out.

"What's your name?" she asked her passenger.

The girl met her eyes in the rearview mirror. "Gabi. My name's Gabi."

"I'm Ester."

"I never saw a girl drive a taxi before."

"We all got to make a living somehow." The light changed and Emilia drove on. "So, where are you headed today?"

Gabi picked at her nail polish. "Didn't he give you the address?"

Second gear stuck. Emilia pumped the clutch and managed to shift into third before the RPMs went into the red zone. "Yeah, I meant, what's the place? School? Sports club?"

There was a long pause. "My father is waiting for me," Gabi said finally.

"Sure." Emilia glanced at the rearview again. Gabi had no

idea where she was going.

The girl peeled polish off her thumbnail. A knee bounced nervously.

"Does your father know you're coming?" Emilia asked.

"My father?"

"Does he know you're coming? In a taxi?"

"The other drivers never ask questions," Gabi said pointedly. She pulled a cell phone out of her skirt pocket and proceeded to tap on the screen.

Emilia drove on, torn between seeing this through to protect the cover job and pulling over, arresting Gabi, and confiscating what was probably half a million pesos worth of cocaine.

Gabi scrolled through some never-ending string of interest. The knee continued to betray her, pumping up and down like a piston.

The address turned out to be a bar called La Tumba. *The Grave*. It was located on a fairly wide street, stuffed between a paint store and used clothing market. Some joker had painted the front stucco black.

The wide front door was propped open with a chunk of cinder block. As Emilia braked, she saw flashes of light and color from a television mounted over the beer taps. A bartender leaned against the counter and gazed up at the screen. A window striped with iron bars revealed four *machos* at a table covered with Pacifico beer bottles. An obviously empty knapsack sagged at the foot of each chair.

Couriers, waiting to redistribute Gabi's haul.

"You sure this is the place?" Emilia asked. She turned off the meter. The fare was 400 pesos.

"I guess." Gabi sounded resigned.

"I'll wait for you," Emilia said. "Go in. Talk to your . . . father. I'll wait and take you home."

"No." Fear animated Gabi's face. "You can't do that. Somebody will come out and pay you. You can't come in."

"How are you getting home?"

"What business is it of yours?"

As Gabi reached for the door handle, Emilia shoved one of the Taxis Coco cards under her nose. "Here's my number. Call me if . . . if you need a ride. If things get rough in there."

"I can take care of myself," Gabi said.

"You don't have to do anything you don't want to do," Emilia said, still holding out the card. "You call me. I'll come get you. Doesn't matter where you are or what time it is. I'll come for you."

"You're pushy," Gabi said.

"Take the card."

Gabi stuck the card in her skirt pocket, grabbed the bag, and trudged into the bar.

At the table, the four men drained their beers as one. They all reached for their knapsacks and followed Gabi towards the rear. Emilia knew that when the drugs in Gabi's duffle were apportioned out, at least one of the couriers would use the girl. Give her a line of coke to make her pliant, then treat her like a rag doll.

The bartender came to the doorway. He was a big man in

a stained apron over a tee shirt and jeans. He motioned for Emilia to roll down the passenger side window. When she did, he dropped a rubber band-wrapped roll of peso bills on the seat and jerked his thumb at the street ahead.

Emilia put the car into gear and pulled away. She had never felt so helpless.

She braked behind Juan Miguel at the head of the line. He stood on the sidewalk watching the intersection but strolled over to her taxi as she got out.

"I hear you went to La Tumba," he said in a low voice.

"Rough neighborhood," Emilia replied. La Tumba clearly wasn't a one-time run but a routine other drivers knew well.

"He knows about the *propina*." Juan Miguel cut his eyes to the dispatch booth.

Emilia nodded. Juan Miguel went back to his taxi.

It was an unspoken word of caution not to pocket a cut of the tip for this particular trip. The *propina* from the bartender was enormous. The wad contained 3000 pesos for a 400 pesos ride and strained the zipper on the lockbag.

Emilia wondered if this was a test. Was Don Cisco checking to see if she would steal tips? Or if she would help mule drugs?

Don Cisco didn't say anything as she turned in her earnings for the day. When the gates of the safe house closed with a clang, Emilia inhaled the last whiff of lavender

Fabuloso and pried her hands off the wheel, but her thoughts kept churning.

Dinner was a salad of watermelon chunks topped with shredded *cotija* cheese, a squirt of lime, and a generous salting of Tajin spice mix. The combination of cold tang and warm spice was just what she craved after being cooped up in the taxi with a load of anger and frustration.

As she speared the chunks of watermelon with a fork, Emilia opened the big binder of *Las Perdidas* from her desk in the squadroom.

Las Perdidas. The Lost Ones.

The faces were familiar, not because she personally knew them, but because she'd lived with this record of failure for so long.

The earliest entry was for a fellow beat cop who disappeared from a club not so different from La Tumba. The most recent entry was the daughter of a former hooker who became a cop. The mother made a surprisingly good officer but was no closer to finding her daughter than before.

The binder held more than 40 records. Most began with an official Missing Persons report and expanded as Emilia included bits and pieces. Photographs, morgue reports of unidentified women passed on by Prade, and letters written to the police department by distraught family members too frightened to appear at a police station to file a report. Afraid of retribution, all they could do was plead for someone to find out what happened to their child and offer a picture of a girl whose life had almost certainly ended in a bad way.

Emilia went through all the records, hoping to see Gabi's face in one of the more recent ones. The girl's good muscle tone and clear skin meant she hadn't been on the street long. The lifespan of a pretty drug mule was invariably cut short by pills, alcohol, and hard men. Emilia hadn't seen any needle marks on her arms or legs, so perhaps she wasn't shooting up.

Yet.

She lingered on the entry for Lila Jimenez Lata. The girl was lovely, with short black hair and china doll features. After her father died and her mother, a former hooker named Yolanda Lata, took off to find another man, Lila lived with her fiercely controlling grandmother. The girl ran away, ending up one of El Acólito's human trafficking victims. Yet when Lila had the chance to escape, she chose to stay with the monster.

Lila and Gabi were about the same age. Both should be in school, writing essays about Octavio Paz's poetry and cheating on algebra exams.

Meeting boys named Pablo.

CHAPTER 13

Her last fare of the day was an enormous woman whose knees banged into the glove compartment every time Emilia drove over a bump. With enough padding to protect a polar bear, the woman was too busy bellowing at her husband and three children in the back seat to notice.

The inside of the taxi stank like a poisonous mix of old peas, warm peaches, and sweaty vinyl. Emilia turned the air conditioning to MAX HIGH and hit another pothole.

She dropped them off at a resort on the east side of the bay and they stiffed her on a tip.

The Palacio Réal was only 10 minutes away. Emilia thought longingly of a dip in the waterfall pool and a couple of mojitos in the Pasodoble Bar. Instead, she reluctantly shoved the car into gear and headed west. When she got to the highway the little flip-up door of the glove compartment fell open. Emilia leaned across the console and slapped the door closed. Something rattled like cheap castanets and the door fell open again.

By the time Emilia found a PEMEX station, the entire glove box was hanging onto the dashboard by an act of will. A map and some packets of tissues tumbled out and hit the tire iron on the floor.

Hoping to prevent a total systems failure, Emilia hastily emptied out the box, cursing the detailers who soaked the car in purple Fabuloso but didn't bother to clean out the glove compartment. The dark interior was a graveyard of dirty tissues and crumpled candy wrappers. Batting that detritus aside, Emilia found an expired box of aspirin, a tire pressure gauge, a remote control for a gate, half-melted peppermints, and a crumpled scrap of paper.

Sticky candy stuck to her fingers as Emilia smoothed the paper. Block printing fairly shouted at her.

Stop what you are doing. You know what we mean. Do you want us to teach you a LESSON?

Los Mozos knew who she was. Emilia nearly levitated out of the taxi.

The PEMEX station was busy, cars swinging out of traffic to fuel up, engines constantly coughing to life or shutting down, fuel gauges dinging and gurgling under the awning protecting the pumps from the hot sun. Emilia ignored the noise as she dug her cell phone out of the center console and searched *El Sol de Acapulco's* online archive for a photo of the note left by Los Mozos claiming responsibility for Arrocha's murder. Not a handwriting analyst by any means, but she could see enough similarities to decide the two missives were written by the same hand.

After another rush of panic, Emilia forced herself to think logically. If Los Mozos wanted to send her a message, they wouldn't have wadded it up and stuck it in the back of her glove compartment. No, this had been in Arrocha's taxi for some time. A threat for him? A threat for Don Cisco that

Arrocha found?

If Los Mozos gang members were handing out threats, they had to be around someplace.

A dozen possibilities, none of them good, whirled through her head as Emilia drove back to the *sitio* with the note stashed with her phone in the console. The other contents of the glove compartment swam around the floor of the passenger seat on top of the tire iron.

A dark blue sedan was parked against the curb in the third spot. Emilia coasted to a stop behind it.

Two men dressed in casual office clothing stood by the dispatch booth talking to Don Cisco. As Emilia got out of her vehicle, Don Cisco pointed her out. Both men turned, faces radiating the studied blankness of city bureaucrats.

Or every witness who ever tried to lie their way out of an interview.

She met them on the sidewalk next to the taxi.

"Ester Ruiz Garcia?" the taller one asked but didn't wait for an answer. "We're from the City of Acapulco Department of Transportation Licensing. We need to see your permit."

It was common knowledge that every *taxista* was subject to shakedowns. A *mordita*--little bite--paid to traffic cops or city officials. Even parking lot attendants got a taste by letting drivers run up a meter while taking a nap.

"It's on display for passengers." Emilia folded her arms and rested her backside against the car door. "Same as in every other taxi."

"Get it for us."

Emilia didn't move. "Why does the city of Acapulco need to see my permit?"

"Routine check."

A car door slammed at the head of the line. Juan Miguel circled around and stood on the sidewalk to watch. Ricardo joined him for the show.

"Are you checking every driver's permit?" Emilia asked.

"We're checking yours." The taller man stepped forward, his belt buckle nearly pressing against Emilia's forearm.

Pendejo. Emilia pushed herself off the car, forcing him to take a step back. She swung open the passenger door and grabbed the plastic document holder. The taller man plucked it out of her hand.

"Invalid," he proclaimed.

"It's brand new," Emilia protested but the game was on. They were following the standard shakedown formula. A couple of hundred pesos would magically cure the problem.

"Wrong safety inspection," the man said.

"Checking permits must be thirsty work," Emilia said. She dug in a pocket. "You must need a coffee? A *refresco*?"

The man wielded a fat marker like a cigar, passing it by his nose as he sniffed the aroma of success. "This is your official notice that your permit is invalid and has been confiscated," the man said. He drew a thick red line across the permit.

"Wait a minute," Emilia protested. A shakedown didn't work this way. "You can't do that."

The shorter man produced a red ticket, inserted it in the now empty plastic sleeve and dropped it on the passenger seat. "It's illegal to accept fares in this vehicle until you have a valid permit."

"Another permit?"

"You can reapply in 90 days."

The two men got into the dark sedan, taking her crucified permit with them. Emilia's brain buzzed with fury but she had the presence of mind to snap a picture of the *placas* before the sedan disappeared around the corner.

Juan Miguel and Ricardo stood rigidly on the sidewalk, emanating confusion and alarm.

Emilia slammed the passenger door as hard as she could. Don Cisco flinched as the sound invaded the sanctity of the dispatch booth, but he didn't lift his eyes from his ever-present notebook.

"Ester," Juan Miguel called.

Emilia didn't wait. She threw herself into the taxi and nearly rammed Ricardo's rear bumper as she pulled away.

What a shit detective you turned out to be.

CHAPTER 14

"More hazing than I expected." The BlackBerry almost vibrated with genuine sympathy from Campos. "We can get a new permit. How are you feeling about the assignment otherwise?"

"Frustrated," Emilia admitted. "Nobody at the *sitio* talks about Los Mozos. The only thing I've gathered so far is that Los Mozos has two enforcers. Even the park vendors know they threatened the dispatcher."

"Two enforcers," Campos echoed. "Corroborates what Donoso Garay told us."

"I've got a lead or two to follow," Emilia said. The note from the glove compartment waited on the pingpong table as she gyrated around the room in a sports bra and shorts. A head-clearing workout on the back patio had generated a new plan of attack to make the most of this unexpected free time. "I found a note that might be from Los Mozos. A couple of old friends might have something for me, too."

"Good work, Detective," Campos said. "Very enterprising. I'll wait for you to pull more threads before nagging for details."

Silvio could learn a lot from Campos. The simple praise put yesterday into perspective. She threw a couple of air punches at the drooping floor lamp with her free hand.

"Will you be talking to Señor Donoso Garay soon?" Emilia asked. "Show him some mug shots?"

"Maybe we'll wait until you have a few more details," Campos said vaguely.

"Something happened that could be related, *teniente*," she continued. "I don't know if it's connected, but cops never like coincidences."

"What's going on?"

"The *sitio* could be muling drugs as a link in a narco distribution operation."

There was a long pause.

"*Teniente*?" Emilia stopped shadowboxing with the floor lamp.

Despite its age, the BlackBerry delivered a clear connection. But as the silence stretched out, Emilia checked the tiny screen to make sure the connection was still live.

"What makes you say that?" Campos asked at length.

"I drove a girl to a bar called La Tumba." Emilia recounted the episode, including the bartender's extravagant overpayment.

"A girl with a bag," Campos said meditatively. "Could have been a waitress. A hooker. Pole dancer."

"Or Los Mozos knows that the *sitio* is distributing," Emilia said. "No wonder the gang's demands keep going up." It was an obvious deduction but Emilia offered it anyway.

"Maybe," Campos said. "But let's keep that thought to ourselves. Relax and I'll be in touch when we get the permit situation resolved."

"Thank you, *teniente*."

Emilia ended the call, hoping she hadn't oversold Campos on the notion that she had leads to follow. It was more like checking on cockroaches.

A couple of years ago, Emilia beat out Omar Montez Serrat in the grueling competition for a detective's badge. He asked her out afterwards and she had a crush on him for about six hours.

He was now an undercover officer with the Organized Crime unit.

Montez walked into the *taqueria* looking like one of the *machos* at La Tumba. Slouchy jeans hung off his hips and an open button-down shirt flapped over a ragged tee. A well-worn knapsack was slung over one shoulder. Montez recognized her immediately and made a beeline for the table where Emilia waited.

He swooped in for a kiss, brown eyes glittering. "*Hola*, Ester," he said. His lips were hot and dry against her cheek.

"Jorge," Emilia said, using his cover name. "It suits you."

"Some days I wake up and wonder who I am today." Montez took a seat, seemingly exhilarated by the tryst.

He was thinner than she remembered, with hair pulled back in a man bun from a low forehead. His eyes darted around the *taqueria*, although it was little more than a collection of plastic tables in a garage open to a side street. Like Emilia, he angled his chair to keep the sidewalk in view.

Organized Crime was the police department's first line of defense against the criminal gangs that were woven through fabric of life in Acapulco. Most of the officers were undercover, like Montez. They drifted through the worst streets, collecting intelligence and following leads back to cartel *sicarios*.

Sometimes they even ran with a gang for a time, creating consequences and moral dilemmas everyone pretended not to see. The dangerous work came with bonus pay, but also the promise of torture, death, and dismemberment if a cover didn't hold up.

"You hungry?" Montez said. He rubbed his hands together, generating a sandpapery sound.

"I'm buying," Emilia said.

"In that case, I'll have whatever he's making." Montez grinned. The rounded cheeks she remembered were hollow now and his teeth were stained.

Every customer had a ringside seat for the grill made from half a barrel sliced lengthwise and stoked with charcoal in the well. A sweaty man with a bloody apron and a cigarette in his mouth flipped chunks of fish and pork onto the sizzling surface with a broad spatula. His assistant, a kid about 10 years old, brought them cans of Pacifico beer, warm tortillas on a paper plate, and plastic-shrouded melamine platters heaped with meat, rice and a pile of coarsely chopped tomatoes, white onions, and cilantro.

In the dim interior, it was impossible to tell if the food was seasoned with cigarette ash. Emilia decided now was not the time to care.

"So word is that Financial Crimes owns the taxi murder near the Cinépolis," Montez said. He shoved a plastic fork into the mound of rice in front of him. Half spilled onto the table. "How did that happen?"

"It started as an extortion case." Emilia scooped salsa and meat into a soft folded tortilla. "Gang bilking the drivers for money."

A woman around Emilia's age shuffled out of a doorway covered with a striped blanket. A polyester skirt hung to her knees and her feet were bare. A baby was cocooned in a sling across her chest, so tightly wrapped in sheeting that all Emilia could see of the child was a thatch of spiky hair.

She called to the kid acting as waiter as he chopped tomatoes and onions. The man at the grill growled a reply. Obviously torn between the two parents, the kid went to the mother. She clouted him on the side of the head, knocking him back a couple of steps.

The father shouted at her, flinging droplets of sweat as he shook his spatula at the woman. At least the boy worked. She was nothing but a *bruja* who drove his customers away. The mother disappeared into the room behind the striped curtain. Emilia's heart went out to the boy as his father barked orders. The kid scurried back to his tomatoes.

Montez ignored the moment of domestic bliss as he shoveled rice into his mouth. "I wouldn't ask around for just anyone," he said. "You're still one hot *chica*."

"You're still good at the bullshit," Emilia said.

The sun was low in the sky and the tempo of the neighborhood was shifting, readying for darkness and the danger that it brought. Workmen in paint-stained coveralls trudged past the restaurant, knapsacks and tools over their shoulders. Mothers called to children from open windows. A couple of working girls loitered across the street, looking none too clean. They were long past their prime but still eking out a living.

Montez guffawed. A grain of rice landed on his arm. He flicked it onto the floor.

"I'm listening," Emilia said.

"I got something. Nothing firm, you know," he said. "But the rumor on the street is that Los Mozos is small. Splinter group. A couple of *sicarios* out of favor with *el jefe*. Executed the driver to show they can pull their weight. That's why they didn't take a trophy. Didn't need to go to all the trouble."

The food was suddenly less appetizing. "All they needed to do was claim responsibility," Emilia guessed.

"Sure. Whoever they're working for says *oye*, maybe these two aren't shit for brains after all. Might be worth keeping them around." Montez assembled a taco. His forehead wore a sheen of sweat.

Killers occasionally took body parts to display and terrify rivals. Indeed, the one and only date Emilia had with Montez ended when a gang tossed severed heads onto the dance floor of the Mercury Club.

"You're sure about this?" Emilia pressed. "The shooter

didn't have time to take a trophy."

Montez reached for Emilia's plastic fork and messed around with her salsa. "We would have made a good team, you know that?"

"Water under the bridge, Jorge." Emilia took the fork out of his hand. Montez's fingers were ice-cold. "Who are these jokers working for?"

"Like who's the *jefe*?"

"Yes. Who were they trying to impress?"

"No idea." Montez took a bite of his taco.

"What about names?"

"Nobody's got names. Los Mozos keeps a real low profile." He snorted at his own joke. "Until they didn't."

"Is that all you've got?"

"Fucking late," Montez muttered as he let his half-eaten taco slide out of his fingers.

A whip-thin man wearing the requisite *macho* uniform and carrying a knapsack threaded his way past the other table to take a seat at theirs. "Jorge," he grunted and thumped fists with Montez.

"This is Ester." Montez cocked his head in Emilia's direction.

"Girl taxi driver from Taxis Coco." The *macho* leered at her. "Everybody's heard of you."

"You got a name?" Emilia asked.

"They call me El Gatito." He licked his lips. "I'm a little cat with nine lives."

"You need a beer?"

"I like this one," El Gatito said to Montez.

As the two men talked in low tones, using cryptic shorthand she didn't catch, Emilia bought a beer for the newcomer and a second for Montez. She didn't like either El Gatito or the situation Montez had put her in. To add to her discomfort, she was beginning to dislike the way Montez was sweating.

Everybody's heard of you. Montez might think he was doing her a favor by putting her in touch with his source, but he'd compromised her cover.

"Time's wasting," she interrupted.

"Tell Ester what you found out," Montez said.

El Gatito licked his lips again. "You're asking about Los Mozos, yeah?"

"You got some names for me?" Emilia asked.

"No names," El Gatito said. "Something better."

"Go on."

"Say, 500 pesos better."

Emilia shrugged.

"There's a contract out on Los Mozos." El Gatito leaned in. "That *sitio* has a godfather. Those *pendejos* from Los Mozos what killed that driver? They moved in on his territory. They're over. Bang, bang. Los Mozos is going down."

"A contract is a good way to start a street war," Emilia said.

"The *sitio* would be the prize." El Gatito gave her a ferrety grin. "If there are any drivers left."

"I need names," Emilia said. "Whose name is on the contract?"

"How about Señor Encapuchado?" El Gatito guffawed and took a long pull of his beer.

Emilia flipped the mangy *macho* a small smile and fanned out 500 pesos worth of *taxista* tips. "What about a name for this godfather?"

"That was for the tidbit about the contract." The man snatched up the cash. "I find out the name of the godfather, it'll cost the same."

Emilia tossed the plastic fork on her half-empty platter. This *pendejo* probably made up his story out of thin air. "Nice chat," she said to Montez. She stuffed 200 pesos in his shirt pocket for the meal and headed for the street.

"Ester!" Montez caught up with her on the sidewalk. "*Oye*, why'd you leave so fast?"

"You fucked with my cover," Emilia said, keeping her voice low as she pulled him into the twilight shadow cast by an awning. "Your boy Gatito is going to tell everybody that he met the famous girl taxi driver so he can pump himself up like a big man. What were you thinking?"

"Yeah, about that." Montez swung around to block her way. "He likes you. Really likes you."

"Great." Emilia unconsciously drew back.

"He's willing to do a deal."

"What kind of a deal?"

"The three of us go to my place. It's not far. You spread your legs and he'll give me a real sweet deal on some *queso blanco.*"

"You want me to fuck your source so you can score cheap *queso*?" Emilia asked in disbelief.

Queso blanco, or white cheese, was slang for cocaine.

"Come on." Montez peered around Emilia's shoulder to make sure El Gatito was still in the *taqueria*. "He won't last three minutes. Then you and me can take up where we left off."

"You're a cop," Emilia sputtered. "Not some coked up pimp."

Montez plucked at her tee shirt. "Come on, *chica*. You owe me."

Emilia batted his hand away "I'll get you help. Rehab. Whatever it takes."

Montez threw his head back to howl with laughter. "Are you my *mami*?" he said. "If I need a little joy now and then, who gets hurt?"

There were needle marks on his neck. He was shooting straight into his veins.

"You stay safe, *amigo*," Emilia said.

She ran across the street and kept going until she was sure no one had followed her.

Emilia sat on the porch and put her aching feet up on the railing. After the encounter with Montez and El Gatito, she had walked the length and breadth of Parque Bellavista. No one recognized the name Los Mozos, except for a woman in a *papelería* who had once sold Pablo Arrocha a set of colored pencils. Over a rack of postcards and souvenir pens, she told Emilia that she was grateful that her store had so far been spared.

A copy of *La Jornada* from the man selling newspapers at the kiosk earned her a click of the tongue and a meandering story about a gang who'd threatened a friend who lived in Ixtapa. The boy who shined shoes at the top of the park whispered that she should talk to Ignacio on Friday.

Her phone beeped with a text from Kurt. He missed her. Missed Mexican food. Protests continued in Hong Kong.

She texted him back, mindful not to reveal anything about her assignment that would compromise her cover even more than Montez already had. But she couldn't resist tossing out a subtle reference to Laura in *Diamond Run.* Kurt caught it right away. *Madre de Dios*, she missed him.

As promised, neither mentioned the half-spoken proposal.

Kurt signed off, reminding her that Hong Kong was 13 hours ahead and he had to work. Emilia sent him a heart emoji and stayed on the porch.

Maybe the day hadn't been a total loss. Maybe Montez's source was onto something.

She mulled over the scant information she had collected so far on Los Mozos. The gang had at least two enforcers. Perhaps one of them was the shooter, whose ambition outstripped his smarts. Montez thought they tried to prove their usefulness to a *jefe*. Maybe, but by killing Arrocha, the gang had come to the attention of a godfather; someone who considered the *sitio* to be under his protection. A contract was out, but Los Mozos was at least savvy enough to keep the names of its members a secret.

Gota a gota. Emilia wondered if Los Mozos was a Colombian bunch. If they had a shred of sense, they'd go back to Bogota and hope this godfather didn't have a long arm.

A *sitio* with a godfather, running couriers to a bar called La Tumba. An invisible gang with two enforcers and a price on at least one head.

It wasn't much, but it was a start.

Gota a gota.

CHAPTER 15

"Viva Taxis?" The twin caterpillars smooching on Don Cisco's upper lip twitched in fury. "The rotten scoundrels who want to put me out of business?"

"That's what I heard," Emilia offered. "The owner of Viva Taxis bribed the city to invalidate my permit."

"A thieving villain," Don Cisco sputtered.

Not only did the dispatcher resemble Tin Tan, but he sounded like the movie actor, circa 1960.

"I found out because I have a friend who works in an office . . ." Emilia trailed off with a shrug.

The drivers clustered around the dispatch booth muttered and shuffled their feet. They understood how the system worked.

"In these trying times." Don Cisco threw his hands up. "This is what happens to an honest businessman."

"I submitted a complaint and they gave me a new one." Emilia hoped she sounded convincing.

In reality, Lieutenant Campos had squeezed somebody, who squeezed somebody else, who squeezed somebody else, until the truth popped out. The new permit, an exact copy of the original, was delivered to the safe house by a messenger service.

Her swift return caused a ripple of excitement albeit disguised by manly snorts of incredulity and off-color jokes about favors only women could do. Emilia let it wash over her, detecting an undercurrent of respect. In the eyes of the other drivers, she'd confronted the system and won, while poking a sharp stick in a rival's eye at the same time.

"So now what?" Don Cisco demanded. He waved his pencil. "Are all of you here to pose for pictures? Move along."

He included Emilia, but the corners of his eyes crinkled in a silent message. *Welcome back.*

Juan Miguel caught up with Emilia as she headed for her taxi at the end of the line. "Ester!" He took her hands in both of his and gave her a traditional kiss on each cheek. "Very impressive. You are a problem solver."

"That's some story." Ricardo slouched in the other man's wake.

"Ester, you seem very fit," Juan Miguel said, taking a step back. "Do you play basketball?"

It was an odd question. "In school," Emilia replied. "I played center. Why do you ask?"

"You see?" Juan Miguel pumped a fist in triumph towards Ricardo. "It is the Virgin's hand, sending Ester to us."

"What's going on?" Emilia asked warily.

"Will you practice with us?" Juan Miguel's face lit with enthusiasm. "We play in the men's three on three basketball league. We need six to practice and Lobo sprained his wrist."

"This is professional level," Ricardo scoffed.

"Ester can practice with us," Juan Miguel reasoned. "She's tall."

"When?"

"Tonight," Juan Miguel said. "At the Escuela Maria Regina. You know the school?"

"I know where it is," Emilia said. "I'll be there."

Don Cisco gave a shout to Juan Miguel. He saw a tourist waiting and trotted off.

"You shouldn't have agreed to play," Ricardo said, his eyes narrowed at Emilia. "It's not for girls."

"I'll let you know if I can't keep up," Emilia said. "So what did I miss? Los Mozos make an appearance?"

Ricardo whipped an unlit cigarette out of his mouth, his lighter in the other hand. "Shut up," he said fiercely, his voice low. "Do you want things to get worse? We don't talk about them."

"How come nobody has heard of them?" Emilia pressed.

Juan Miguel's taxi drove off. Felipe moved into the first position and immediately got out of the car. Paco drove into the second spot.

"Fuck, a crazy woman." Ricardo dropped his voice even further. "We've all heard of Los Mozos. You think we can't read?"

"No other business is paying protection money to Los Mozos." Emilia matched his hush. "Just the *sitio*."

"I told you to shut up," Ricardo said savagely. He flicked his unlit cigarette into the gutter and jumped into his taxi to cruise forward.

Emilia started her engine and eased along until she was barely a breath away from his bumper.

Ricardo spun out of his car and squatted by her open

driver's window. "Two things, Ester," he said. His breath stank like nicotine. "One, we don't talk about Los Mozos. Two, you can forget about going to La Tumba again."

"La Tumba? What's so special about that place?"

Ricardo jabbed a finger at her. "I didn't say there was anything special about it."

"No? What about the bartender and his wad of pesos?"

"The money isn't the point. It's a bad place. You stay away."

"Don Cisco told me to go," Emilia countered.

"You're a woman. He wasn't thinking."

"Thinking? I think there's a connection between Los Mozos and La Tumba that nobody wants to talk about."

"Women should stay home," Ricardo snapped. "Be a teacher. Or a nurse."

He was an idiot.

"See you tonight," Emilia said sweetly. She hit the button and the window went up, sliding past Ricardo's face.

"Fuck you, Ester," Ricardo said, his voice muted by the glass. He went back to his own taxi.

Ricardo wasn't finished being angry with her, which Emilia knew she could use to her advantage. After she ran him and the other *taxistas* into an exhausted heap of gristle, she'd use a cooler full of snacks and sports drinks to get them talking. The dynamic had worked when she was a relatively new detective and appointed acting lieutenant over the heads of more senior officers, including Silvio. At Kurt's suggestion, she fed her sullen colleagues premium coffee and breakfast pastries until they stopped sabotaging the investigation and began to cooperate.

She had a hunch the drivers would react the same way. But more importantly, Don Cisco wouldn't be looking over their shoulders.

CHAPTER 16

By the time she got to Escuela Salve Regina that evening, Emilia was ready to leave it all on the basketball court.

The day shift drivers were there, even Lobo whose wrist was in a compression bandage, and Gennaro who took classes at night. Ricardo didn't speak as Emilia hefted the cooler full of sport drinks onto a bench. Gennaro, who was razor-thin with an Elvis-style quiff of black hair, gave Emilia's midriff-baring compression top and copped leggings an appreciative look. Paco slapped the younger man on the side of the head. Ricardo gave a bark of laughter.

The sun wouldn't set for another two hours but mercury lights already illuminated the white lines of the court enclosed by a chain link fence. Juan Miguel was the coach as well as a player. They started with dribbling sprints up and down the length of the court.

Emilia concentrated on running and controlling the ball while also ignoring the thunder of five other balls banging against the blacktop. Her ball seemed to have a will of its own, never bouncing straight up from the rough asphalt court.

She kept pace, although Ricardo stayed half a court in front of the pack. By the third lap, Emilia felt her muscles loosen and settled into the rhythm. Juan Miguel called a halt after six laps and they moved on to passing sprints. Dribble halfway down the court. Pass to the player on the left. Turn.

Dribble. Pass to the player on the right.

Emilia waited for one of the men to throw the ball at her head or deliberately overshoot. Surprisingly, none of them did. They were wholly focused on honing their skills and agility.

They moved on to layouts and three-pointers. Ricardo was the tallest and the most consistent shooter. She studied his approach, determined not to mess up. He always stepped on the lane with his right foot, then lifted off from his left. Gennaro also scored each time he went in for a layup shot. Juan Miguel, the oldest man there, was a powerful three-point shooter.

They took a break after an hour of drills, but it wasn't a time for conversation. Emilia pulled a towel out of her sports bag and mopped her face. When she opened the cooler and offered drinks, only Gennaro took a bottle.

After five minutes of rest, Juan Miguel divided them into teams to play 3-on-3. Emilia was with Felipe and Paco. She played center, facing off against Ricardo, Gennaro, and Juan Miguel. Lobo and his bandaged wrist kept score.

From the beginning, it was a hard fought game played with speed and dirty tricks.

It took a couple of minutes for Emilia to realize she wasn't being singled out. This was the norm for these players. Everybody played dirty and everybody defended dirty, too. Emilia found herself back in high school, shouting at her teammates and brawling for the ball.

Her team was up by five after Emilia made an unexpected

three point jump shot that stunned Paco and Felipe. Lobo snarled and paced from the sidelines as Ricardo swiped the ball and the tempo intensified. He passed to Gennaro, who snaked around Felipe to score. Twice.

Emilia's team was clinging to the lead when Paco threw to her. She charged down the court. Ricardo rushed to meet her with an elbow to the ribs and the heel of his hand to her ear. Emilia saw stars but got under his guard and slammed her head into the soft spot under his chin in a move worthy of Laura in *Diamond Run*. Ricardo's head whipped back and he landed on his backside as Emilia put her hands on her knees and struggled to catch her breath in time with the bell clanging inside her skull.

Lobo called time out.

Ricardo struggled to a sitting position as the rest of the players gathered around.

"Ester?" Juan Miguel peered at her. "Are you all right."

"How's the weather down there, Ricardo?" Felipe chortled.

Ricardo glared at Emilia as he checked his teeth.

The ringing in her head subsided. "Sorry about that," Emilia said.

She held out a hand to help him up. His face tightened but he took it. Emilia felt him yank hard and stumbled forward. But before Ricardo could pull her off her feet, Felipe grabbed Emilia around the waist and acted as a counterweight.

Ricardo spilled backwards again amid roars of laughter.

"Ester, you're a real find," Juan Miguel declared as they gathered courtside after the game. This time her cooler of sports drinks was emptied by the sweaty men. The sun had set but the court and school property beyond the chain link buzzed with the blue glow of mercury lights mounted on tall poles.

"I didn't think you would be so good," Emilia confessed. They were all lightning fast.

"We're serious," Felipe said. "If 3-on-3 makes it to the Olympics, we want to be there."

Emilia wasn't sure they were up to Olympic standards but she found herself warming to Felipe and the rest of them. "I heard Pablo Arrocha was good, too."

"Not as good as me," Ricardo growled.

"What was he like?" Emilia ventured. "If his ghost turns up what's he going to talk about?"

"Himself," Paco said immediately as he rubbed his calf muscles.

Somebody chuckled.

"Poor Pablo," Juan Miguel said. "His soul rests in peace, thanks to Los Mozos. We should not make jokes."

"Maria's doing better," Ricardo said. "Doctors finally decided to put a metal pin in her arm to fix the break."

"She has a broken arm?" Emilia asked. "I thought she had a miscarriage."

"She fell down the stairs," Juan Miguel said, as if that explained everything.

"Then Pablo died," Paco added.

Emilia shivered, the sweat cool on her skin. "Do you think the police will ever find his killer?" she asked.

The question threw a pall over the conversation. Ricardo looked down. Lobo knuckled an eye. Gennaro trotted over to a metal trash bin and chucked in their empty bottles.

"The police aren't going to do anything," Felipe said. "We have to protect ourselves."

"That's enough sad talk," Juan Miguel said.

The group broke up after that and straggled out to the parking lot where their taxis waited. There was laughter as they figured out which taxi belonged to which driver. Emilia got into her vehicle and nodded as Juan Miguel mimed that she should lock her doors.

Back at the safe house she eased herself into a hot bath. Maybe the oaf who ran Viva Taxis had done her a favor by showing her fellow *taxistas* that they couldn't chuck her out of the club so easily. Ester Ruiz Garcia could hold her own.

Nobody was going to scare her off.

CHAPTER 17

There was something about the man that made Emilia look twice as he left Café Coco across the street. Maybe it was the natty tan suit or the blonde hair.

He had a confident loose-limbed stride that reminded her of Kurt.

Leaning on the rear fender, Emilia scanned the intersection, the now-familiar frisson of dread at being first in line playing up and down her spine. She longed for the seclusion of the safe house where she could sit on the porch and text with Kurt. Mark off another day in which she'd found out exactly nothing about Los Mozos or Pablo Arrocha's killer.

She'd driven up and down La Costera a million times already. It might be Acapulco's lifeline, filled with a colorful jumble of stores and sights to see, but Emilia no longer appreciated the lush green of the median separating the six lanes of traffic or how the mountains shimmered in the distance. The giant Coca Cola bottle near the convention center was just another billboard. Too many kids earned too few pesos washing car windshields or selling bottled water at busy intersections. She never realized how many tourists wandered around like lost souls or the number of morons on scooters willing to risk life and limb by constantly weaving in and out of lanes.

The man in the tan suit waited to cross the street. He held

a cell phone to his ear, obscuring his face.

Juan Miguel pulled up behind her. "A long day, Ester?"

"A bit," Emilia admitted. "How about you?"

"I got lucky," he said. Juan Miguel might have been behind the wheel all day but the wiry older man was still freshly pressed. His hair was neatly combed and shone like patent leather. "I played chauffeur to a couple of tourist ladies. Took them all over. Very generous tip, too."

He grinned knowingly.

Emilia had yet to snag a big client, the kind that wanted the taxi to be their personal car service for hours at a time. The money from days like that were the best, according to the other *taxistas*, because the meter ran while the driver waited.

Juan Miguel pointed with his thumb. "There you go."

The man in the tan suit hopped in the back of her taxi.

Emilia gave Juan Miguel a thumbs up, trotted to the driver's side and slid behind the wheel.

"Hotel Torre Ventura," the man said, briefly lowering the cell phone to give the destination. His voice was deep and languorous and hauntingly familiar.

Emilia threw her eyes to the rearview mirror and froze.

It was him. Rafa Gamboa. El Acólito.

Maybe.

She remembered those cheekbones and jaw, but the wavy sun-streaked hair was nothing like El Acólito's shoulder-sweeping dark locks. The fine wool suit rivaled anything in Kurt's closet but was a far cry from the loose cotton trousers that the Santa Muerte priest wore on stage as he exhorted his followers into a religious frenzy and his cohorts picked out women in the audience to drug for his sex trafficking operation.

If only Emilia could see the tattoo of a black-robed Santa Muerte on his naked chest, she would know for sure, but of course, she couldn't.

"Hotel Torre Ventura," he repeated. "The hotel with the big neon palm tree. Do you know the one I mean?"

Maybe it was El Acólito's voice. Maybe it wasn't. The blood pounded in Emilia's ears, distorting every sound.

"*Si*, señor," she breathed.

Hotel Torre Ventura was just off La Costera, on the west side of the bay. The towering white hotel anchored a wide swath of beach.

Emilia reached for her seat belt with a shaking hand and found that her shoulder was up against the window. Without realizing it, she'd wedged herself, as far as she could get from her passenger without falling out of the car.

Once in traffic, he made a phone call. "Manolo Bernal calling for Señor Hathaway," he said in English.

Señor Hathaway was not available? Could Señor Bernal make an appointment? Yes, yes, he completely understood. Señor Hathaway could call back at his convenience.

Emilia risked a glance in the rearview mirror. He was broad and strong, with a weight lifter's shoulders.

His phone played a soft electronic chime. "*Bueno*," he said to the caller, in Spanish. "Yes, some random taxi. Sure,

I'm sure."

Emilia drove, all but paralyzed by the notion of her rapist sitting behind her. He had drugged her and abused her and chained her like an animal. She wasn't the only one.

If the man was El Acólito, he knew what happened to Lila Jimenez Lata and all the other girls. Surely, he'd recognize Emilia as the woman who led a revolt against El Acólito's human trafficking operation and forced him to flee his hideaway in the hills of Guerrero. In the process, Gamboa had killed one of his own men, a guard whom the women had overpowered, with absolutely no hesitation.

But her passenger ignored her as he continued his cell phone conversation.

"I'm going to scout locations this week," he said. "Got half a dozen lined up. Just got to find the right place. Something impressive, but not overboard."

A red light gave Emilia a moment to assess her options. She could pull out the BlackBerry and send the alert code or drive to the closest police station to bust the gate before her passenger grabbed her from behind and snapped her neck like a dry twig. She could be at her own police station in fifteen minutes if the traffic stayed light.

If it wasn't Gamboa, she'd think of some lie for the detour. The light changed. Emilia turned right and headed away from the beach.

"I'll let you know," the man said "Maybe. You know how I roll." He gave a laugh.

Emilia heard the ping as he ended the call.

"This isn't the way to Torre Ventura," he said before they went another block. "You're going the wrong way."

"Excuse me, señor?"

"Hotel Torre Ventura," he said sharply. "Where are you going?"

"There was a big accident. I had to go around." The lie came out in a panicky blurt. "My apologies, señor."

They were two blocks from the police station. Emilia could have wept with fear and fury. She circled the block and headed for La Costera.

The man reached over the center console and grabbed the *sitio* permit, pulling the tape off the dashboard. "You're a girl," he exclaimed. "Ester Ruiz Garcia."

"*Si*, señor," Emilia murmured.

"Acapulco is more modern than I thought. What does your husband think of you driving a taxi?"

He'd noticed Isabel's ring. Whoever he was, the man had sharp eyes.

"My husband is dead," Emilia said.

"Ah." He dropped the permit on the passenger seat and leaned back again. "My condolences."

The white spire of the Hotel Torre Ventura came into view as they kept pace with the early evening traffic. Emilia wracked her brain for some way to prove his identity but panic obliterated any semblance of linear thinking.

She headed into the circular drive in front of the Hotel Torre Ventura. The famous neon palm tree, with a blue trunk and green fronds, soared ten stories up the side of the building.

"How much do I owe you, Ester Ruiz Garcia?" he asked.

"Four hundred pesos, señor," Emilia said.

"Is that all?" He tossed 600 pesos on the front seat.

"Do you need a driver while you're in Acapulco?" Emilia blurted. She grabbed one of the Taxis Coco cards. "I know Acapulco very well. I can take you anywhere you need to go, señor."

She held out the card, desperately trying to keep her hand from shaking. "I'm very reliable, señor. And discreet."

He tucked her card inside his suit jacket, slammed the car door, and disappeared into the hotel.

CHAPTER 18

Emilia paced the kitchen of the safe house, her stomach roiling. Had she just driven the man who raped her to a luxury hotel? Or was this businessman with blonde hair and designer clothes simply a dead ringer for a fugitive criminal?

A trick of fate, simple bad luck.

Besides, how could a notorious criminal walk around Acapulco as if he owned it? Gamboa was a wanted man, with the *federales* hunting for him across Mexico. He was born and raised in the city. Karina, Sophia's sister, had raised him and still lived in Las Brisas, high on a hill where she could curl her lip at the rest of humanity. Dozens of people would recognize him.

Emilia wanted to know for sure, yet she didn't want to encounter him again, either. For months she'd wanted to kill Rafa Gamboa. But when she saw him, her reaction was primal, unadulterated fear.

How many times had she thought about the day she met Gamboa?

If only she'd refused the offer to talk to him after the Santa Muerte rally. She could have refused, walked away, met Silvio at the rendezvous point and shared the pittance she'd learned.

If only she'd refused the soda Gamboa offered her. She didn't examine it. Why did she think it was an unopened bottle?

If only she'd known it was laced with a date rape drug.

But *if only* never solved anything.

Emilia went outside. The taxi was a ghostly outline in the darkness. The street on the other side of the courtyard was quiet. The streetlight silhouetted a trumpet of hibiscus as it dared to venture between the spikes topping the wall.

"It's not him," Emilia said out loud. "Wrong hair. Wrong clothes."

There was no conviction in her voice. None of the reasons why Manolo Bernal wasn't Rafa Gamboa were as compelling as her memories.

If she never found out who her passenger really was, she would always think of herself as a coward. A perpetual victim who would rather live in chains than risk losing the black hole that let her hide her heart from Kurt and commitment. For the rest of her life, she'd always hear that frightened whisper in the back of her head.

Go. Hide. Never come out. Stay safe.

"What would Franco Silvio do?" Emilia actually laughed, startling herself. Silvio would make sure he knew who the fuck the *cabrón* really was instead of whimpering like a frightened puppy in the dark. And if the *cabrón* turned out to be Gamboa, he'd arrest his ass and make sure every *maldita federale* knew that Lieutenant Franco Silvio of the Acapulco police department did the job they couldn't.

Thirty minutes later, wearing skinny jeans, a black tee, and her moto jacket with the asymmetrical zipper, Emilia tipped the driver of an unlicensed taxi and walked past the doorman into the Hotel Torre Ventura with a plan. All she had to do is ask the front desk to call Señor Bernal's room and say he had a visitor in the lobby. When he appeared, she would claim that he left money in the taxi. As an honest *taxista*, she was there to return it. Taxis Coco drivers were nothing if not honest.

Once they were face to face, she'd know if he was Gamboa or not.

The lobby of the Hotel Torre Ventura was a noisy warehouse of industry, with a terrazzo floor that amplified footsteps and a pale wood customer service desk that snaked along one wall. It was immediately apparent that this was a city hotel for business travelers and Japanese tour groups. A dozen small shops and the standard-issue hotel bar robbed the place of anything approaching the expensive intimacy of the Palacio Réal. Sandwich boards in front of the shops badgered hotel patrons in English and Spanish about snorkeling trips, today's exchange rate, and 2-for-1 margaritas.

"Welcome to Hotel Torre Ventura." The girl behind the desk wore a polyester blazer that pulled tight across the bosom, puckering the hotel logo emblazoned on the breast pocket. She gave Emilia a brief smile. "Are you checking in?"

"No, I have to speak to a guest," Emilia said. "Could you please call up to Señor Manolo Bernal's room?"

"You can use the house phone over there." The girl pointed to an old-fashioned push-button phone sitting in the middle of the long counter.

"I don't know the room number," Emilia said.

The girl's smile faded. "What did you say the name was?"

"Señor Bernal."

The girl plucked at the tight jacket with one hand as she tapped on a keyboard with the other. "Bernal?"

"Yes, Manolo Bernal," Emilia said.

"I'm sorry, señora." The girl's expression was professionally sympathetic, the kind patented by Christine at the Palacio Réal. "We don't have a guest by that name."

"Are you sure?" Emilia pressed. "Bernal."

"There's no one named Bernal staying with us tonight."

"Perhaps I got the name wrong," Emilia managed. "Is Señor Rafael Gamboa here?"

The hotel staffer tapped on the keyboard again, but with markedly less enthusiasm than before.

Emilia waited, not caring if the girl obviously thought she was a hooker.

"I'm sorry. He's not a guest here, either."

"What about Escobar? Gamboa Escobar?"

The tapping slowed. "No, señora. We have no guest with that name. Perhaps your friend just came in for a drink in the bar."

"Maybe." Emilia thought fast. "Did he check out today? Is that why he's not here?"

"Who are you asking about?" Any helpfulness the girl had worn on her face was gone and she regarded Emilia with justifiable suspicion.

"Bernal." Emilia took a steadying breath. "Could you check if Señor Bernal checked out earlier today. Just a few hours ago. Please, it's very important."

More tapping and another suspicious look. "No one by that name checked in or out today," the girl said. "Perhaps you can come back in fifteen minutes to speak to the manager."

Fifteen minutes. The standard Mexican euphemism for *Go away*.

"I must have misunderstood," Emilia said. "Thank you for your time." She forced herself to leave the hotel with some semblance of dignity.

Later that night, as she lay sleeplessly under the chandelier in the former dining room, Emilia tried to think rationally. Maybe like the clerk said, this Bernal person had a date for drinks in the bar of the Hotel Torre Ventura. Maybe she had completely overreacted.

On the other hand, if this Bernal was Gamboa, one of Mexico's most wanted fugitives had slipped through her fingers. Emilia cycled through endless worst case scenarios.

Fear and inaction poisons her relationship with Kurt. She grows old and sour alone, a constant hostage to not only El Acólito, but to her own dark recriminations.

Her career goes down in flames, too. Silvio takes it as a personal and professional embarrassment that his former partner wasn't bright enough to make it to a police station when she had the great luck to chauffeur around one of Mexico's most wanted fugitives. The first and so-far only female police detective in Acapulco is a laughingstock. No other woman is ever promoted into the squadroom.

Emilia sat up suddenly, nearly smacking her head into the chandelier. There was at least one person in Acapulco who would know if Rafa Gamboa was there or not.

CHAPTER 19

Emilia figured she'd have better luck in La Brisas if she didn't bang on the door at the crack of dawn. She headed to the *sitio* at the usual time and took her place in the rotation for the morning rush hour. Under a cerulean sky, Emilia made half a dozen trips up and down La Costera. The new city hall, a giant windowless white box near the cruise ship dock, was a popular destination that morning.

Near the Bali Hai bungalow resort, with its overpriced tourist market jammed against the curb, Emilia passed two buses. The mayor's patronizing *re-elect me* smile was plastered over the rear of both. Carlota's teeth were stained by exhaust.

In between trips, Emilia enjoyed a growing sense of camaraderie with the other *sitio* drivers. Dull Ester had gotten her permit back, bested Ricardo on the basketball court, and brought in new business. She had proven herself worthy.

Emilia was first in line after Paco drove off with a fare. Before she could start getting edgy about being first in line, Gabi opened the door and shoved her heavy sports bag onto the back seat. The teen climbed in after it, lank hair swinging like a curtain over her shoulder. The denim miniskirt did nothing to hide the bruises mottling her long bare legs.

"It's Gabi, right?" Emilia asked, trying to sound casual.

"I remember you." Gabi leaned forward. "You're that girl

driver."

"Ester."

"Take me here." Gabi held her phone over the seat and waggled it.

Emilia caught the edge of the phone to hold it steady and saw the address for La Tumba.

The traffic going north on Avenida Farallón del Obispo was heavy. "What do you do all day?" Emilia asked, glancing at the rearview mirror. "Ride around in taxis?"

"I got a boyfriend," Gabi said. "We do stuff."

"Great." Emilia tried to sound enthusiastic. "You live around Café Coco?"

"Sometimes."

"Where's your family?"

Gabi wrinkled her nose. "You ask a lot of questions for a taxi driver."

"Hey, one *chica* to another." Emilia passed the Mega Soriana supermarket and its parking lot overlooking hills dotted with white sugar cube houses. "Tell me about your boyfriend."

"He's all right," Gabi said with real indifference.

"He shouldn't let you do what you're doing, Gabi," Emilia said. "It's not safe. I can help you."

"You got a boyfriend?" Gabi interrupted.

Emilia nearly said yes, but bit it back just in time. "My husband died," she said.

"Were you married to Pablo?" Gabi asked. "You know, the driver who got shot."

The girl said it with such a lack of emotion that she might have said *the driver who wore a black tie* or *the driver who smoked.*

"No, I wasn't married to Pablo," Emilia said.

"Yeah, he was a *pendejo*, right?"

Emilia glanced in the rearview mirror. The girl was texting. "Was he?"

"Who?"

"Pablo."

"Oh. Yeah. He got whacked by a gang."

"Los Mozos." Emilia checked the rearview again.

"Yeah." Gabi bobbed her head and tapped her phone's screen again. "Them."

"What do you know about them?"

Gabi remained focused on her phone.

"I think you know something about Los Mozos, Gabi." Emilia kept one hand on the gear shift. Second and third gears still didn't like each other

"Hey." Gabi's head jerked up from her phone. "Don't say that. Are you trying to get me in trouble?"

"No." Emilia caught the girl's eye in the mirror and decided to test a theory. "I think somebody from Los Mozos gave you that bag."

"I don't know anything about Los Mozos." The girl's lip trembled and for a moment she looked very, very young. "Those fuckers are like the wind. Nobody sees them, but we all know they're out there."

La Tumba was just ahead. Emilia downshifted and tapped

the brake. "Who told you about them?" she asked.

"The *taxistas*." Gabi bent her head to her phone again.

"Besides them," Emilia prompted.

Gabi didn't reply.

Emilia couldn't go any slower without parking the taxi in the middle of the street. She coasted to a stop in front of the big black entrance. As before, the door was propped open with a chunk of cement block and four *machos* sat at the table in the window. One of them poked another when he saw the taxi.

"Do you still have my card?" Emilia asked as Gabi.

"Yeah. Ester the taxi lady. Shut up now."

Gabi hoisted the heavy bag over her shoulder and shuffled in. The men at the table followed her into the back, empty knapsacks in tow. The bartender came out. Emilia hit the button for the passenger side window. He tossed in a wad of bills.

Emilia was tempted to break cover, call Dispatch and report a drug deal in progress. But she also knew how it would go. Gabi was on the bottom of the distribution pyramid and would be thrown to the wolves. Instead of the *machos* or the bartender, the girl would end up in jail. Either she'd get out and go to ground or be stuck inside and raped to death in a week.

There was nothing Emilia could do right now except head to Las Brisas.

☼

Rafa Gamboa's boyhood home was a cubist showplace high in the Las Brisas hills on the extreme eastern end of Acapulco Bay. His foster mother Karina Escobar de la Vega still lived there with her second husband, Hector Gamboa Proctor, president of an investment bank. The house was surrounded by a white iron fence topped with square finials that matched the architecture. The taxi robbed Emilia of any authority she had as a cop, but to her surprise the private security guard recognized her from previous visits and opened the gate.

He evidently never got his employer's memo barring Emilia from the property. The last time there, she and Karina nearly came to blows over the discovery that Karina was her aunt, Sophia's older sister who had been in love with Sophia's husband. When the husbands of both Karina and Sophia died, Karina helped herself to Sophia's son Ernesto Cruz Encinos, Junior; the spitting image of his father. Karma delivered vengeance, however, because the child Karina renamed Rafael Gamboa Escobar turned out to be the monster known as El Acólito.

A maid in a gray dress and white apron opened the front door and delivered the message that la señora was unavailable.

"Is Señor Rafael here?" Emilia asked in reply.

The maid's eyes widened and she shook her head vigorously. "No, no, Señor Rafael has not been here for a very long time."

"Tell la señora I'll wait for her by the pool," Emilia said. She stalked through the dramatic foyer with its floating glass and mahogany stairway to the sunny room at the rear of the house where Karina had received her in the past.

The pale aqua room once seemed like a palace to Emilia, complete with pale silk upholstery and gilt furniture, but now she thought of it as a gilded cage. Karina was trapped there with her money and her twisted memories.

French doors led to a limestone patio where a huge turquoise pool twinkled in the midday sun, flanked by chaise lounges and market umbrellas. The infinity edge gave the illusion of a waterfall spilling onto the city below. The view from Las Brisas was breathtaking, with the blue bay, tan beaches, and white skyscrapers spread out like a picture postcard.

Heels rapped a staccato rhythm and Karina Escobar de la Vega swept through the French doors, eyes and diamonds flashing. In her late 50s, but looking a decade younger, her shoulder-length auburn hair was pulled into a low ponytail that brushed the neckline of a white cashmere tee. Only a person that thin and that rich could get away with pleated silk pants.

"What are you doing here?" she snapped.

"Is Rafa here?" Emilia responded just as abruptly.

"Rafa?"

"You heard me." Emilia gestured at the house.

"I don't know where Rafa is," Karina said.

"Have you seen him lately?" Emilia pressed.

"I haven't seen him in years. You know that."

The pool lay between them, endlessly baptizing the chaos far below. "Have you sent him money?" Emilia asked.

"No, of course not." Karina's unlined face had too much filler in it to register surprise, but her sudden hand-wringing served notice. "Why are you asking me these questions?"

"Have you left messages at a hotel for him?" Emilia went on. "Maybe at the Hotel Torre Ventura? Or did a friend of a friend meet him there for drinks?"

"He's in Acapulco?" Karina asked hoarsely. One perfectly manicured hand squeezed the other.

"Has he been in touch?"

Karina shook her head.

"What about your husband?"

"He would tell me if Rafa reached out to him."

Emilia squinted at the glare coming off the turquoise water. She was already out of both questions and bravado. "If he shows up," she said. "You have to call the police. Otherwise, you're harboring a criminal fugitive."

"Don't you think I know that?" Karina sank onto a chaise lounge.

"Ask for Lieutenant Franco Silvio," Emilia continued. "Don't put yourself in danger because you're mad at me."

Karina pressed her lips together.

Emilia took a deep breath and realized there was nothing left to say. If Rafa Gamboa was in Acapulco pretending to be someone named Bernal, he had not sought refuge in his boyhood home. "Thank you for seeing me."

"I never meant to hurt your mother, you know," Karina said, halting Emilia in her tracks as she headed for the French doors.

"You took your sister's son," Emilia replied with her back to the other woman. "Did you think she wouldn't notice?"

"It was the fair thing to do," Karina said, with a tremble in her voice. "We were both widows. Sophia was a teenager with two children and I didn't have any."

"That's not how it works, Karina."

"Don't you think I've been punished enough?" Karina demanded. "My son is a criminal. I don't know where he is. He hates me."

Emilia turned around. This woman was her aunt, after all.

For all her privilege and wealth, Karina was pathetic figure. Alone in her mansion, standing by a pool that was just for show, and wearing the same hostage chains that bound Emilia.

These were different. Karina had forged them herself.

"I'm sorry for your loss," Emilia said.

CHAPTER 20

"It's Thursday, Ester," Juan Miguel said. "Basketball tonight."

"I'll be there," she promised.

Her taxi was at the end of the line and she waited on the bench in front of the dispatch booth as Don Cisco pored over his notebook. In three hours she'd swing by the store, fill her cooler, and sweat out all her troubles on the court. Forget Bernal and Gamboa and Karina. Forget Los Mozos and godfathers and contracts to kill invisible men. Even forget Gabi and what the teenager might be doing right now.

Tomorrow would be a fresh start. She'd go back to Parque Bellavista. Confront the shake down artist calling himself Ignacio.

"Got a minute, Ester?" Ricardo didn't wait for her to reply but caught her by the upper arm. Emilia swung around, Ricardo jerked back to dodge her fist, and they yanked each other to the relative privacy of the ATM machine.

"What's your problem?" Emilia snarled, breathing hard.

"Are you deaf, Ester? I told you not to go to La Tumba again."

Emilia massaged her bicep. He had dodged her fist with the speed of a whippet. "Have you told Don Cisco that you want to be the new dispatcher?"

"Funny, Ester." Ricardo's lips twisted in mock mirth. "Don't go there again. It's not a place for a woman."

"Tell me, what kind of a place is it exactly?"

"All you need to know is that you shouldn't be there." Ricardo wiped the back of his hand across his mouth. "Don't go back again."

"Or what?" Emilia challenged. "You'll teach me a lesson?"

"What's that supposed to mean?"

Ricardo trailed Emilia back to her taxi. She plucked the glove compartment note from an inside pocket of her shoulder bag and held it out for him to read. "What do you know about this?" she asked.

"Where did you get that?" Ricardo asked, his voice suddenly subdued.

"Stuck in the glove compartment."

"What's going on?" Juan Miguel trotted up. "You two should save your energy for basketball."

"She found a note," Ricardo said.

Emilia handed it to the older man.

Juan Miguel studied it. "Where did you get it, Ester?" he asked without looking at her.

"It was wadded up in my glove compartment. It looks a lot like the one Los Mozos left after the shooting."

"Pablo must have found it." Ricardo put an unlit cigarette in his mouth and patted his pockets to find his lighter.

"Do you think Pablo was deliberately targeted?" Emilia asked. "Maybe he wasn't killed just because he was the first in line."

"No, poor Pablo was killed because he was first in line,"

Juan Miguel said sternly. "Everyone knows that."

"Maybe it was meant for Don Cisco," Ricardo said, the unlit cigarette bobbing from the corner of his mouth. "Pablo found it instead."

All three looked toward the dispatch booth where Don Cisco was bent over his notebook."

"Of course," Juan Miguel said. "That must be it."

A couple ran up to Ricardo's taxi parked at the head of the line. He headed to his vehicle.

Juan Miguel squeezed the note into a tiny spitball and stuffed it into his pocket. "I'll throw it away and we'll never speak of it again," he said to Emilia. "Knowing that poor Pablo took the threat meant for him would kill Don Cisco."

"Don't throw it away," Emilia protested. "It could be evidence,"

Juan Miguel grimaced. "For the police? Don Cisco already talked to the police. They're good for nothing."

"When did he talk to the police?" Emilia followed Juan Miguel to the line of cars.

Juan Miguel waved a hand to indicate a time frame of *before now.*

"You could do worse, Ester," he said as Ricardo's taxi turned north onto Avenida Farallón del Obispo.

"You mean me and Ricardo?" Emilia's eyebrows raced for her hairline. "Are you trying to play matchmaker?"

"He has a good job. He goes to church. He's good to his mother. Not a drinker."

Emilia sent a silent thanks to Silvio as she held up her

hand to show off Isabel's ring. "I just lost my husband. I'm not looking for another one."

"A woman as pretty as you should not be alone," Juan Miguel said gravely. "This is a dangerous time. A young woman needs a man to protect her."

He left her to drive forward. A man with a hefty messenger bag hustled over and Juan Miguel headed into traffic.

Emilia replaced him at the head of the line.

She got out of the taxi and felt dread settle over her like a coat of liquid lead. Traffic moved north along Avenida Farallón del Obispo at a good clip but the southbound lanes headed toward the Diana monument were sluggish. Emilia got a lungful of exhaust fumes as she stood on the sidewalk.

She should not have let Juan Miguel confiscate the note, although she'd taken the precaution of snapping a picture of it. The way the drivers protected Don Cisco was unexpectedly touching. They were a loyal bunch.

A gaggle of people went into Café Coco. Across the intersection, Parque Bellavista began to fill with small children and nannies in pink uniforms. One of the popular puppet shows, Emilia guessed. Or a magician. Her cousin Alvaro's kids loved magicians.

Two men with briefcases left Café Coco and crossed Avenida Bellavista at the light. One of them held up a finger to Emilia as she stood by her taxi. They kept talking to each other as they settled into the back seat. Emilia closed the door and swung around the front of the taxi to get behind the wheel.

"*Oye,* the lady taxi driver," one of her passengers exclaimed as she adjusted the rearview mirror.

"*Si,* señor." Emilia said. "Where can I take you?"

Both men chuckled "You're very pretty. How about I take you, instead?"

As Emilia gritted her teeth and started the engine, a figure with a man's stride and face obscured by a hood ran diagonally across Avenida Farallón del Obispo. The *encapuchado* came at the *sitio* like a rocket. Hidden hands were thrust into the kangaroo pocket of his hoodie. Cars braked and swerved to avoid him as sunlight glinted off hoods and mirrors, creating sudden angles of laser brightness.

It was the same *encapuchado* who'd murdered Pablo Arrocha and Emilia was the first taxi in line.

Instinct took over. Emilia kicked her door open as he neared the taxi. It slammed into his legs like a cannon and she heard a guttural pop as air left his lungs.

The *encapuchado* grabbed the door frame and his weight caused the car to shudder. Emilia kicked out again and he staggered back, the hood still hiding his face. As horns blared and tires squealed across the intersection, a passing sedan scooped him up with the dull thud of a side of beef hitting the slaughterhouse. He cartwheeled across the windshield, as a confetti of bright blue brochures rained out of the kangaroo pockets.

The next second the *encapuchado* splattered against the

side of a red delivery truck trying to catch the green light at the intersection. The truck rumbled on, leaving behind a crumpled heap of dark sweatshirt and faded jeans.

Emilia clapped a hand over her slack-jawed mouth. Her passengers screamed.

CHAPTER 21

"I was never completely in favor of this type of operation," said Chief of Police Rodrigo Salazar Robelo said, tapping ash off the end of his cigarette. Bald as a cue ball, he reminded Emilia of old pictures of Spanish dons.

He didn't invite any of them to sit down. Emilia and the two bickering lieutenants stood in front of the chief's desk like truant schoolchildren awaiting punishment. Campos kept nodding at her, as if she needed reassurance. Silvio glowered, but that was normal for him.

"Detective Cruz thought she was preventing a second attack from Los Mozos," Campos said in a conciliatory tone. "The episode may well have strengthened her position at the *sitio*."

"An innocent young man is in the hospital," Chief Salazar said wearily. "Detective Cruz's judgement is seriously in question. And not for the first time."

Salazar had given Emilia her detective badge. At the graduation ceremony, he had to be embarrassed into shaking her hand. Police work had taken a toll on both of them since that awkward moment, especially during the investigation into the murder of Silvio's wife, when Emilia and Silvio caught him laundering money through a casino with the head of the police union. Things ended in a draw with Emilia hanging onto the proof and Silvio eventually promoted to lieutenant.

"*Mi jefe*, I didn't know it was some teenager passing out brochures for a beach bar," Emilia said. The kid had four broken bones and would be in the hospital for weeks. The last 24 hours were a blur of exhausted explanations, culminating in this conversation with the chief of police. "It was the exact same situation as when the gang shot the *taxista*."

"Were there emergency protocols in place for this assignment?" Salazar asked.

"Yes, of course," Emilia began."

"Then why didn't you abide by the established guidelines?" Salazar barked at Emilia.

"I had a split second to decide," Emilia said, keeping her temper in check. "His face was hidden and his hands were in his pockets. He cut across the intersection and came straight at the taxi, exactly like the shooter."

"Detective Cruz would have been justified in using lethal force," Campos interjected. "He'll recover."

"At the police department's expense," Salazar pointed out.

"Financial Crimes will manage payments," Campos said. They all knew that under Mexican law responsibility for medical bills fell on the person accountable for the accident.

"If he'd turned out to be the Los Mozos shooter, this would be a very different conversation, *mi jefe*," Emilia said.

Chief Salazar glowered at the lineup in front of his desk. "It would have been easier if he'd been killed. End of responsibility. Fewer questions. But we must deal with the situation as it is."

His implication was clear. Emilia was negligent for not finishing off the kid.

"Instead of blaming Detective Cruz, we should be congratulating her for staying completely in character." Campos pointed out. "She didn't break cover at all. She merely did what any quick thinking driver would have done. We'll take care of the bills and proceed with the assignment as planned."

Silvio squinted at the other lieutenant. "It's over, *champ*," he said, with enough topspin on the nickname to serve Campos into next week. "There have been a dozen homicides since Pablo Arrocha was killed. I need Cruz back in the squadroom."

"May I remind you that this is my decision, Lieutenant Silvio," Chief Salazar rasped and stubbed out his cigarette in an overflowing glass ashtray.

Her big mistake, Emilia now realized, was to have pulled out the BlackBerry and punched in the emergency code. But hindsight being 20/20, as the saying went, at the time she didn't know that the *encapuchado* was simply a clueless teenager with pockets full of coupons for a new bar on Playa Hornitos.

"It is extremely important that Detective Cruz return to the assignment," Campos said. "She is far from finished collecting intelligence on Los Mozos. We don't know enough about the gang to determine how much of a threat they pose to the people of Acapulco. Her undercover work is the best chance we have of finding out."

Silvio rolled his eyes. "If my unit had the case from the beginning, this never would have happened."

"This is an extension of the extortion investigation," Campos said, his ever-resent good nature slipping.

Chief Salazar held up his hand for quiet. "What about this Los Mozos?" he asked Emilia. "What do you have so far?"

"The *sitio* appears to be the gang's only target so far," Emilia said. "They haven't hit any other businesses in the area or even the vendors in the nearby park. Organized Crime doesn't have anything specific on them, either. Word on the street is that Los Mozos has two enforcers. One of them was probably the shooter. I've also got reason to believe that the *sitio* has a godfather and he's looking to punish them. If we can find out who the enforcers are and pull them in, we can stop another gang war."

"Do we know who this godfather is?" Chief Salazar asked.

"Not yet," Emilia admitted.

"We're also waiting for account details from the bank, *jefe*," Campos interjected.

"This doesn't merit the full time use of one of my detectives," Silvio snapped.

Chief Salazar opened a desk drawer and took out a roll of antacid tablets. "Anything else, Detective?" he asked tiredly.

"The *sitio* is involved in a distribution operation," Emilia said. "I've identified one transit point, but there could be others. My guess is that Los Mozos knows and is taking a cut by squeezing the *sitio*. But I don't know yet who the *sitio* is working for." She took a deep breath. "I really think it's important for me to remain in the assignment long enough to find out."

"Just about every taxi in this city is involved in moving shit from one distribution point to another," Silvio said dryly. "It's not a reason to tie up one detective for weeks at a time."

"Los Mozos is an extortion gang that resorted to murder even when they were being paid off. Campos countered. He leaned on Chief Salazar's desk. "It's not a trend we can allow to take hold. We all know that financial crimes are ballooning in the state of Guerrero. Detective Cruz is burnishing those skills. She'll be a better detective when she eventually returns to duties with Lieutenant Silvio."

Emilia wondered what skills Campos thought she was acquiring, besides how to pocket tips and curse at that *maldita* second gear.

"I propose a solution," Silvio said. "My unit takes point, in coordination with Organized Crime. We can roll up both the *narcotaxi* operation and the gang at the same time."

"This is not a counterdrug investigation," Campos reminded him.

"Not yet," Silvio sneered. "Your gang is targeting a *sitio* made fat from hauling dope."

Emilia couldn't believe the way the conversation was going. She elbowed Silvio to the side. "*Mi jefe*," she said to Salazar, who thumbed a tablet out of the antacid roll. "This operation depends on a good cover story and what happened this morning has only bolstered it. The drivers are all terrified of Los Mozos. They think another driver will be killed just because they were first in line. I just demonstrated that I do, too."

"What have they said about the city's effort to catch the killer?" Salazar asked thoughtfully.

"To be honest, they haven't said anything at all," Emilia admitted. "They're all so afraid we're driving around with tire irons in the front seat."

The lines in Salazar's face deepened with the ghost of a smile. "So we should be grateful that you didn't hit this boy with a tire iron. Is that what you're saying?"

"I think, *jefe*, that we need to stay on this," Emilia said honestly.

Campos gave her a conspiratorial smile. Silvio's eyes said *what the fuck*?

If they each had yanked an arm, Emilia could not have felt more pulled between the two lieutenants. Campos was adamant that the undercover operation continue on his terms, which meant forgetting the *narcotaxi* operation. Silvio was willing to take on both the Arrocha homicide and the *narcotaxi* operation to get her back in the squadroom.

Emilia was wanted, but not in a good way.

"The real issue here," Chief Salazar said and raised the cigarette in the air. "Is that we have made a mistake in thinking that a female detective is required for this situation. As you continually prove, Detective Cruz, a female detective is a risk to this entire department."

"This is an exceptional situation, as you're well aware, *mi jefe*," Campos began.

Salazar cut him off. "Detective Cruz can continue in the assignment if, as she claims, the other drivers perceive her to be in keeping with their fear of another assault by Los Mozos."

Campos nodded. "Thank you, *jefe*--."

"Given the investment already made in this operation, I approve a one month extension," Salazar continued. He burped softly and thumbed another antacid out of the roll. "But if there's been no progress on the case by then, it gets turned over to Organized Crime."

Emilia's quick intake of breath was audible. Silvio folded his arms, his forearms as thick as slabs of jamón Serrano. Campos pulled at his chin, but his easy stance suggested he knew he'd won the day.

Salazar glared at Emilia as he raised the tablet to his mouth. "Go back to your assignment, Detective so I can talk to your superior officers. Try not to get in any more trouble. I can't keep overlooking your female lack of sound judgment."

She was dismissed with a roll of his hand; a perennially troublesome fly needing to be shooed away.

Emilia leaned against Silvio's official sedan and waited.

Ten minutes later he came out of the building, the white shirt making him immediately recognizable in the glow of the mercury lights casting a blue haze over the mostly empty parking lot. As soon as he saw Emilia, he shook his head. "You got a knack for shit, Cruz."

"Like you wouldn't have done the same thing."

"If it was me, I would have made sure he was dead," Silvio said. "Saved us all a shitload of trouble."

"Saved Campos a shitload," Emilia corrected him. "He's the one inventing Ester's bank account."

"Maybe you did him a favor. Last time he volunteers to take on a murder case." Silvio circled around to the driver's side of his sedan. "You need a ride?"

"Sure, if it's on your way." Cover being paramount, the taxi was at the safe house.

"It's not." Silvio went to the driver's side and aimed his key fob at his sedan. A bleep unlocked the doors. "So what's the deal with this godfather shit?"

"Do you know Montez?" Emilia asked, her hand on the door handle. "Been with Organized Crime a couple of years."

Silvio shook his head. "No."

"Well, I got that from one of his sources. Skinny dealer named El Gatito."

"Is that why you're so fucking hot to keep driving a taxi?"

"I didn't say that."

"Sounded like that to me." Silvio paused. "Campos promise you something out of this? Promotion or a seat in his shop?"

"No." Emilia laughed. "But what if he did?"

"You'd be bored," Silvio said dismissively.

Emilia was warmed by the thought that he didn't want to lose her from his stable of detectives. "The *narcotaxi* thing is bothering me," she said. "There's a girl in the middle of it. Her name's Gabi. A mule. If I could get her out, she might know something she'd not telling about Los Mozos."

"Or maybe you just want to get her out."

"Like that's a bad thing."

Silvio leaned his forearms on the roof of the car. "Campos doesn't give a shit about drug mules, Cruz."

"Sure he does, *champ*."

Silvio snorted.

"How many homicides in Acapulco since the Los Mozos shooting?" Emilia asked.

Silvio squinted at her across the roof. "Fourteen. Why?"

"There's an angle nobody brought up in Chief Salazar's office," Emilia said. "Maybe the godfather already killed the Los Mozos shooter and his enforcer buddy. I heard there's a contract out for the Arrocha shooter."

"Retaliation," Silvio said. "Does that mean the *sitio* stopped paying?"

Emilia shook her head. "Don Cisco would have told the drivers if the threat was gone."

"So bring in this Don Cisco character to look at pictures of every *sicario* scraped off the sidewalk since Arrocha."

"I suggested to Campos that we make him look at mug

shots," Emilia said. "But Campos is dragging his feet. Maybe he's afraid it'll blow my cover or something."

"Speak of the devil." Silvio swiveled toward the building entrance.

Campos trotted down the steps. A car waited for him, the engine running.

"You know why he doesn't want you working the *narcotaxi* angle, don't you?" Silvio asked as they watched the taillights of the car with Campos and his driver disappear beyond the gate to the parking lot. "Anybody who can throw a rock will find drugs moving across this city. But solving a murder is like finding gold. If Campos finds out who killed that driver, Financial Crimes is Acapulco's new hero. You go running after a taxi distro outfit, nobody's gonna care. It's just another rock." He paused. "Get yourself out of there, Cruz, before something else happens."

It didn't matter that Chief Salazar had shown himself to be an ossified idiot. It didn't matter that Silvio and Campos disliked each other so much that if they went at it any longer, only dogs would be able to hear them. Maybe one good thing could come of this whole mess.

"I want to get the girl out of there," Emilia said stubbornly.

"Just once, Cruz," Silvio sighed. "Could you take my advice?"

"Already did." Emilia stuck out her hand and showed him the wedding band.

It no longer felt so tight.

CHAPTER 22

The next morning, the man calling himself Manolo Bernal strode out of Café Coco and got into her back seat.

"Good morning, señor," Emilia managed. He looked like a movie star in a pale gray suit with a heathered tee under the tailored jacket. His shoes were gray suede with red soles. Aviator sunglasses with silver frames hid his eyes and accentuated the blonde streaks in his wavy hair. "Where can I take you?"

"Good morning, Ester," he said. "Did I get that right?"

"*Si*, señor."

He gave her an address just off Ruta 200, where it was called the Carretera Cayaco highway.

Ruta 200 was the main artery running north-south on the east side of the bay. It originated near the coastline above the Palacio Réal and snaked through hilly neighborhoods like El Coloso before merging into an even bigger highway.

Emilia put the taxi in gear and headed out.

Gamboa--if it was Gamboa--kept his sunglasses on. Every time Emilia checked him out in the rearview mirror, he seemed to know it. He adjusted the sunglasses and his mouth curved in a half smile.

"How long have you been driving a taxi?" he asked as they sped east toward the interchange.

"Not so long," Emilia admitted. "But I know the city, señor. I don't get lost."

"It's very rare to see a female driver," he said.

"I'm the first."

"Wasn't a driver killed at your *sitio*?" he asked.

"Yes," Emilia said. "Did you read about it in the paper?"

"Like everyone else," he said casually. "What was his name?"

"Pablo Arrocha." Emilia downshifted to get around a truck full of workers standing in the bed.

They passed the big signs for the airport and Emilia took the exit for Ruta 200. They didn't speak again as she navigated the crazy mixing bowl. Emilia was grateful that Arrocha had invested in a vehicle with enough horsepower to pass delivery trucks and rattletrap minivans full of tourists. Eventually they left the mad scramble of the highway exchange and continued north.

The house was in a residential pocket off the Carretera Cayaco. Emilia pulled to the curb in front of a tall salmon-colored wall topped with loops of razor wire. The gates were painted brown with a discreet *Se Vende* sign attached to the left side. The house could be clearly seen through the gates, the stucco the same pinkish tone as the surrounding wall.

Gamboa got out of the taxi and came around to the driver's side. When Emilia rolled down her window, he took off the aviator sunglasses and El Acólito's eyes met hers. "Wait right here," he said. "I'll only be 10 minutes."

Emilia nodded numbly, too paralyzed to do anything else. Face to face, she was sure. Manolo Bernal was Rafael Gamboa Escobar, aka Rafa Gamboa, aka El Acólito.

Rapist. Murderer. Human trafficker.

Brother.

A man with a clipboard got out of a nearby SUV and the two men went through the brown gates, leaving them open.

The BlackBerry was in her hip pocket but she didn't want to use that *maldita* emergency code again. Instead, she could call Silvio using her own cell phone. Tell him that she was driving El Acólito in her taxi today and that he was touring a house for sale.

Before Emilia could summon the courage, the two men came out of the house, passed through the gates, shook hands, and parted ways. Gamboa headed for the taxi, crossing the street with a bounce in his step that caused the lightweight fabric of his suit jacket to flutter against his torso.

"Well, that was a disappointment," Gamboa said as he got into the taxi. "Have you ever bought a house, Ester?"

"A house?" Emilia was momentarily seized with fear that he was a plant so Diego Barrielos Luna could steal information about the new house where her mother and Ernesto enjoyed relative anonymity.

"Yes, a house." Gamboa tapped on his phone, only partially paying attention to her.

"I rent."

"Ah. Well, if you ever do, be noticeably clear as to what you want," he said. "I want modern appliances, privacy, and a pool. Is that so much to ask?"

"You're looking to buy a house, señor? To live in?"

Emilia was amazed that he'd risk buying a house in Acapulco with a fake name. Of course he could simply pay cash, just like Silvio did to buy the house for Sophia and Ernesto. Cash bought off questions that the rest of the world had to answer.

"A business investment," he said. He gave her another address, one that would take them across the city to the southwest side of the bay.

"Did you know the driver who was killed?" Gamboa asked as Emilia headed south, retracing their route. "What was his name again?"

"Arrocha. Pablo Arrocha." Emilia settled into the right lane. "I didn't know him."

"Why not?"

"I wasn't driving then," she explained.

"What about his taxi?" Gamboa asked.

"This was his taxi," Emilia said. "I bought it."

"You weren't worried about driving a dead man's car? Finding the odds and ends that he left behind?"

"It's been cleaned with Fabuloso." The idiotic words tumbled out before Emilia could stop herself.

"You're a very funny girl, Ester," he said.

The Colonia Progreso neighborhood on the west side of Acapulco was one of the few spots in the entire city laid out in an orderly grid. While the colorful houses were packed close together and Progreso lacked the airy spaciousness of Las Brisas on the east side of the bay, the neighborhood's high elevation meant that most houses had an ocean view of Playa Hornitos, even if the view was confined to the upper floors.

Emilia slowed as they travelled the grid, looking for the address Gamboa gave her. The houses pressed close to the street, creating a warm mosaic of ochre, amber, and rust stucco against a bright blue sky.

When they finally found the big corner lot, Gamboa clicked his tongue in disapproval.

Gray walls were pocked with bare patches where stucco cladding had fallen away to reveal raw cinder block construction. The walls were topped with jagged shards of glass cemented into place to dissuade anyone who wanted to climb over. Separated by a meter-wide spiderweb of cracks, two brass letters hung crookedly on the stucco. *C. L.*

Perhaps the building once had a name but was too ashamed to claim it now.

"Go around the block," Gamboa ordered.

Emilia drove slowly past dark corrugated metal gates set into a deep niche. The property took up most of the block, yet no house peeped over the top of the wall. The only ocean view would be from the roof.

She parked around the corner from the entrance. The streets were wide, but there was no curb, just drainage grates to mark the territory between vehicles and pedestrians. The street was lined with parked cars, including a big black

BMW sedan with tinted windows. Colonia Progreso must be the new residential neighborhood of choice for cartel *jefes.*

Gamboa trotted around the corner to the gates they'd passed before. When he was out of sight, Emilia got out of the taxi. The street was a friendly mix of residence and storefronts, although the sidewalks were deserted.

Emilia tipped her head to the sun and breathed in a lungful of high altitude. The sensible thing would be to call Silvio. She wiped sweaty palms on the thighs of her pants.

If Gamboa came out of the building before the police showed up, they'd end up playing a deadly game of cat and mouse until Gamboa figured out what was going on and killed her.

He came around the corner five excruciating minutes later. The opportunity for a decision was gone.

"Well, Ester," he said as Emilia slid behind the wheel again. "Let's keep looking."

This time they headed south. She picked up the wide Pie de la Cuesta boulevard and headed west toward the beach of the same name.

The road scrolled around hills, high rise apartment buildings, and the irregular coastline. Emilia drove swiftly but carefully, not wanting to rattle the taxi into pieces. Gamboa stared silently out the window. She noticed that he sat with the right side of his torso slightly angled away from the seat.

It took more than 45 minutes before Emilia turned right off Pie de la Cuesta into the Jardin Azteca neighborhood.

The streets were narrow and residential here, with the uphill slant that reminded her how close they were to the mountains that guarded the city.

The address wasn't another high rise, however, but a house in a *privada,* an enclosed neighborhood. Gamboa gave his name as Bernal to the guard at the entrance to the *privada*, the name was compared to a checklist, and the barrier swung up. Emilia drove into an enclave of single residences, each a different pastel stucco decorated with a vertical line of stone geckos climbing to the second story. One had a large *Se Vende* sign in front.

Emilia thought the motif quite clever but it was immediately apparent that Gamboa did not. "Are you sure this is the right address?" he asked, looking around. "The houses are very close together."

"A bit," Emilia admitted. She drove slowly around the circular street, found the correct house number and parked in front.

A late model minivan with *Pacific Realty* emblazoned across the side tucked in behind the taxi.

Gamboa got out and conferred with the driver of the minivan. As Emilia watched him point to the house. Eventually the two men went into the house.

Emilia got out of the taxi with her phone and searched against the name of the realty company and was rewarded with the listing of properties for sale. The lizard house was one of them. According to the listing it was a new construction, with four bedrooms, five bathrooms, and attached quarters for servants. It shared a pool with other residences in the *privada.* The price was astronomical.

She hastily closed out her search as Gamboa hustled out of the house.

"The inside of the house was decorated with lizards, too," he said. "Could you believe that, Ester? Lizards."

"You don't like lizards, señor?"

"I didn't know it, but apparently not." He grinned, disarmingly handsome behind the aviator sunglasses. The blonde streaks in his hair glinted in the midday sun. His cologne was a subtle blend of lime and musk as he slid into the back seat. "Crank that air conditioning, okay?"

Emilia slid behind the wheel and blasted cold air. Maybe it would wake up her courage.

They stopped at an outdoor place on Playa Olvidada and he bought them both iced coffees. They stood in front of the bar instead of grabbing the requisite plastic chairs. Gamboa held out his clear plastic cup full of frothy caffeine and ice cubes in a toast. "To poor Pablo Arrocha and his taxi."

"To Pablo Arrocha." Emilia touched the rim of her cup to his.

"Did he have family?" Gamboa asked. The aviator sunglasses stayed fixed on her. "He must have left someone behind."

"A wife and daughter," Emilia said sipping from the

straw. "But I never met either of them."

"A family man, eh?"

Gamboa asked her a few more questions about the dead driver, apparently just making conversation, before giving Emilia another address. She drove him to see two more houses in neighborhoods further west along the Pie de la Cuesta boulevard. The same realtor met them at both locations.

He had her drop him off at the Hotel Mirador near the cliffs of La Quebrada. "Are you going to watch the divers tonight, señor?" Emilia asked.

"Doesn't everyone?" Gamboa replied. He paid Emilia the amount on the meter, plus a 600-peso tip.

"Do you need a driver tomorrow, too, señor?" Emilia winced at the sound of her voice. Breathless, whiney, and grasping but she couldn't help it. After a whole day with him, was El Acólito going to slip through her fingers again?

"I'll let you know." Gamboa lowered the sunglasses and gave her a wink. A minute later he was gone, swallowed by a swarm of tourists intent on getting to the next cliff diving spectacle.

CHAPTER 23

Emilia sat alone on the porch of the safe house that night, listening to the rustle of insects in the foliage lining the perimeter walls and occasionally dashing away tears with the back of her hand.

But mostly, she just sat and hated herself.

As far as Emilia could tell, the only thing she did right the whole day was to maintain her cover. Meek and plain Ester Ruiz Garcia murmured *Si, señor* to everything Gamboa said just like any driver hoping for a fat *propina* would do. Answered questions about a dead taxi driver she never met and earned an extra 600 pesos.

Once she was sure that Bernal was Gamboa, why didn't she call Dispatch and demand a dozen squad cars to arrest El Acólito? Yes, it would have meant breaking cover and torpedoing Lieutenant Campos's operation but wasn't catching El Acólito ten times more important?

So why didn't she call? Or tap the emergency code into the BlackBerry? Why hadn't she texted Silvio during the day, instead of passively waiting while Gamboa toured houses and complained that none suited his needs?

The only viable answer was that she let Manolo Bernal, aka Rafa Gamboa, aka El Acólito, slip through her fingers because she was afraid of him. Paralyzed by what he did to her. Seeing him again, Emilia was right back in that place, raped and chained like a dog. All of her power surrendered to his brutality.

She was still El Acólito's hostage.

CHAPTER 24

The next day, Emilia cruised around the Fuerte San Diego fortress until she saw the dwarf who pimped out most of the girls who worked the streets around the vast colonial fortress. Thanks to his stable, Chavito had tentacles that reached across Acapulco. He paid protection money to a dozen gangs and twice as many probably paid the same to him. He had dirt on everyone, which was the most effective currency in Acapulco.

She slowed the taxi by the intersection of Hornitos and Morelos, and spotted the improbable figure. Chavito had a broad, flat face with a high forehead and a spill of oiled rasta braids that fell almost to his waist. In custom jeans and half a dozen fake gold chains, he attracted nervous attention from tourists and used it to good effect, keeping up a sales patter as he handed out flyers advertising a Playa Tamarindos beach bar where his girls hung out between tricks.

The second time Emilia passed there was a break in the traffic and she stopped. "*Oye*, Chavito," she called. "Come take a ride with me."

He recognized her immediately and came over to the passenger window. "Well, a girl driving a taxi. It's the end of the world. Somebody steal your badge, *puta*?"

"Get in and I'll tell you all about it."

Chavito riffled the sheaf of brochures in his hand. "I got business going on here. Can't just leave it to go joyriding with strange women."

Emilia held up a roll of tips. "This is better business."

He snorted a laugh and opened the front door. "Nice welcome mat," he said, as he boosted himself onto the seat, using the center of the tire iron as a footstool.

"Times are hard," Emilia said shortly.

"Gotta have a side hustle," Chavito said. He sniffed. "This thing reeks. You got a dead cat in here someplace?"

"We're talking business, remember?" Emilia shifted gears. "Ever heard of a guy named Manolo Bernal? Tall, good looking. Blonde hair like a rock star. Fancy dresser, too."

"Local?"

"Says no." Emilia headed east on La Costera. The boulevard narrowed as it dipped and rose with the hills. The stores got smaller and dingier.

"Meaning he might be?"

"Meaning I want to know and I'm willing to pay." Second gear stuck again. Emilia rode the clutch, finally shifted into third, and hit the accelerator.

"You better get your transmission looked at," Chavito said. "I know a guy."

"Yeah, hold that thought," Emilia said. "Bernal. Sound like somebody you've heard of?"

"Bernal," Chavito repeated. "That's not much to go on. Who is he?"

"That's what I'm asking you," Emilia parried. "You know everybody who's worth knowing in Acapulco."

"Checking on a new boyfriend?" he asked.

If only Chavito knew the irony in his question. Emilia shook her head. "Let's just say he's a person of interest."

"He beat up girls or what?" Chavito's face clouded with concern. "Likes the rough stuff? My girls don't like that. He'll have to pay double."

"That's your problem," Emilia said. "I'm paying for information and I'm feeling generous."

Chavito hooted. "What's he done?"

"You tell me." Emilia glanced in the rearview mirror. "The deal is a thousand pesos. Find out what he's doing in Acapulco. Where he hangs out. His friends. Double if you find out where he lives."

Chavito raised his eyebrows. "You want this guy bad, eh?"

Emilia passed him a picture of Gamboa she'd printed out from an entertainment website. "That's him from a couple of years ago."

Chavito whistled. "Pretty."

"What do you know about a gang called Los Mozos? Controls the territory around Café Coco."

"Not my patch," said Chavito. "That's big money territory. My, ah, business interests are of the more immediately local variety."

"You know everybody who has an itch to scratch," Emilia said.

Chavito rattled the picture. "He's part of it?"

"No, different problem."

"So, tell Chavito everything."

"Los Mozos is the gang that executed the *taxista* by Parque Bellavista. It was in the newspaper."

"I remember." Chavito tucked Gamboa's picture into a pocket. "Walked up to the first taxi and shot him in the head."

"I want names." Emilia downshifted to go over a *tope* speedbump. "Who claims to be part of Los Mozos? Has anybody in the gang been killed?"

"You think somebody is trying to get rid of them?"

"Like a godfather."

"Never heard of them before," Chavito said seriously. "Haven't heard of them since."

"You hear anything about that *sitio* at all?" Emilia asked.

"Like what?"

"Distributing, maybe? A girl named Gabi mules for them."

"Let me get this straight." Chavito ran a hand over his chains, rattling the loops of fake gold. "You want me to dig up something on this Bernal character. Plus Los Mozos. And a girl named Gabi."

"Generous," Emilia reminded him. "Exceptionally generous."

CHAPTER 25

She would find him, Emilia vowed to herself. Turn over every rock in Acapulco until Gamboa crawled out. She prayed that Chavito dug up something, but fury at her fears spurred her on.

For the next two days, Emilia called the realtors, pretending that she was a friend of client Manolo Bernal, but none would pass along his telephone number or address. She hit a dozen hotels on La Costera, but he wasn't a guest at any of them. She cruised by bars and restaurants but didn't see him again. The taxi helped her stay anonymous, blending into every cityscape.

Eventually, before Don Cisco got suspicious and questioned her cover, Emilia had to show up at the *sitio* and drive passengers around.

The tall woman was in Acapulco for a tennis event at the Fairmont Acapulco Princess, the huge pyramid-shaped hotel where the Mexican Open was held every year. As Emilia drove along La Costera in the middle lane, they conversed in English. The woman was a sports agent from Canada, an occupation Emilia didn't even know existed. The conversation was the most interesting one she'd had in days.

Emilia slowed to a stop at an intersection behind a silver hatchback. Her rearview mirror immediately filled with the white hood and yellow fenders of another *sitio* taxi. It wasn't a Taxis Coco vehicle.

The *taxista* behind the wheel noticed her noticing him and blew her a kiss. Emilia scowled and looked away just as the other taxi rolled into her rear, tapping it hard enough to give both women a noticeable jolt.

"Sorry," Emilia muttered. "Traffic in Acapulco is crazy sometimes." She nudged forward but there was only so far to go before riding the hatchback.

The *pendejo* deliberately collided with her bumper again, giving Emilia a jangle of whiplash.

Her passenger cried out and clutched her neck. "What the hell?"

"Hold on," Emilia said shortly. Forcing her car into traffic was infinitely more dangerous than invalidating her permit or even slashing her tire.

She took her foot off the brake, rolled forward until she kissed the hatchback, then shifted into reverse and stamped on the accelerator. Tires chirped and the taxi careened into the one behind with a healthy thud. Eyes glued to the rearview mirror, Emilia saw sunglasses, CD cases, and holy cards rain down from the *taxista's* visor as his car rocked backwards. His mouth worked with curses Emilia couldn't hear as he blasted the horn.

He tried to counter her vehicle's momentum but Emilia was ready. Her RPMs swung into the red zone as she fought the other car's acceleration to a standstill. Locked together, tires screaming and smoking, the two taxis chewed the pavement in an even match of resolve and horsepower. The light changed. The hatchback moved ahead. Traffic streamed by to the right and left. Emilia ignored the cacophony of honking horns, held her ground, and counted the seconds.

Just before the light changed, she shifted out of reverse. Propelled by her adversary, Emilia's taxi shot through the intersection like a stone from a slingshot. Emilia's foot pounded the clutch and she raced through the gears like a qualifier at the Autódromo Hermanos Rodríguez in Mexico City.

The other taxi was left behind, unable to make it through the intersection before being hemmed in by traffic coming from the other direction.

"Does that happen often here?" her passenger sputtered.

"I'm the only female taxi driver in Acapulco," Emilia explained.

Emilia found the entrance to the vast Fairmont Acapulco Princess complex. The 15-story pyramid hotel was an Acapulco icon, with numerous pools, two golf courses, huge swath of beach, and a famous rock garden, all fringed with banana palms.

Her passenger hesitated before getting out. "Seriously," she said, handing Emilia a generous *propina*. "If the taxi gig doesn't work out, you might want to consider a job as a professional daredevil. That was a gutsy move."

Professional daredevil. Emilia liked the sound of it. Flashier than *cop in Acapulco*, although it meant the same thing.

☼

By the third day of fruitless hunting, her stomach was so cramped Emilia couldn't force down more than a bite or two. She knew she wasn't thinking clearly and grasping at options that didn't exist.

Telling Campos was out of the question, he had no interest in capturing El Acólito. Trying to decide whether or not to tell Silvio was agony.

It was painfully obvious to her that Gamboa had bought off enough cops across Mexico to go where he wanted without fear of capture. Acapulco was his hometown; no doubt he had dozens of informers on his payroll. Once Silvio put the word out that the police had reason to believe El Acólito was in Acapulco, the man would slip through the net like smoke.

So she made small talk with her passengers, memorized the blue landmark signs pointing along La Costera, admired the flowers in the median, and prayed harder than ever that Chavito would come through for her.

"Are you all right, Ester?" Juan Miguel asked as she sat on the bench idly twisting Isabel's wedding band. Her car was third in line.

"I'm fine," Emilia said automatically.

"Thinking about him?" Juan Miguel smiled sadly at the ring.

"A little."

"You must miss him very much."

"It's our anniversary." Emilia's lies amazed even herself sometimes.

"How many years?"

"Um, five."

They both stood as Paco's taxi left the head of the line and moved into traffic.

"Will you still come to basketball practice tonight?" Juan Miguel asked.

Emilia nodded. "But I think I'll take tomorrow off," she said and let him think he knew the reason why.

She poured her frustration onto the basketball court that night at Escuela Maria Regina. The youngers players were fast, accurate, and fearless. Maybe it wasn't so crazy to think a few of them could make it into FIBA's 3-on-3 league. At first, she'd thought they were foolish dreamers; none were professional athletes. But as she continued to practice with them, her pessimism faded.

Ricardo was good, too, although he'd be a better player if he stopped smoking. In a couple of years he was going to turn into Chief Salazar, with antacids mixing with the smoke in his mouth.

She was red-faced with embarrassment after the game when the drivers presented her with an anniversary cake from a *pastelería*. Emilia choked down sugary frosting and let them think they'd solved Ester's problems.

"Hey, Bino!"

The man turned around and scanned the second floor of the parking garage. The dim afternoon light barely penetrated the concrete structure, casting a grayish haze over the rows of cars.

Emilia stepped out of the shadows by the open stairwell door. "Hey, Bino," she said again.

She'd trailed the cop calling himself Ignacio through the park all Friday afternoon, watching him crack jokes and reassure the vendors in Parque Bellavista as they slipped him folded peso notes. He made his rounds like a legitimate businessman, oblivious to Emilia in her sundress and cloth tote. If he noticed her at all, she'd register as just another young mother letting her kids run wild around the playground.

"Well, if it isn't Detective High and Mighty," Bino said, recognizing her.

"Been awhile, Bino." Emilia had served in the same unit with him before she became a detective. Aurelia Balbino was a thickheaded lunk who spent about as much time in the gym as Silvio. Everyone called him Bino.

He once tried for a detective badge but had to withdraw after accidentally shooting himself in the leg during target practice. He still walked with the hint of a limp.

"Cruz, right?" he asked.

"Yeah." Emilia stayed by the stairwell. "You still working for Sergeant Orozco?"

"Can't complain." Bino's meaty shoulders shrugged

toward his ears. The man had left his neck in the weight room years ago.

"So I hear some cop named Ignacio is shaking down vendors in Parque Bellavista," Emilia said. "Collects every Friday. You know anything about that?"

Bino made a sound, somewhere between a chuckle and a cough. "Not a thing."

"That's not what I heard," Emilia said.

"What's it to you?"

"What do you know about Los Mozos?"

"The gang that killed the driver near that swank French restaurant?"

"Yeah."

"They got everybody scared," Bino said. "Not much besides that."

"Come on, Bino," Emilia said. She pushed herself past the stairwell doorway to the first row of cars. "Everybody's paying you but they don't know more than that? I want names. Where they hang out."

The man shook a bovine head. "Don't got no names. Nothing."

"What about a contract out on the shooter?"

"Somebody's got a contract out on the shooter?" Bino asked, clearly surprised.

Madre de Dios. Emilia didn't think he was lying. The man drove around in his patrol car, collected his police salary on Tuesdays, a second salary on Fridays, and went to the gym in between. Crime wasn't his problem. Life was good.

"If you had to guess, who would do that?"

"Some cop who's pissed he didn't get a cut." Bino walked towards her.

"What about a godfather?" Emilia asked. She stayed where she was.

"You mean the guy who owns Viva Taxis?"

"Maybe," she said, not sure what he meant. "What's up with Viva Taxis?"

Bino stopped a few paces away from Emilia, his back to a numbered row marker on a painted concrete pillar.

"The owner," he said. "Lanza. He's godfather to the kids of the guy who owns Taxis Coco."

"Godfather to Don Cisco's kids?" Emilia was dumbfounded. A *padrino* or godfather was an important role in Mexican society. A host of traditions went along with the role. "Then why are they bitter enemies?"

Bino laughed. "Lanza slept with the other guy's wife."

Don Cisco's wife had an affair with the owner of Viva Taxis? No wonder Don Cisco called the man a thieving villain.

"What's that got to do with Los Mozos?" Emilia circled around to make sure she had a clear line of retreat.

"I don't know but they're good for business," Bino said. He slouched a few steps closer. "They showed up and now everybody's ready to pay double."

"You're already paid to protect these people, Bino," Emilia said in disgust. "But you're no better than some extortion gang."

"Hey, Cruz." Bino narrowed his eyes at her. "You working for Internal Affairs?"

"Maybe." Emilia shifted the cloth tote to her other hand.

"I'll give you half," Bino said and reached for her.

Emilia slammed the tote, heavy with two bricks from the safe house patio, into Bino's bad knee. A sickening crunch echoed off the hard surfaces of the garage. Bino let out a bellow and canted sideways. Emilia hit the leg again and he fell to the concrete.

"You're out of the collection business, Bino," she yelled. "You understand? Done!"

"You fucking *puta*." Bino flailed at the nearest vehicle for support as he labored to rise.

Emilia fled down the stairwell, just as a car alarm went off.

CHAPTER 26

The taxi engine idled roughly, the pitch rising and falling. Emilia squirmed impatiently behind the wheel as she watched Chavito hand out flyers to a gaggle of tourists who clearly didn't speak Spanish but were fascinated by the little man. Apart from the waist-length dreadlocks, their eyes focused on a tee shirt with a vulgar logo and his shiny silver high tops.

Clutching their brochures, the tourists continued toward the entrance to the Fuerte San Diego. Emilia tapped the horn. Chavito glanced around, saw no other customers, and hustled toward the taxi. Emilia unlocked the door and he climbed in, once again using the tire iron to boost himself onto the front seat.

"You'd better have something good for me," Emilia said.

"*Oye*," Chavito exclaimed. "Where are your manners, Detective. No greeting? No kind words to someone who risks his life for you? No compliments on my fashion?"

"Sure. *Hola*, Chavito, your shirt is disgusting and I've got no time." Emilia swung onto La Costera and stayed in the right lane. "Start talking."

"You like this?" Chavito stretched the fabric of his tee, making the sequined silhouette of a naked woman dance across his chest. Two black tassels suggested the more voluptuous parts of her anatomy. "I wore it for you."

"Don't think I don't appreciate it, *pendejo*." Emilia took

a right on Avenida Serdan and headed north. The left turn onto Barrio del Panteón would come up fast, providing a circuitous route into Colonia Carabali, a neighborhood of confusing little streets northwest of the Fuerte San Diego. It was a nicely anonymous place to roam through.

"Chavito has a smorgasbord of secrets for you today." He opened the glove compartment and rooted through it. "You like that word? Smorgasbord. I learned it from a Swedish girl."

"Spare me your vocabulary lessons," Emilia said. "And close that."

Chavito pocketed the blister pack of aspirins but tossed the remote control back into the box before shutting the compartment door. "You know why nobody has seen Los Mozos?"

"No, why?"

"Because Los Mozos has been taught a lesson," Chavito said. "What do you think about that?"

"I think your smorgasbord sucks," Emilia said. "I drive all the way out to Fuerte San Diego and you talk in riddles."

Emilia drove around the little green park in the middle of Colonia Carabali and headed east on Avenida 16 de Septiembre. The skinny street curved to the north until it straightened into Avenida Durango with a wide, grassy median. The less concerned she had to be about her driving, the more energy she could focus on Chavito and what he had to say.

"Taught them a lesson," Chavito shook his head in sorrow

at her obtuseness. "Two kills. Retaliation for Los Mozos hitting the driver."

"There was a contract?" Did this validate the rumor from Montez's source?

"That's the rumor."

"Okay, so who paid for the contract?"

Chavito held up the packet of aspirin. "How old is this?"

Emilia snapped her fingers. "Contract, *pendejo*. Who paid?"

"Hey, nobody knows," Chavito stuffed the aspirin in a pocket again. "I'm telling you what people are saying, not that anybody really cares about Los Mozos. They're small beans."

"But somebody cared enough to put out the contract," Emilia countered. "Who?"

"Why should anybody care about one shitty *sitio*?" Chavito turned on the radio and a driving beat filled the taxi.

"Who took the money for the kill?" Emilia slapped her hand on the dial to get rid of the music.

"Don't know that either."

This line of attack wasn't going anyplace and Emilia decided to move on. "What about Gabi? The girl I asked you about. What did you find out?"

"Ah, Gabi." Chavito stretched to flip down mirror in the visor and preened at himself. "She came to Acapulco a couple of months ago. Story goes that she followed some boy who thought he'd find his fortune here. He disappeared. Now she does odd jobs for whoever will pay."

"What's her full name?"

Emilia stopped at an intersection. A grassy valley separated the opposing lanes of Avenida Delgado; a fresh green slice through the blocky gray and white cityscape.

"Rubio. Gabriela Rubio Saravia." Chavito blew a kiss to his reflection. "Nice, eh?"

"What about a home? Where does she sleep?"

"No fixed address."

"Okay." Emilia parked on Durango and handed him 400 pesos. "That's for the girl's name."

Chavito snatched up the peso bills. "What about Los Mozos? That was solid."

"You gave me an empty rumor about Los Mozos." Emilia fanned herself with more 200-peso bills. "What do you have on Bernal?"

"Ah, your friend Señor Manolo Bernal," Chavito said. He settled against the seat as if the taxi was a limousine.

Not my friend. Emilia bit back the words. "Go on."

"I have to know that my information is really worth the effort I went to." Chavito waved a small hand. "The risk, Detective. Imagine my risk."

"How many dragons did you have to slay?"

Chavito considered. "Five thousand."

"There aren't that many dragons in Acapulco," Emilia countered. "Two thousand."

"You wound me, Detective." Chavito clapped a hand to his heart, inadvertently covering up half of the silver lady's bosom. "Two thousand does not begin to address the risks I took for you. Four and a half."

"Three."

"Four."

"Three and a half, if it's good."

"Four."

"Did you get Bernal's address?"

Chavito squirmed. "The risks to my life don't have a price—," he began.

"You don't have an address!"

"Three thousand," Chavito countered.

"Three," Emilia agreed, knowing he was robbing her. "Tell me about Señor Bernal. What's he doing here in Acapulco?"

"He's a big time movie producer," Chavito crowed.

"Movie producer?"

"Bernal works for a company called Copa Multimedia. He's scouting locations for a new movie."

"What else?" Emilia's thoughts raced ahead. Gamboa had been an actor in Mexico City and the country's film industry was well known for being an incestuous cesspool. Was this a scam using old film connections? "Who does he work with? Does this Copa Multimedia company have an address?"

"*Oye!*" Chavito held up both hands to slow her down. "One question at a time."

"Names," Emilia barked.

"No names," Chavito admitted. "He's working alone. A low profile."

"What about the movie company?"

"Copa Multimedia. Rumor says it's a Spanish company. Or Florida." Chavito frowned. "Maybe the investors are from Florida. Maybe some Cubanos. Lots of different stories out there."

"Okay." Emilia gripped the steering wheel in frustration so hard that her knuckles turned white. "What about the movie? What's it about?"

"An action film." Chavito nodded energetically, making the beads woven into his dreadlocks click together. "This is very solid information. An exciting, big budget film. Lots of action. He's looking for helicopters to rent. And pilots."

"Helicopters?"

"And many, many extras. Bernal is looking for a certain type of extra, too. You know the kind."

"*Sicarios*?" Film companies shooting crime-on-the-beach stories in Acapulco often hired extras who looked like *narco* assassins, probably because they were *narco* assassins.

Chavito settled back in his seat. Now that he'd delivered his big news, the limousine effect was kicking in again. "Sure. Tough guys."

"Just extras? That's it?"

"I hear your Señor Bernal is handsome enough to be a leading man himself."

What Chavito was telling her made sense, but it was astoundingly hard to believe. Amazingly, no one had recognized him as either Catholic schoolboy Rafael Gamboa Escobar, *telenovela* star Rafa Gamboa, or Santa Muerte priest El Acólito. Was Gamboa boldly cruising through Acapulco, where he'd grown up and could be recognized? How could the criminal fugitive become a filmmaker named Manolo Bernal while on the run from the *federales*?

"Tell me about the film company," Emilia said. She started the engine and headed back to Fuerte San Diego. She wanted time alone to digest this unexpected gold mine of information on Gamboa. "Copa Pictures?"

"Copa Multimedia," Chavito corrected her.

"How did the word get around that he's looking to hire extras? Is he working with legit film companies in Acapulco?"

"The information came to me by the usual way."

Emilia grimaced. Chavito's hookers serviced their fair share of *sicarios* as well as tourists. "What you mean is that Bernal is buying drinks and spreading the word about his action movie. Where?"

"Mostly bars in rough parts."

"Any place specific?" Emilia pressed. "Tell me one place where he's been."

Chavito shrugged. "Those kinds of places don't have names. Word is getting out but he hasn't hired anybody yet."

"Where are they making the movie?" Emilia's thoughts churned.

"Oye!" Chavito yelped "Watch out!"

Emilia slammed on the brakes to avoid a slowing truck ahead. "Fuck," she muttered as the taxi stalled.

"You drive like shit," Chavito exclaimed.

"You didn't die." Emilia stamped on the clutch and restarted the engine. "So what else did you get?"

"I heard Bernal carries a gun," Chavito said.

CHAPTER 27

The next morning, Gamboa strolled down Avenida Bellavista and got into her taxi. Once again, she drove him to see houses for sale. He was in and out of each one so quickly, she couldn't have called for help even if she'd wanted to. One house was too small, another too close to its neighbor, another required too many upgrades.

"Do you know a decent beach bar?" he asked, back in the taxi after the last viewing. "Not a tourist joint like Planet Hollywood. Just a real local place for real people."

"You want some fish tacos?" Emilia asked. "Grilled camarones on a stick?"

He was on the edge of the back seat, practically draped over the console. Emilia's muscles were clenched so tightly her back hurt. *Get away from me. Don't assume you can touch me.*

"You know exactly what I want," Gamboa said.

"I know a place." Emilia put the car in gear and he sat back.

A few turns and she was on La Costera, heading southwest where the bay hooked into Boca Chica, literally, "the Little Mouth." Hugging the inner side, halfway down the hook, la Costera turned into Avenida Casa Blanca. The shank of the hook narrowed to a bottleneck where a little turnoff called Avenida Las Playas led across to the Pacific side.

"You really know Acapulco," Gamboa said admiringly as Emilia navigated the narrow street.

"The place is at the tip of Punta Pilares, señor," Emilia said. "I think you will like it."

The Pacific side of this particular spit of land was made of rocky cliffs and stunning panoramas. They were south of La Quebrada, where the famed cliff divers put on their shows, but the ocean was too rough here for tourist traps.

She drove through the intersection with Avenida Adolfo Los Mateos and cruised slowly to the end of the street. Avendida Explanada stretched to the right but Emilia turned left toward the ocean and turned down a crushed coral road that threaded between two low walls. It ended in small lot next to an outdoor restaurant painted sky blue. A painted sign below the thatched palapa roof proclaimed Casa San Blas. *Cervezas. Mariscos. Ensaladas. Ambiente Campestre.*

The ocean roared below the verandah fronting the single-story cinder block restaurant. The entire front was open, with rusty metal accordion doors framing both sides. The obligatory white plastic tables on the verandah were topped with yellow umbrellas touting Corona beer, while pots of red and pink geraniums bolstered the impression of dramatic color poised above the wild ocean.

Emilia stayed by the taxi, keeping it between her and Gamboa. When he went inside, she'd call Silvio. "They have very good food here, señor. You will enjoy it."

"Country atmosphere." Gamboa grinned as he read the sign. "I think this will do just fine."

He started for the restaurant, his designer shoes crunching on the coral. When Emilia didn't follow, he turned around. "You must be hungry," Gamboa said. "Don't you eat?"

"A taxi driver must be like a camel."

He made an elaborate bow. "I insist," he said.

As if by mutual unspoken agreement, they chose to sit on the verandah. Emilia could watch either Gamboa or the salt spray as the ocean threw itself against the giant rocks. She wondered if he could sense her nervousness. Would it trigger his memory or simply be attributed to a lowly taxi driver overcome with awe because she'd been invited to share a meal with El Señor?

Gamboa was relaxed and pleasant as he ordered them both the special of the day, plus a Pacifico beer for himself and *agua de jamaica* for Emilia.

"So, a lady *taxista*," Gamboa said after a long pull at his beer. "You are the first one I've ever met. Does everyone say that?"

"Now and then." Emilia kept her hands in her lap. He sat sideways in his chair, no doubt to keep the gun from digging into his hip, just like in the taxi.

Below the verandah, the ocean surged and roared, sending frothy spumes into the air. The crash of water against the rocky cliff was loud and insistent.

The nagging suspicion that she was committing a serious error had mushroomed into absolute conviction. A sign for the restrooms beckoned. She could excuse herself, go into the restroom and call Silvio. Stay on the toilet until a dozen patrol cars showed up to arrest him. But Gamboa wasn't a fool. After five minutes he'd know something was up and kill her in the stall. The dual hands of fear and curiosity kept her in her seat.

"You told me your husband is dead." Gamboa glanced meaningfully at Isabel's ring on Emilia's finger. "How did it happen?"

"What happens to most men in Acapulco," Emilia said.

"Ah." Gamboa nodded knowingly. "So now you drive a taxi."

"It's good money." For some absurd reason, Emilia felt the need to defend her fictitious decision. "I know the city and . . . and I can come and go. Not spend the day stuffed into a shop or an office."

"But aren't you afraid?" Gamboa asked. "After all, that other driver was killed."

"He was executed by a gang."

"Why? What did he do?"

"Nothing." Emilia shrugged. "The *sitio* didn't pay enough protection money and the gang decided to kill the driver at the head of the line."

"He was the driver at the head of the line," Gamboa repeated.

"Yes," Emilia said. "They killed him because he was at the head of the line and now the *sitio* pays them more so nobody else dies. It's the way things work in Acapulco, señor. You should know that if you are doing business here."

Gamboa rubbed at the condensation on his beer bottle.

"Do you believe that the gang killed him?"

"Everybody does, señor," she said. "They left a message."

"Has there been a police investigation?"

"The police in Acapulco are clowns," Emilia said and threw up her hands. "They couldn't make an arrest if the man sat down and sold them the gun in his hand."

Gamboa threw his head back and laughed, the sun glinting off the yellow streaks in his wavy hair. Emilia couldn't help but smile at the irony of the situation, but he mistook it for mirth at her own wit. "You're very funny, Ester. You're wasted as a taxi driver."

His cell phone chimed from the inside pocket of his jacket. Gamboa grimaced and checked his watch before pulling out the phone and answering the call.

Emilia anchored her crumpled paper napkin under the edge of her plate to keep it from blowing away and eased herself around so that she was looking out at the ocean but could still hear Gamboa's side of the conversation.

She heard him snort in exasperation. "What do you mean Alejandra's not there?" Gamboa barked into the phone.

There was a pause, while the caller evidently tried to mollify him. Gamboa snorted again. "What about her stunt double?"

Gamboa threw his own crumpled napkin on the table. It sailed past Emilia and disappeared over the edge of the wall and was snatched away by the crest of a wave breaking against the seawall.

"Wait," Emilia heard Gamboa say. "Set up the scene for Alejandra. I think I have a solution." He chuckled. "Yeah, you're going to love me even more."

He tapped the phone screen, dropped it back in his pocket, and snapped his fingers at the waiter. When the bill was paid, Gamboa stood up. "Ester, have you ever wanted to be in a movie?"

CHAPTER 28

Perched on the Punta la Prietilla promontory, not far from the divers at La Quebrada, the fan-shaped Sinfonia del Mar amphitheater was designed to appreciate Acapulco's dramatic sunsets. As the sky blazed with ribbons of crimson and gold, the sun sank into the ocean and spectators were enveloped in the transition from day to night. A huge red mosaic of the sun covered the circular stage at the bottom of the tiers, distinguishing the Mexican outdoor theater from its Greek ancestors.

The last time she was there, Emilia mistook a woman for missing teen Lila Jimenez Lata. The woman panicked before Emilia could explain her mistake, causing a stampede up the narrow aisles.

Getting drunk in the amphitheater's parking lot was a rite of passage, as was making out on the curved stone benches. Usually the parking lot was littered with wrappers, bottles, and newspapers despite the mayor's trash bins.

But that afternoon, Sinfonia del Mar's parking lot was swept clean and transformed into a bustling Hollywood film set.

Instead of the usual throng of cars and picnickers getting ready to enjoy the sunset in a few hours, the parking lot was dominated by four enormous silvery trailers. A generator the size of a refrigerator hummed loudly, feeding a winding canal of cables that disappeared into the descending rows of the amphitheater. People jostled by with pieces of equipment that Emilia couldn't identify. Gamboa was greeted as Manolo Bernal. He led Emilia to the largest trailer.

The door popped open. A long-haired *gringo* in skinny white jeans and a black polo shirt stepped out.

"Ester, this is Bob, our director," Gamboa said.

Bob gave Emilia a nod. Watery blue eyes raked her from head to toe before he turned to Gamboa. "Where'd you get her?" he asked in English.

"She's the taxi driver I told you about," Gamboa replied in a crisp, unaccented version of the same language. "Needed a local. Hired her to drive me around for a couple of days."

Bob continued to assess Emilia as if pricing her by the pound. "Can she act?"

"She doesn't have to." Gamboa gave Emilia a reassuring smile, obviously assuming she didn't understand the conversation. "We'll use her as Alejandra's stand-in. Take some long shots. Use a filter for anything closer. It'll work. Trust me."

It was just like one of Sophia's movie magazines. Hollywood people and cameras and scripts and big lights. Chavito was right.

The two men talked about blocking and B-roll and other things Emilia didn't understand. Her brain tried to absorb the sights and sounds of a Hollywood movie production spreading out against the backdrop of the Pacific.

Amid the chatter and bustle, she wondered if she could

tell Gamboa that she forgot something. Go back to the taxi, slump down and call Silvio. How long would it take for a couple of patrol cars to get to Sinfonia del Mar? Ten minutes? Twenty?

No, it would be safer to play sick and ditch him. Blame it on the fish tacos and pretend to be desperate for some antacid. Drive downtown, stop at a gas station, and call Silvio once she was out of Gamboa's reach.

A woman with a mass of frizzy yellow hair stepped out of the trailer, improbably dressed in an embroidered muslin top and full skirt like a secondhand Frida Kahlo.

"Ester, this is Lora," Gamboa said.

He was back to Spanish, brimming with excitement and enthusiasm. "She's in charge of hair and makeup," he said to Emilia. "Go with her. I'll meet you down on the stage when you're ready."

Emilia knew she shouldn't be this starstruck. She had to do something now or be a paralyzed hostage forever. A wounded bird, unable to flap her way out.

"Okay," she heard herself say.

An hour later, Lora plucked a black top and matching silk trousers off a hangar labelled "Alejandra Messi" and held the items out to Emilia. Once in costume, Emilia hardly recognized the woman in the mirror.

Her eyes were bigger, rimmed with false eyelashes and

smudged with dark shadow. Her lips matched her dark red nail polish and were shaped into Alejandra Messi's signature pout by some wonder chemical Lora painted on before applying the lipstick.

Instead of Ester's braid, Emilia's hair was as flat and shiny as a satin sheet. It spilled over her shoulders and swayed with the slightest movement of her head.

She was no longer a cop or a taxi driver. She was a glamorous, sulky *telenovela* star, ready for the movie role of a lifetime.

All she needed was a pink house and a poodle. The resemblance was uncanny.

Her top had shoulder pads the size of aircraft wings. The trousers were nearly a second skin. Emilia wore flipflops to mince her way down the stone steps of the amphitheater to the stage. Lora followed, carrying a pair of black stiletto sandals, various hats, and a selection of sunglasses.

Everyone gaped as they slowly descended. Emilia did her best to ignore the stares ranging from outright shock to hungry satisfaction. She wondered how many of the crew thought she was really Alejandra Messi.

Gamboa. A movie set. It was dangerously surreal.

"Remarkable," Bob said when she finally got to the stage.

Gamboa was there, wearing black linen trousers and a white band collar shirt open at the throat, but Emilia almost didn't recognize him. His hair was coal black now, marcelled into glossy ridges that matched heavily darkened eyebrows. Clever shading appeared to make his face narrower. His cheekbones were less prominent. A male makeup artist hovered by his elbow.

Gamboa snapped his fingers at Bob. "What did I tell you?"

"This could work, Manolo," Bob said. Again, the two men conversed in English, shutting out Emilia. "We'll get some stills of her, see how to set this up. Let's get your scenes first, but yeah, I like it."

Lora helped Emilia trade the flipflops for the high heeled sandals. They fastened around her ankles with a bow that kissed the hem of the pants. If she tripped on the uneven mosaic, she'd break a leg. A folding chair was produced for her and she sat while Gamboa stood in the center of the sun mosaic and struck a pose.

One of Bob's minions darted in front of the camera, snapped the top to the bottom of a black and white digital clapper, and stepped away.

"Action," Bob said.

"I love my country," Gamboa exclaimed with sudden passion. Emilia gave a start.

Manly and determined against the dramatic backdrop of soaring sky and restless ocean, Gamboa proceeded to deliver a ringing speech about being a simple seller of oranges whose heart bled for the people of Mexico. It was up to him to save the country from its patriarchal past. At the end, he shook his fist in defiance.

The words were second rate but Gamboa turned them into a riveting performance. Emilia's skin turned to gooseflesh.

His performance as El Acólito had ignited the same sense of passion.

Bob yelled "Cut." Gamboa hustled over to the camera and the two men appeared to watch what had just been filmed.

They filmed the speech again, with minor adjustments to where Gamboa was standing, and again reviewed the digital footage. Gamboa filmed it three more times until he and Bob were satisfied.

The crew produced a folding chair for Gamboa and his makeup artist proceeded to fuss with the perfectly coifed black hair. Emilia was led over to the seawall and positioned with her hands on the rough stone and her chin high. As she gazed over the ocean, somebody tilted her head, splayed her fingers, and adjusted her shoulder as if she was a store mannequin. A wind machine blew her hair in the right direction. Out of the corner of her eye she saw a photographer circle around, snapping pictures.

After five minutes, Gamboa joined her. He didn't touch her but he was close enough for her to feel his body heat. Emilia started to tremble.

Bob yelled directions. Lora rushed over and sprayed something on Emilia's hair. Someone else steadied Emilia's chin, murmuring, "Just like that."

Gamboa got a spritz of hairspray, too. When the makeup people moved away, the photographer took pictures of the two of them looking over the ocean.

Finally it was done. Gamboa rubbed his hands together. "Can you give it another thirty minutes, Ester? We need to shoot a very simple scene."

"This is too much, señor," Emilia blurted. She was acutely aware that she was in over her head and needed to end this. Now.

"You'll be fine," Gamboa said confidently. "It's a really simple scene. You get in and out of a car."

"That's all?" Emilia quavered.

"That's all," Gamboa promised.

It took far longer than 30 minutes for the scene to be set up. During the wait, Emilia was photographed wearing different combinations of hat and sunglasses so Bob could decide what to use in the shot. They decided on a broadbrimmed straw hat and an oversized pair of sunglasses with dark lenses and rhinestones on the corners. With her face all but covered, no one could prove Ester the *taxista* wasn't Alejandra Messi.

The scene was filmed in the parking lot at the top of the amphitheater. Two hefty cars were parked side by side, their front bumpers nosing the unruly foliage that bordered that side of the lot. A Buick and a Cadillac, both at least 30 years old and covered in chrome.

Emilia was introduced to Patricia, an older woman who could play the matriarch in every *telenovela* ever made. Patricia wore a tweed suit reminiscent of the 1980's with a short jacket and ropes of pearls, as well as a honey-blonde updo and enough makeup to fill a cement mixer.

Gamboa was still in costume but not in the scene. "You are Victoria," he explained to Emilia. "Patricia is your mother. You want to get married but she doesn't like your boyfriend. The two of you just argued and you walked out of the house."

"What's wrong with him?" Emilia interrupted. "The boyfriend, I mean."

"Patricia doesn't think he'll treat her right," Gamboa said.

"Okay."

Behind Emilia, Patricia murmured something about working with Alejandra Messi. Bob closed in on the older actress.

Gamboa beckoned for Emilia to walk over to the Cadillac. "Now, you're going to walk from that line, over to this door," he explained as they stood by the driver's side. "Open the car door but don't get in. Patricia will follow you and say her lines as you two stand between the cars. When she's done, you get in the car, close the door. You're upset that she doesn't like your boyfriend, so you do this."

Gamboa pantomimed taking off the sunglasses, casting them aside, and dropping his head in his hands.

"I'm supposed to cry?" Emilia asked doubtfully. Did he really expect her to be an actress?

"Just pretend," Gamboa said. "Shake your shoulders a little."

They ran through the scene several times so that Emilia could get the blocking and pacing right, without toppling off her stilettos or banging the *maldita* hat into the doorframe of the Cadillac.

After three dry runs, Bob decided that the sunglasses hid enough of Emilia's face. Lora confiscated the hat. The decision forced an angle change to make sure the Alejandra Messi dodge was going to fool audiences.

"Here we go," Gamboa said and moved to stand near the camera.

Emilia adjusted her sunglasses. Lora arranged her hair.

"Action," Bob yelled.

Emilia walked to the car.

Patricia rushed up behind her. "Victoria, wait!"

Emilia turned to the woman who was supposed to be her mother.

"Cut!" Bob yelled.

Emilia pulled her sunglasses down on her nose. "What's wrong?"

"You're supposed to open the car door," Gamboa explained as Patricia flounced back to her mark.

The next time the camera rolled, Patricia gushed her lines and Emilia dutifully opened the door on cue.

"Victoria, listen to me. You are involved with the wrong man." Patricia knew how to wring drama out of her lines, delivering each like a punch to the heart. "Yes, he has money. Gives you things. But he's not the one for you. Anything could happen with a man like that."

Emilia's own mother had said the same thing about Kurt.

"But I love him," Emilia blurted. She didn't know if she

was saying it to Sophia or the battleship in tweed.

"If you love him that much, go," Patricia declared, pearls swinging across her bosom. "Goodbye, *m'ija.*"

Patricia stalked off. Emilia got into the Cadillac. The cameraman came around the rear of the car and approached the driver's side, the camera protruding from a harness like an alien pregnancy. Just in time, Emilia remembered to get rid of the sunglasses and drop her head into her hands. She jogged her shoulders up and down.

Just the way a hostage would cry.

"Cut!" Bob yelled.

"Was that in the script?" someone asked. "Alejandra's extra line."

"No, but it was perfect," Gamboa said.

"I agree," said Bob. "Really gave the scene extra heft."

Emilia stayed in the car until Lora came to get her.

Just the way a hostage would wait.

CHAPTER 29

Gamboa didn't speak to her again after the filming except to let her know she didn't need to drive him anymore that day. Emilia got out of there as fast as she could, checked out for the day with Don Cisco, and picked up a six-pack of beer on her way back to the safe house.

She drank the first beer before she got in the shower and the second as hot water pounded her back. The third slipped down as she stood next to the open refrigerator door and tore meat off the carcass of a roast chicken.

It tasted like salt.

Halfway through the last beer, Emilia's knees gave out and she slid to the floor, her back against the wall as the room tilted around her. Laughter came next, tinged with beer-flavored burps and the warmth of recycled anger.

For a week she'd played a game with a rapist, murderer, and human trafficker named Rafa Gamboa. And at the end of their time together, all she knew was that he was an artful actor. As El Acólito, he killed to continue playing that role. When it was no longer possible and he was a wanted fugitive, he reinvented himself as a producer and cheesy romantic lead named Manolo Bernal.

He was a chameleon she had no hope of outwitting. He used people in ways they didn't expect. Over and over, his acting skills gave him the power of surprise.

Gamboa was never going to tell her what happened to

Lila and the other girls, because she was never going to be brave enough to ask.

Emilia knew she had to call Silvio. She groped for her phone, too drunk to remember where she left it, and sprawled over the floor like a sodden *borracho*. With her cheek pressed against the tiles, Emilia watched as chair spindles and table legs spun by in a slow-moving tornado.

Sunlight streamed in the kitchen window. Emilia's mouth tasted like bile. Her neck was permanently twisted and her cheek sore from resting on the tile all night.

Her phone was on the kitchen table, next to a cluster of empty beer bottles. The ringtone drilled into her skull like a jackhammer.

It was Gamboa.

CHAPTER 30

"Another location scouting day," Gamboa said as he settled into the back seat of the taxi. "Take me to a bar, Emilia."

"What kind of bar?" Emilia rubbed the back of her neck. She was a bloodshot wreck, but Gamboa was completely at ease.

"Someplace with good atmosphere," he replied. "Not some new, shiny place full of tourists. I want gritty."

"Tequila in a dirty glass?"

"Exactly." Gamboa shifted on the seat so that his right hip didn't brush against the upholstery. "Local color. Drinkers from the *barrio*. Someplace rough that will hold its own on film. You know what I want, Ester."

You know what I want.

"All right." Emilia swallowed just to get some moisture into her dry mouth and counter the hangover taste of used cotton sock. "You know a part of the city called El Roble?"

"I've heard of it."

Gamboa tapped his phone screen as Emilia drove. The midday traffic was light. Fifteen minutes later she pulled to the curb next to a yellow stucco building. *Cantina Pico* was written above the door in scratched red paint. A skinny boy, no more than 10 or 12 years old, stood with his back against the stucco wall. He wore a dirty tee shirt, baggy jeans, and plastic sandals. One hand clutched a bottle of beer like it was a trophy.

Two other boys, younger and therefore less entitled to the prize, squatted on their haunches. Their eyes were vacant and their hands empty. The kid with the beer stared at the taxi. He took a slug from the bottle, lurched off the wall and went into the bar. The other boys tittered aimlessly.

This was life in El Roble, where nobody walked the streets at night, not even Silvio, who lived a block away. Homicides were commonplace and virtually all unsolved.

"What's with the soda bottles?" Gamboa asked abruptly.

Both younger boys wore clear plastic soda bottles suspended by string to make a necklace.

"Homeless kids put glue in the bottom of empty plastic bottles," Emilia said. "Sniff the fumes all day. The high keeps them from getting hungry."

She glanced at Gamboa in the rearview mirror, willing him to get out of the taxi and go into the bar. Give her a minute alone to call Silvio. But Gamboa did nothing more than survey the street, displaying neither fear nor compassion.

An enormously fat man appeared in the door to the bar, one hand latched onto the skinny kid. The other hand was down by his side and hidden from view.

"Let's go," Gamboa said.

Emilia peeled away from the curb as the bartender shoved the kid away from himself, revealing a dark handgun held against a meaty thigh.

The taxi's engine strained as Emilia spun the wheel into

a sharp left turn. They skidded into El Roble's oldest section. It was a messy web of narrow streets where the unwary were soon lost.

Every block was a mirror image of the one before. Peeling stucco dripped rust from rooftop condensers. Graffiti taunts were illegible, written by the illiterate. Wrought iron barred every door and window.

El Roble hid a hundred personal prisons.

"What about a place with a little less local color?" Gamboa leaned forward and put his forearms on the back of her seat.

Emilia drove him to La Tumba.

CHAPTER 31

"Well done," Gamboa said. "This looks good, real good."

Emilia cut the engine as he got out of the taxi. Like before, the door to La Tumba was propped open. The television over the bar was on again. A tennis match.

Back to the door, the bartender leaned against the bar to watch. Otherwise, the place appeared deserted. The barstools nearest the door were empty. No one sat at the table in the window.

Gamboa surveyed the exterior, obviously intrigued by the cemetery theme. Emilia could tell that it appealed. He took out his phone and began taking pictures.

"Hurry up," Emilia muttered. "Go inside."

Gamboa finally pocketed the phone and tapped on the passenger window to get Emilia's attention. When she nodded, he gave her the traditional sign for wait a few minutes, holding his thumb and forefinger slightly apart. Emilia nodded and he passed into La Tumba.

Emilia leaned forward over the wheel to watch him. The bartender gave Gamboa a once-over, taking in the expensive suit. Both men passed beyond Emilia's line of vision.

Two minutes, maybe three. It would hardly take him any longer to assess the bar's film potential and work out some deal with the bartender.

Emilia grabbed her phone out of the glove compartment. She was about to open the contact list when Gabi lurched out of La Tumba, wearing the same short denim skirt and cross trainers as before. The teen promptly tripped on a crack on the sidewalk, overbalanced, and fetched up against the taxi's yellow fender.

"Gabi!" Emilia dropped her phone on the seat and rocketed out of the taxi. "Are you all right?"

"I remember you," Gabi slurred. She stood up straight and grinned glassily at Emilia. "Esterrrrr. The lady driver. Taxi driver."

"That's right." Emilia picked up a cheap string bag the girl had dropped.

Gabi grabbed the bag and held it against her pink tee shirt, hiding a brown stain. Held back by a plastic alligator clip, the girl's hair was greasy and lank. "Got your card."

"That's great, you keep it safe." Emilia glanced through La Tumba's open door. The television was on, but neither the bartender nor Gamboa were to be seen. "How about I give you a ride?"

"Where's my phone?" Gabi leaned against the taxi and began to paw through the string bag, the mouth of the bag gaping wide enough for Emilia to see a worn zippered change purse, a package of breath mints, a wad of plastic bags, and a couple of tampons.

"Gabi, let me take you home." Emilia reached around the girl for the door handle. "No charge."

"Why?" Gabi found her phone but wasn't sure what to do with it.

Emilia gently eased the phone out of the girl's hand and

back into the bag. "You're drunk and you're in trouble."

"You think I don't got places to go?" Gabi demanded. "I got friends, you know."

"Sure." Emilia managed to bump Gabi out of the way and get the passenger door open.

Gamboa stepped out of the bar. "Who do we have here?" he asked, his eyes drinking in the girl and resting on the hem of the very short skirt.

"This is Gabi," Emilia said. "I'm taking her home."

Gabi gave Gamboa a loopy smile. "*Hola*, handsome señor. She's Esterrrrr."

A barrel-chested man came out of La Tumba. Emilia couldn't be sure, but he had the same coarseness about him, the same readiness to inflict pain as the *machos* she'd seen sitting at the table waiting for the latest haul. A knapsack slung on one shoulder was packed so tightly the zippers strained against the fabric.

"She's with me," he said with a jerk of his chin at Gabi.

Gamboa raised his hands to signal that he had no claim on the girl. "Lucky man, *amigo*."

"I promised to take her home," Emilia said. "She's drunk."

Two steps and the *macho* was at the curb. "She don't need no taxi," he sneered. The girl was his bonus. Or maybe it was just his turn.

Gabi tossed her head and gave a snuffling giggle as he grabbed her wrist. She knew the routine and was already subservient to it.

"Let me take her home," Emilia said to the *macho*. "I'll pay you for the drinks you bought her."

"Fuck off, *puta*." The man threw his arm around Gabi's shoulders and pulled her away from Emilia. The teen stumbled on legs made of jelly but he kept her upright. Gabi didn't resist as he kissed her neck with the impatience of a thirsty vampire.

"Look." Emilia rushed to follow the *macho*. "The girl's drunk. She's going to be sick."

"Get your *puta* away from me," the *macho* snarled over Emilia's head to Gamboa.

"Hey, *amigo*," Gamboa said pleasantly. "I got no quarrel with you or your girl."

"Gabi," Emilia said urgently. "You don't have to do this."

"Bye, Esterrrrr."

Gamboa licked his lips in appreciation of Gabi's barely-covered backside as she was propelled away.

Rage surged through Emilia's veins. How many girls like Gabi had Gamboa bought and sold and fucked? Sun-streaked hair and designer clothes and a new name, but still El Acólito.

"Do you still need a house?" Emilia improvised.

"Why?" he asked, oblivious to the anger boiling around him.

"I know a place," Emilia said recklessly. "A perfect place. Private. With a pool. I can take you there now."

CHAPTER 32

Emilia hit the button for the remote control. The metal gates opened slowly. She had never realized how slow they were.

Her heart raced, frantic that Gamboa knew what she was doing.

In the back seat, he craned his neck to get a better view. Emilia gunned the engine as soon as the gates were wide enough. The taxi shot through the opening and she immediately hit the remote again. The gates shuddered and reversed. The two metal plates clanged together behind the taxi like the closing of a trap.

She cut the engine.

Gamboa opened his door and swung out of the taxi. "This is not what I expected," he said sulkily, looking at the safe house's plain porch and rusty iron fixtures.

Emilia was fast, but he heard her running footsteps. As Gamboa turned, she scythed the cross-shaped tire iron into the side of his head. Blood flew from an immediate gash in his temple, the skin flayed open by the sharp metal flare at the end of one of the spokes.

Gamboa stumbled backwards. Emilia chased after him, all rational thought swept away by a hurricane of revenge. She racked her weapon into the air with both hands and momentum slammed five pounds of iron into his face. Again, Gamboa didn't go down, but bellowed like an animal and came at her like a prizefighter.

Emilia parried his fists with the tire iron, catching him across the knuckles. But he got inside her defenses and punched her on the cheekbone with a left-handed jab that momentarily blurred her vision. Emilia staggered and felt him grab an end of the tire iron.

She had to hang on with both hands to counter his strength. Gamboa wrenched her towards the porch and she tripped over the step. Emilia nearly lost her grip, but then he trod into a thicket of bird of paradise and stumbled. Emilia pulled back and they both ended up by the porch. The tire iron seesawed between them. Her adversary was close enough for her to smell sweat and cologne and the cinnamon scent of his breath.

Gamboa grunted with effort, let go of the tire iron with one hand, and cuffed her on the side of the head with the other. Emilia lunged back but the blow still burned her ear. Her hands strained to hold onto the tire iron as Gamboa reeled her in and they careened around the taxi and the foliage, each desperate for possession. Gamboa used his superior weight to smash Emilia into the wall by the gate. The shoulders of her blouse tore and Emilia nearly lost her footing as she trampled the plants but she didn't let go.

Her stumble let Gamboa loom over her for a nanosecond, teeth bared in a killing grimace. She ducked, straining every sinew. The skin of her hands rubbed raw but she still clung to the two flanged ends of the tire iron. Terror gave Emilia strength and she twisted herself away from the wall before he could flatten her. Gamboa kept his grip on a third spoke.

The mad struggle took them across the drive, primal beasts snorting and gasping in some hideous ritual. They flailed into the taxi, tripping around the end and banging against the doors. The tire iron gyrated between them like a live thing, ravaging the vehicle with a volley of sacrificial metal. A taillight exploded with a burst of brittle plastic.

Emilia knew if Gamboa got the tire iron out of her grasp he'd kill her.

He managed to slap her face and the afternoon glazed over. He hit her again, a blow to the chest that stopped her heart. Emilia's lungs emptied and the sky swam around her as she felt the rough edge of the porch against the back of her legs. Only the cement footing kept her upright as Emilia kicked out blindly. She missed his balls but got Gamboa's thigh hard enough to make him wobble.

The next kick landed in the sweet spot and Gamboa pitched to his knees, sucking wind as if his ribs had collapsed. Emilia tore the tire iron out of his grasp and slammed it into his jaw.

Gamboa went down on all fours. The next blow sent him sprawling.

She hit him again as he lay on the concrete. Again and again and again. Her movements were clumsier with each blow as weight and sweat and heat took their toll. Sparks leaped off the driveway on every down stroke, as if the tire iron was tipped with matches. The leading spokes of the tool turned red. Blood spattered across the hood of the taxi.

Emilia stumbled back. The tire iron was suddenly so heavy she couldn't raise it again. Gamboa's body lay on the driveway in an ungainly sprawl, suit jacket half off, one hand outstretched and slick with blood. His face was meat cut by a butcher's cleaver.

"Get up, *pendejo*," Emilia shouted.

He didn't move.

Her breathing came in ragged gulps. The neighborhood beyond the blossoming foliage and the spike-tipped walls was a planet away.

She took a hesitant step forward and tapped Gamboa's leg with her toe. No reaction. Emilia kicked him in the ribs hard enough to bump his torso off the concrete. Gamboa made a muffled sound, like air going out of a child's balloon. Emilia kept one hand wrapped around the tire iron as she used a foot to roll him over and ease his suit jacket away to expose a small pistol in a leather holster. She darted forward, snatched the pistol and trained it on him as if she was a modern day *soldadera*, ready to wage the revolution.

Gamboa didn't move.

Her rage was spent. Emilia stood doused in exhaustion and uncertainty as she stood over Gamboa with the gun in her hand.

Gamboa still didn't move.

After a time, she wondered if he was dead. But no, there was a barely discernable rise and fall as he breathed. She put down the tire iron, tucked the pistol into her back pocket, ripped off her skinny black tie, and used it to bind the unconscious man's hands behind his back.

Her teeth chattered and Emilia knew she was on the edge of shock. She got into the taxi but left the car door open.

Silvio picked up on the third ring.

"I have a problem," Emilia said.

CHAPTER 33

"*Rayos*, Cruz," Silvio said. He took in the blood spattered ground and the man lying face down on the driveway with his hands tied behind his back. "You caught the Los Mozos shooter?"

"No, it's him." Emilia was spent. Twilight had happened while she sat in the taxi and waited for Silvio. The sticky tire iron offered a feast for flies. Their drone would live in her memory forever.

"What happened?" Silvio squatted down next to Gamboa and felt for a pulse. Gamboa moaned as Silvio's hand touched his neck, but didn't regain consciousness.

"I hit him with my tire iron," Emilia said. "He was looking at the house and I hit him from behind."

"*Rayos*, Cruz," Silvio said again, but there was a touch of admiration in the words this time. He stood. "Wraps up this case. Campos is going to shit himself with happiness."

"This is nothing to Campos," Emilia said dully. "He's not the shooter."

"What do you mean? He try to rob you?"

"Didn't you hear me?" Emilia glared at her former partner. "It's *him*."

"Him." Silvio repeated the word, completely clueless.

Emilia blinked, only now recalling that Silvio had never seen the man in person, only pictures of a younger Rafa Gamboa. "That's El Acólito," she said.

"El Acólito," Silvio exclaimed. "You're shitting me."

"He got into the taxi," Emilia said.

She explained what happened from the first day that Gamboa got into her taxi as she waited at the head of the line, to the movie set at Sinfonia del Mar, to the encounter with Gabi at La Tumba. Emilia heard Silvio catch his breath and he shook his head once or twice, but otherwise he caught each detail like a boxer absorbing a body blow. *Take it, forget the pain, keep going.*

"All I could think of was what he'd done," she finished with an exhausted shrug. "Taken girls like Gabi. Did things to them . . . used them . . ."

And me.

"How did you get him here?" Silvio prompted brusquely.

"I told him I had a friend selling a house," Emilia said. "I said it was just what he was looking for. You know, private. With a pool."

The counterpunch was coming, she knew. Silvio was going to say that he could never trust her again. She'd had a thousand opportunities to tell him what was going on.

Silvio rubbed a hand across his bristly crew cut and frowned. "I didn't know this house had a pool."

"I lied," Emilia said.

To her surprise, Silvio gave a loud guffaw and suddenly they were both shaking with laughter and stumbling around the bloody driveway like a couple of idiots. High emotion roiled out in great gusts at the absurd situation. One of the most wanted men in Mexico lay on the ground in front of a police safe house like a cartoon image of crude vengeance.

"You fucking beat him with a tire iron," Silvio roared. "Fucking shit, Cruz. That's the ballsiest thing I ever heard of and I've been around awhile."

"I was supposed to beat up the Los Mozos shooter," Emilia chortled. "I bagged El Acólito instead."

Silvio's laughter ran down and he prodded Gamboa's chest with the tip of his boot. "He probably needs an ambulance."

"Probably." The notion produced another bout of laughter. The great El Acólito brought down by a snip of a girl with a tire iron!

"You're under cover in a safe house," Silvio pointed out. "This isn't going to be easy to explain."

Emilia swung from hysterical glee to sober reality in the blink of an eye. "I fucked up, didn't I?"

"We've got to keep you out of it or else your cover is going to blow sky high."

"He'll know it was me. I mean, Ester."

Silvio raised his eyebrows and Emilia immediately knew what he was thinking as if Chief Salazar was there to repeat himself. *It would have been easier if he'd been killed. End of responsibility. Fewer questions.*

"Lawyers will argue his rights were violated," Emilia said slowly. "They'll say he was tricked."

Silvio nodded. "If we take him in like this. But I'm not feeling so official right now, come to think of it. I mean, what's the rush?"

He cocked an eyebrow at her. Emilia considered what to do with the respite he was offering.

"I want one thing," she said. "One thing. After that, we'll play it any way you want."

Gamboa chose that moment to groan. His expensive leather shoes scuffed the stones.

Emilia handed Gamboa's gun to Silvio. "I want him to admit it," she said. "Admit it to my face. What he did to those girls. What he did to me."

Silvio replaced Emilia's tie with a pair of handcuffs. Emilia watched as Silvio dug through Gamboa's pockets, finding a wallet and cell phone.

Gamboa was still half conscious and mumbled indistinctly as they wrestled him through the house. His head lolled, chin to chest. The fancy shirt was stained and slick with blood and snot. His knuckles were scored and grimy.

As Emilia propped him against a wall, Silvio dragged a chair from the kitchen table to the sink. They plopped Gamboa into it. He was as limp as a rag doll.

"Looks like he went the distance." Silvio ran a towel under the tap and wiped off Gamboa's face. "You busted him up good. Probably got a concussion. Nose is broken. Maybe a busted cheekbone, too."

"Serves him right," Emilia said and opened the wallet.

All the slots in the leather were filled. According to his

cédula, Manolo Bernal lived in Toluca, state of Mexico. The picture on the identity card showed a smiling Gamboa with blonde highlights in his hair.

Emilia pulled out everything. Bernal had a Banco Azteca credit card, a store card for shopping at the Palacio de Hierro department store, a Santander Bank ATM card, and a driver's license with the same Toluca address. Printed on thick cardstock, his business cards featured a globe logo for Copa Multimedia and a Mexico City business address, with Manolo Bernal listed as Executive Producer.

The wallet yielded three thousand pesos in bills of various sizes and a hotel keycard from the Hotel Torre Ventura. Emilia scratched at the lining of the empty wallet. A corner peeled back, the edge cleverly hidden by the leather seam, to reveal another slot.

"Jackpot," Emilia breathed.

A second *cédula* in the name of Omar Rodriguez Reyes showed a photo of Gamboa with uniformly dark hair and silver framed glasses and an address in Veracruz. The same name was on a driver's license and an American Express platinum card.

"He must be checked into the Hotel Torre Ventura as Rodriguez," Emilia said. No wonder the desk clerk couldn't find Manolo Bernal in the hotel's reservations system.

Silvio took his jacket off and sat down to examine the documents. The big gun in the shoulder holster he wore on the left side was clearly visible against the white cotton of his shirt. His lieutenant's badge hung from a lanyard around his neck.

He picked up the *cédula* in the name of Manolo Bernal. "This is the real thing. If it's a fake, it's a damn good one."

"Of course it's fake," Emilia snapped.

"No, it's real," Silvio said, and tapped both *cédulas*. "All of it. Our boy knows somebody inside."

"Ester," Gamboa croaked.

Emilia jumped at the sound of his voice. Gamboa's body sagged against the sink cupboard, but he was anchored to the chair. Silvio had pulled his arms around the seat back and cuffed his hands to it.

"Finally awake, are we?" Emilia stood over him to inspect her handiwork.

Gamboa's face was a pulpy mess. Blood and snot trickled out of both nostrils, his lips were cut to ribbons, and one side of his head was red and wet. One eye was already closed, and surrounded by swelling puffs of flesh that obscured his eyelashes.

"Ester, please." Gamboa took a gurgling breath. "Please."

Emilia was exhilarated. The feeling was so intense it frightened her.

She'd broken his bones, battered his brain. Made him beg.

"Do you want money?" Gamboa asked. "I can pay."

"I don't think she wants your money, *pendejo*," Silvio said.

Her senses were supercharged with the taste of revenge. It was pure, sharp, electric, and any more was going to kill her. Emilia went to the counter and filled the coffeemaker carafe with water from the big *garrafon*. Poured it into the machine. She didn't know if Silvio wanted coffee but the motions were safe and normal and gave her time to think.

"Everybody wants money." Gamboa coughed and spit up a gout of blood. It landed on the leg of his trousers. "Talk to me, Ester. Please."

Emilia found a filter. As she measured out coffee, the scent was rich and heady. She pressed the button. The light went on.

"Ester."

"Shut up." Emilia sat at the table, keeping it between herself and the drooping figure at the sink, and aligned the various cards from Gamboa's wallet. So many different types of documentation meant that he'd paid off officials at city, state, and national levels.

El Acólito had influence. And money.

Silvio poured himself a cup of coffee and drank it standing up. Gamboa raised his head in mute appeal to the other man.

"Look at me," Emilia snapped and Gamboa slowly turned his head. He was pathetic.

She wanted to hurt him over and over.

"Your real name is Rafael Gamboa Escobar," she said. "Not Manolo Bernal or Omar Rodriguez Reyes. You're not a movie producer from Toluca or whatever story you've got going for Rodriguez. I know you're from Acapulco. Grew up in Las Brisas. Now you're a murderer and a rapist."

"You're confused." Gamboa's voice was gummy.

"Five years ago, you shortened your name to Rafa Gamboa," Emilia went on. "Started acting in Mexico City. The boyfriend in *Rosa Quintana*."

Gamboa made a gurgling noise.

"Rafa Gamboa," Emilia snapped. "Wanted to be in movies but you were such a *pendejo* that you got kicked off a movie set and beat up your girlfriend the director. Left Mexico City and turned yourself into El Acólito. The great high priest of Santa Muerte."

"Feel sick," Gamboa rasped.

Emilia slammed her hand on the kitchen table, making the credit cards and *cédulas* jump. "Rallies up and down Mexico to cover up a human smuggling operation. Young women scooped up, sold over the border to buyers in *El Norte*."

Gamboa abruptly vomited all over himself, swaying as far forward as the handcuffs allowed.

"*Madre de Dios*," Emilia exclaimed. The smell was rank.

His eyes rolled back and Gamboa passed out, slithering halfway off the chair seat but pinned to it by the handcuffs. The shift in weight caused the chair to tip forward on one leg, hovering like a circus trick, until it crashed to the floor with Gamboa's arms still looped around the back. His head hit the tile floor with a resounding crack.

The buttons on his shirt gave way. The fabric split, baring his chest and revealing a tattoo of Santa Muerte, resplendent in black robe and leering skeleton face.

"Definitely a concussion," Silvio said.

By midnight, three more people knew that Emilia had beat El Acólito into submission with a tire iron. Macias, Sandor, and a paramedic who owed Silvio a favor.

Emilia hit the remote control to close the gates as the last vehicle backed into the street. Silvio's sedan led the parade of vehicles to his house in El Roble. Gamboa was in the back of the paramedic's van, strapped to a gurney. Macias and Sandor played caboose in their own unmarked official sedan.

The hastily conceived plan was to keep Gamboa at Silvio's house there until he was sufficiently coherent to answer questions. After all, as the paramedic said, there wasn't much to do for a concussion except keep the patient awake for a few hours.

"And make sure he doesn't escape," Silvio had added darkly.

Emilia stood in the pool of light thrown out by the porch fixture and relived the struggle for possession of the tire iron. Would Gamboa have killed her if he'd won? Probably. She'd glimpsed the same wild ruthlessness in his eyes the day he killed that *sicario* in cold blood, right in front of her and half a dozen of his human trafficking victims.

There was still some bleach left in the bottle she'd used to clean the kitchen. She dumped the rest on the driveway next to the taxi, grabbed a broom and began to scrub. As Emilia hosed off the drive, finally feeling the adrenaline ebb and fatigue drag her down, she saw Gamboa's suit jacket stuck in the giant hibiscus plants below the porch.

Emilia carried it into the kitchen, tossed it on the table, and searched the pockets. All empty except for the inside breast pocket. Emilia pulled out 400 pesos, a pair of silver glasses with plain glass lenses, and a glossy plastic keycard.

This one had a colorful picture on it instead of a hotel logo. A cartoon mermaid beckoned from the prow of a boat called *La Feliz. Present this for 20% off Acapulco's best yacht tour!*

Emilia stared blearily at the mix of cards on the table. She'd lived with an image of El Acólito in her head for months, tearing up Kurt and her family in the process. The display in front of her didn't align with that image at all.

False identities, multiple hotels, and a movie production. Puzzle pieces Emilia didn't know how to fit together.

The aftertaste of revenge lingered, sweet and sharp.

CHAPTER 34

Sometime during the night, Emilia was hit by a freight train.

Getting out of bed was a lesson in muscle pain and sore ribs. Not that she'd slept. Instead, Emilia spent the night with an all too vivid memory, reliving every second of the struggle with Gamboa. Heard his guttural grunts and felt the eddy of his breath on her cheek as they wrestled for control. Saw his eyes widen in surprise as the iron connected. Watched the blonde hair ripple like water as he fell to the ground.

A hot shower revived her enough to call her apologies to Don Cisco, then contemplate Gamboa's phone on the kitchen table. It used the same power cord as her own. As it recharged, Emilia made coffee and figured out her plan of attack.

The police liaison officer to Telmex, the national Mexican phone company, was in the office early and checked the number for her. Gamboa's phone was registered to Manolo Bernal at the same address in Toluca as Bernal's *cédula*. Promising to repay the favor someday, Emilia scrolled through Gamboa's contact list.

Ester was a contact. Emilia erased the entry.

She recognized names from the movie crew, who'd need an explanation for Gamboa's absence. Emilia texted Bob, the director. *Slight accident in taxi last night. Need a couple of days to recover. Nothing serious. Pass the word. Talk soon.*

That done, Emilia turned her attention to Gamboa's call log. Most of the calls were to or from someone in the Contact list. Several to Bob. Just as many to realty companies.

On the day Gamboa first got into her taxi, he made a 22-second call to an unidentified number and received a call from a different, also unidentified, number less than a minute later.

Manolo Bernal calling for Señor Hathaway . . .

Emilia poured herself another cup of coffee, composed a lie remarkably close to the truth, and hit redial for the first number.

"How may I direct your call?" a female voice answered in English with the cadence of the professionally bored secretary. It competed with the faint buzz of static.

"Señor Hathaway, please," Emilia said.

"Who is calling?"

"Ester Ruiz Garcia."

"What is the nature of your call?"

"I work for Manolo Bernal," Emilia said over the background warbling. "I'm his driver."

"Señor Hathaway isn't in right now." The secretary gave no indication that the name Bernal held any significance. "May I take a message?"

"Señor Bernal's been in an accident," Emilia said. "Nothing serious, but he'll be recuperating for a few days and out of touch. He wanted Señor Bernal to know."

"Thank you," the secretary said blandly. "Is that all?"

"Yes, that's all."

The call ended, leaving Emilia with Gamboa's phone in her hand and no more information than before. She redialed the second unidentified number. It rang once and then emitted the tone for a voicemail. Emilia didn't leave a message.

As she dressed, gingerly mindful of several new bruises, Emilia tried to decide if the secretary's voice was familiar or not. It wasn't the voice of a young woman, nor was it an older woman. Emilia didn't know many women who spoke English without any trace of an accent.

The fuzzy connection didn't help.

The heels of Emilia's navy sandals rang on the terrazzo floor as she strode across the lobby of the Hotel Torre Ventura in her matching linen sheath, praying that she looked the part this time. The hotel was busy in the morning, with business travelers checking out in time to catch taxis and shuttles to the airport. The tour place was open and booking people for tonight's cliff diver show at La Quebrada and boat rides in the lagoon where Sylvester Stallone filmed *Rambo*. No doubt, the ability to get lost in the crowd was exactly why Gamboa used it.

Her target was easy to choose. The man behind the concierge desk was young and so eager to please as he spoke to an older couple that he reminded Emilia of a puppy.

Maybe this was her lucky day.

She clutched her shoulder bag, marched up to the desk as the couple moved away, and narrowed her eyes at the young man. According to the tag on his jacket, his name was Saul.

"I'm meeting Señor Rodriguez Reyes for a meeting, but he's late," Emilia declared, channeling every loud *gringa* who had irritated the Palacio Réal staff. "I need you to call his room."

To his credit, Saul didn't lose his smile. "Of course. El señor is a guest?"

"Señor Rodriguez Reyes," Emilia said impatiently. "Señor Omar Rodriguez Reyes. From Veracruz."

"Of course." A few taps on his computer and Saul's head bobbed in relief. "Señor Rodriguez Reyes is in room 302. Who shall I say is waiting for him?"

"Never mind." Emilia waved her cell phone at Saul, trying to stay in character with a display of high dudgeon. "He just texted me."

She turned on her heel and strode off, tapping furiously on her phone's screen.

"Have a good day, señora," Saul called after her.

Emilia's heart pounded as she stowed the phone, found the elevator and used the keycard from Gamboa's wallet to activate the elevator and take her to the third floor. When she slipped the keycard into the slot by the door handle, the light flashed green and the lock clicked off. Emilia slipped inside, flipped the deadbolt and leaned against the door.

The room was a standard-issue hotel accommodation, designed for a conference attendee rather than a beach-going tourist planning a drunken spree aboard *La Feliz*. Neatly made bed with a floral coverlet. Television on a low laminate dresser with matching bedside tables. Narrow desk and chair.

Emilia found the phone. No blinking light. No message from someone who would help solve the riddle of Rafa Gamboa.

She checked out the bathroom. Neatly folded towels awaited use. The complimentary bottles of shampoo and conditioner were unopened, although the Hotel Torre Ventura probably provided fresh ones every day. A small nylon kit bag on the counter by the sink was the only thing not provided by the hotel. Emilia unzipped it to find a toothbrush, toothpaste, a razor, deodorant, and a package of aspirin.

Razor but no shave gel or cream. Kurt never shaved without it.

Emilia threw open the drawers under the television and was rewarded with a pair of bathing trunks and two pairs of stretchy boxer shorts. She moved onto the closet where two pairs of pants and two guayabera shirts hung neatly on wooden hangers. An empty nylon duffel bag sat on the floor next to a pair of flipflops and a pair of brown shoes with rubber soles.

Where were his designer suits? The fancy shirts? A book? A laptop?

With the growing suspicion that she was wasting her time, Emilia searched the room again, opening every drawer, peering behind the curtains, feeling behind the toilet tank and under the bed. After an hour, she came to the inescapable conclusion that Gamboa's room in the Hotel Torre Ventura was a fake set up by a clever fugitive, a deliberate detour meant to take the unwanted down the wrong road.

For 500 pesos or 35 dollars, tourists could cram onto the *La Feliz* with 450 of their closest friends for a sunset cruise to La Roqueta Island and back. Open bar and live music guaranteed a great time and a pounding headache the next morning.

"Just one ticket?" the girl behind the counter asked. "Tonight's cruise?"

"No, I'm not here for a ticket today. I have a silly question." Emilia smiled and put the cartoon keycard on the counter. The place opened at noon, which meant that Emilia had to cool her heels for an hour before charging in and now her impatience spilled over. "Do you know which hotel in Acapulco uses keycards with an ad for your tours?"

The girl frowned at the bit of colorful plastic. Behind her, big posters shouted the excitement and ocean vistas of a ride aboard Acapulco's most memorable cruise. The corners of the posters fluttered as a ceiling fan whirred.

The office was little more than a closet tucked into the

Acapulco Yacht Club on the west side of the bay. A rack of brochures ate up a third of the floor space next to an enticing photo montage of girls in bikini tops holding frothy drinks, an Elvis impersonator in front of a three-piece band, and *La Feliz* herself churning past the Acapulco skyline. *La Feliz* catered to the spring break crowd from *El Norte* and rich kids from Mexico City who wanted to evade their parents' watchful eye for a week of sun and fun.

"You can only use one discount per ticket," the girl informed Emilia. Her eyes were red, bleary no doubt from last night's good time, and her hair was a sloppy updo secured with steel bobby pins. "It doesn't matter how many coupons you have."

Emilia nodded, trying to exude friendliness. "Of course. That makes perfect sense."

"So one ticket?"

"No, I need to know which hotel uses this kind of keycard."

"Are you a tour guide?"

"Yes," Emilia lied, chagrined she hadn't thought of the excuse herself. "Do you have a list of hotels in Acapulco that offer a tour discount on their keycards?"

The girl sighed. "They don't have to tell us to get the discount."

"Sure." Emilia's smile began to slip. "Do you have a list?"

"Of what?"

"Hotels," Emilia reminded her. "Hotels that use keycards

promoting your tours."

An electronic ping prompted the girl to turn her attention to the computer screen. She gave a smirk at whatever she saw there.

Emilia cleared her throat. "What if I wanted a hotel to offer your discount? Who would I talk to?"

"About what?" The girl tapped on a hidden keyboard.

Emilia repeated her question.

"The manager will be in tomorrow." The girl glanced at Emilia, clearly surprised that this nosy, nonpaying interloper was still there. "You can ask him then."

CHAPTER 35

Emilia went back to the Hotel Torre Ventura and found a quiet corner of the lobby. Silvio texted her that the paramedic had come back, filled Gamboa full of pain relievers and antibiotics, and retaped his nose. Gamboa apparently was made of stern stuff because nothing else was broken.

She watched the swirl of business travelers. This wasn't the typical *La Feliz* crowd. Hotel Torre Ventura guests got drunk in Playa Condesa restaurants and splurged on jewelry at Joyas Alameda.

When Emilia dropped Gamboa off or picked him up from the Hotel Torre Ventura, he either got into another taxi or walked to a hotel that used keycards advertising rides on *La Feliz*. It followed that the second hotel served a younger, less well-heeled crowd.

"No." Emilia said aloud, surprising herself, but no one heard her.

Gamboa would not have taken a taxi from the *sitio* serving the Hotel Torre Ventura to go to another hotel. There was a risk, however slight, that one of the regular drivers would recognize him as the guest named Omar Rodriguez Reyes and be suspicious if a doorman at a different hotel addressed him as Manolo Bernal.

Each time Emilia had entered the Hotel Torre Ventura she'd used the hotel's main entrance on Calle Ventura. But from her quiet vantage point across the lobby from the bar, she could see another way in and out of the place.

On the far end of the lobby, a coffee shop invited hotel guests to stop, relax, and enjoy a latte. Or take a coffee to go.

Foot traffic also came that way. The must be another entrance to the hotel.

Gamboa had chosen well. The Hotel Torre Ventura was centrally located and big enough to guarantee anonymity. If Omar Rodriguez Reyes walked through the lobby and out a back door, he'd end up on the street running parallel to Calle Ventura.

Emilia scrambled out of the chair. There were a dozen hotels within walking distance for a fit and clever person.

She tried the same ruse at three hotels about a man missing a meeting. Each time she was told Manolo Bernal wasn't a guest, leading Emilia to apologize, scurry out, and kick herself for thinking that walking around downtown Acapulco in the middle of the day was a good idea. The neckline of her dress was soaked with sweat. Her shoulder bag weighed a ton.

Hotel Dominga was a yellow box of a place, with a fountain and a grove of palms in front. Emilia trudged up the drive, sure she had a blister from her navy sandals. A doorman pursed his lips in pity as she passed into the lobby. The blast of air conditioning nearly knocked her sideways.

Without any conference facilities, Hotel Dominga was much more of an economical tourist haven than Hotel Torre Ventura. A familiar rack of brochures stood in for a concierge desk. A big sign pointed guests towards the pool, bar and restaurant. Floor to ceiling windows faced a long check-in desk. The floor was patterned with random stripes of sunshine, thanks to the missing vanes of the vertical blinds.

Emilia delivered her pitch, wondering if she sounded too well-rehearsed.

"Señor Bernal? Let me check."

Emilia waited, anticipating another brush-off.

"He's in room 215," the clerk said. "Do you want me to call?"

"No, don't bother," Emilia said. "I'll go up."

The clerk gave her a thin smile of gratitude and Emilia found the elevators. Unlike more upscale hotels, she didn't need a keycard to start the ascent.

Room 215 wasn't quite as tidy as the room in the other hotel. A wide assortment of toiletries were lined up on the bathroom vanity. Moisturizers, face masks, eye creams, exfoliating oil. Cologne, scented deodorant, shower gel. A fancy razor and shaving cream in a fancy tube. Teeth whitening strips.

Gamboa took care of himself.

Emilia found underwear in a drawer along with socks, shorts, polo shirts. The closet was loaded with expensive clothing, most of it shrouded in dry cleaning bags. Half a dozen pairs of shoes were lined up, including the gray pair with the red soles.

A rolling suitcase was hidden behind the clothes in the closet. Emilia wrestled it out, hearing something slide to the bottom with a thump. The suitcase nearly pulled out of her hand as the weight shifted.

A small combination padlock protected the suitcase's contents. Emilia set the case on the floor, grabbed a small Swiss army knife from her shoulder bag, and jabbed the longest blade into the thick nylon fabric.

The suitcase put up a good fight but Emilia sawed an opening big enough to pull out a sweatshirt, a pair of dark jeans, an iPad, and a thick brown accordion file.

The iPad was charged but required an access code. Emilia put it aside, and cut the twine binding the accordion file. Dozens of newspaper and magazine clippings fell out, along with a thick book the size of a magazine.

Emilia sifted through the articles. Some were brittle with age, others had the gloss of new magazines. One after another, she found headlines about Diego Barrielos Luna. A tattered newspaper report praised the orange crop on his hacienda in Michoacán. It was more than 20 years old. Another article announced his wedding, with a picture of the bride holding an enormous bouquet of roses. A more recent article was all about the distribution of global wealth. Barrielos Luna was listed as the tenth richest man in the world.

Several of the clippings were about Barrielos Luna's first

arrest. His stint in Mexico's maximum security prison. His escape. The man hunt which brought him down. The most recent were about his daring escape from the extradition convoy. Thanks to Barrielos Luna, Mexico was now a failed state, ripe for cartel takeover.

Emilia set the clippings aside and picked up the heavy volume. It wasn't a book so much as a bundle of typewritten pages sandwiched between red cardboard covers and secured with three old fashioned brass brads. She opened it to see a title page.

A Misunderstood Man
by
Diego Barrielos Luna

Emilia's hand shook as she flipped through the pages. It was a movie script, written by the man who'd engineered her stepfather's kidnapping, killed every member of her extradition team, and murdered so many people by stuffing them in vats of acid that he was known as the Barrel Bomber.

Her last conversation with Barrielos Luna came back to Emilia in a dazed rush. As if it was happening now, she could smell the blood and the lead. Hear the crackle of the flames as the extradition convoy burned. Members of the paramilitary team taking him to prison in *El Norte* lay dying, gunned down in a bold daylight rescue that involved a blockaded road, a helicopter attack with rockets, and swarms of armed *sicarios*. She was the only one left alive. Barrielos

Luna knew that Emilia was looking for El Acólito. The cartel kingpin's words, as he got rid of his shackles, were written on her soul.

When it's time, I'll bring you El Acólito. In return, you'll do me a favor. Whatever El Acólito is to you, you want him that much.

How did the so-called Manolo Bernal get this screenplay? Did Barrielos Luna and Gamboa have a relationship she knew nothing about?

It took Emilia a few minutes before she had the courage to read any of it. The drama focused on Diego's rise from penniless farmer to successful businessman, although the type of business was never actually mentioned.

Along the way, Diego falls in love with proud heiress Victoria, who abandons her wealthy family to be with him, only to die at the hands of a business rival. But Diego finds love a second time with a much younger woman named Emilia.

Feeling sick to her stomach, Emilia leafed through the pages, skimming over treacly *telenovela* dialogue and chunky monologues for the Diego character. On the last page, Diego and his new love drive off in a red convertible in an ending stolen straight from *Diamond Run*.

A cast of characters was scribbled at the bottom.

Enrique – Gael Villahermosa Villas
Banjo – Alex Escobedo
Patricia – Catherine Bey Benitez

Victoria/Emilia – Alejandra Messi
Diego – Rafa Gamboa

The screenplay retold a tale that was almost a modern Mexican legend. Diego Barrielos Luna married Victoria Coronel Rivera when he was still a small player. The Coronel family had made its money in the banking business and looked on Barrielos Luna as an uncouth peasant. Nonetheless, Victoria was by his side, dripping with diamonds bought with blood money, as he killed off his rivals. By the time they had been married five years, he controlled the most lucrative smuggling routes into *El Norte* and was one of the richest men in the world.

Victoria was murdered by his so-called business rivals. As she and her bodyguards left a clothing store in Guadalajara, they were shredded by automatic gunfire. Barrielos Luna struck back. Mexico reeled under the onslaught for over a year.

Emilia scrambled through the clippings until she found the wedding announcement. Despite the yellowed and cracked newsprint, Victoria Coronel Rivera was Emilia's mirror image.

CHAPTER 36

"Where did you get this?" Emilia threw the script on the table in front of Gamboa.

His face wasn't quite the dish of ground meat as it was 36 hours ago. The right cheek was lumpy and splotched with purple bruises. One eye was swollen shut, his nose was taped straight, and his jaw and chin were crisscrossed with scratches from the flanged ends of the tire iron. He held an ice pack to his ear. His knuckles were raw and swollen.

Gamboa's working eye went to the red cardboard cover. "I'm a movie producer. I get scripts all the time."

"Cut the crap," Emilia snapped. "We all know your real name is Rafael Gamboa Escobar and that you're not a fucking movie producer. You're El Acólito. A *telenovela* has-been named Rafa Gamboa who chucked it all to run around the country as a Santa Muerte priest to cover for his human smuggling ring. Now apparently, you're back in the acting business, pretending to be three people at once."

"What have you got there?" Silvio asked.

Emilia threw herself into a chair across from him. "See for yourself."

They were in the room at the back of Silvio's house in El Roble that he used as office and storeroom for the trophies, prizefighter belts, and scrap books from his boxing career. Macias and Sandor lounged against the doorway to the kitchen, ready to provide backup.

Silvio pulled the script across the table, opened it, and gave a start when he saw the author's name. "Where did this come from?" he asked Emilia.

"His room at the Hotel Dominga," she said. "He's registered there as Manolo Bernal. The keycard was in his suit jacket. He's also registered as Rodriguez Reyes at the Hotel Torre Ventura. That room is just a decoy."

"Barrielos Luna is branching out." Silvio paged through the script and gave a snort as a phrase caught his eye. "Fucking 'seller of oranges.' Is this supposed to be his autobiography?"

"It's the original script for the movie this *pendejo* is filming at Sinfonia del Mar." Emilia forced herself not to lose control. "Read the last page."

"Victoria. Emilia." Silvio paused and she watched him absorb the implication of the names on the cast list. "The same actress is supposed to play both characters?"

"Apparently there's a certain similarity."

"Ahhh, fuck." Silvio met her eyes. "I get it."

"Actor Rafa Gamboa is starring in a biopic of Diego Barrielos Luna's life," she said bitterly. "With a surprise ending. Some *chica* named Emilia deserts her law enforcement career to run away with him."

Silvio shoved the screenplay at Gamboa. "How the fuck did you get involved in this?"

"I could have both of you charged with kidnapping," Gamboa said. With only one eye tracking, he looked like a cyclops. "Your buddies, too."

"The doctor said he should be kept for observation," Sandor called, earning a snort of laughter from his partner.

"I asked you a question," Silvio said, dangerously calm.

"Ester." Despite the injuries, Gamboa managed to project both strength and sympathy, as well as a hint of forgiveness. "This is a hell of a mistake. Look, I make movies. I'm a producer. I meet a lot of people, a lot of writers."

"I want to know where you got this screenplay," Emilia slammed both fists on the table. "Who gave it to you?"

Her anger washed over Gamboa, leaving nothing behind. No flicker of guilt. No drawing back or tremble of tension.

"I can't help you, Ester," Gamboa said. He dropped the ice pack and attempted a weak smile of sympathy. "This has been a tragic mistake. Let's agree to part friends. I'll take my phone and my wallet and let bygones be bygones."

He was a very good actor.

Emilia dug into her shoulder bag for the other item she'd brought. She dropped the binder of *Las Perdidas*, letting it hit the table with a loud bang. "What happened to Lila Jimenez Lata?"

The abrupt move clearly took Gamboa by surprise. "Who?"

"Lila Jimenez Lata. Sixteen years old, looks older, likes to dance. From Acapulco."

"Never heard of her." Gamboa picked up the ice pack again.

Emilia flipped to Lila's missing persons record with the girl's photograph, and turned the binder to face Gamboa.

"Sometimes she used her mother's name. Yolanda."

The cyclops eye blinked.

"All right. Yolanda. You recognize her. Where is she?"

"You're looking for a girl." Now that they had something tangible to discuss Gamboa seemed to gather himself. "You think I know her? I don't."

"Think harder," Emilia said. "You kidnapped her and kept her like a dog. Raped her and she mistook that for love. Ran away with you when she had a chance to escape. Where is she now?"

"You want the reward for finding El Acólito, is that it?" Gamboa's eye swiveled from Emilia to Silvio and back again. He was used to making deals. "I'll triple the reward. Triple. Think about that. You could buy a fleet of taxis and whatever your boyfriend here wants, too."

"Fuck your money," Silvio said. "We've got El Acólito's DNA and enough of your bloody shit to fill a laboratory. We know that they're a match."

"So you say," Gamboa said, without hesitation.

"How else do you think she found out she's your sister?" Silvio demanded with a jerk of the head at Emilia."

She gaped at him. "Shut the fuck up, Franco."

Silvio held up his hands in mock surrender. "He's got a right to know, Cruz."

"What?" For the first time, Gamboa's composure was shaken. "What are you two, some sort of comedy team?"

"No, two cops who have been looking for your sorry ass," Silvio said.

"Cops?" Gamboa gingerly patted his eye. "All right, now I get it. You want to see how much I'll pay. Triple the reward isn't enough, Ester?"

"Stop calling me Ester," Emilia said. "My name is Detective Emilia Cruz Encinos."

"All right, I'll play whatever game you've got going." Gamboa seemed amused but wary. "Why were you driving a taxi if you're a detective?"

"Investigating the murder of Pablo Arrocha."

Gamboa adjusted the ice pack. "Yet you think I'm El Acólito."

"You were born Ernesto Cruz Encinos, Junior." Emilia folded her arms to hide her trembling. "The DNA proved it. I didn't even know you existed until last year. Your real parents were Sophia Encinos and Ernesto Cruz, Senior. But you were raised by Karina Escobar de la Vega in a big white house in Las Brisas. Pool in the courtyard. A grand piano. Stop me if you've heard all this before. Oh, yes, and Karina is actually your aunt."

The name of his foster mother finally got through Gamboa's defenses. "Why do you think Karina Escobar de la Vega is my aunt?" he asked slowly.

A double wave of calm and weariness washed over Emilia. "She's my mother's older sister. They didn't grow up together and by the time they reconnected, Karina was married to a rich doctor and Sophia was a teenager with two babies. You're a year older than me."

Gamboa's good eye flashed to Silvio, then back to Emilia.

The silence grew heavy and warm.

"What happened to your doll?" Gamboa asked.

"My doll?"

"You had a doll that you carried around by the leg."

Emilia had heard about the doll from Karina but had no memory of it. "I don't know."

"I remember that day," Gamboa said. He put the ice pack down. His hand shook but he didn't notice. "Papi didn't come home. I didn't understand what was happening. La señora took me up to the big house. You stayed behind. I kept asking to go back and get you."

Little Ernesto, looking for little Emilia. Two innocent toddlers who lost their father. Now they were enemies; testing, parrying, and probing for any sign of weakness.

Such as a slight tremor of the hand.

"Karina was in love with our father," Emilia said. "After he died, you were the next best thing. It was supposed to be temporary but she shut us out. Mama never spoke of you again. Nobody did. I never even knew you ever existed. Until El Acólito . . ." She couldn't go on.

"You say you can prove this with DNA results?" Gamboa threw himself against the back of his chair. The moment of weakness was gone and he was ready to contest her tale.

"You held a rally outside Acapulco," Emilia said with great deliberateness. "I was chosen as one of the lucky few who got to pray with the great El Acólito himself. You gave me a bottle of soda full of drugs and then you raped me."

"I didn't rape anybody," Gamboa said dismissively.

"I woke up chained in the middle of nowhere with a bunch of girls," Emilia went on, fighting to stay calm as the fight or flight instinct strained every sinew. "We ganged up on the guard and I thought you were going to shoot me but you shot him instead. Executed him. Right in front of me."

Gamboa breathed hard, the ice pack now clapped to the swollen eye.

"Don't deny it," Emilia said between clenched teeth.

"I did the world a favor," Gamboa retorted. "He liked to stick things up the girls to see how long they could stay still. Knives. Gun. You get the idea."

"He ruined your inventory," Emilia said bitterly.

"Call it what you want. He was a pig."

"If you remember killing him," Emilia went on. "You remember leaving us chained up. All the girls except for Lila. You took her with you."

Gamboa put down the ice pack. "Well, where does this leave us?"

"Same place we were five minutes ago," Emilia said. She was never going to admit out loud that he was her brother. "I'm a cop and you're a criminal."

Gamboa rubbed the side of his neck. "I used to call you Baby," he said.

Emilia found herself remorselessly massaging the web between thumb and forefinger of her left hand with the thumb of her right. The skin was red.

Silvio blew out his breath.

"Kind of funny that we both grew up to be cops," Gamboa

said.

"You're no cop, *pendejo*," Silvio growled.

"I'm a *federale*," Gamboa said. "Pablo Arrocha was my informant."

CHAPTER 37

The bombshell enveloped Emilia in a riptide of churning waves. All logical thought was swept away.

Silvio's snort penetrated but it came from a faraway island battered by her angry current.

"A Santa Muerte worshipper?" the lieutenant charged. "Or was he a movie producer, too?"

"He was my snitch inside the narco distribution operation the Taxis Coco *sitio* is running," Gamboa said, the single open eye swiveling between his two interrogators. "It's a key distribution hub for the Barrielos Luna organization."

"You needed a snitch because Barrielos Luna is bankrolling your film," Silvio said in disgust.

"No," Gamboa said. "Arrocha was my guy inside because I'm a *federale* trying to close down the Barrielos Luna operation."

"*Rayos*," Silvio whooped in admiration. "You got a real pair, *pendejo*, coming up with a story like that."

"The movie is our best chance of luring Barrielos Luna out of hiding," Gamboa said. "In the meantime, we're tracking his distribution organization. Plan B is to gut him that way."

After a few tries, Emilia forced herself to process the information Gamboa was spewing and landed on the most obvious possibility. Barrielos Luna was the godfather that Montez's snitch had talked about. But only if she believed this outrageous story.

After a few tries, Emilia finally found her voice. "You really expect us to believe you're some deep cover *federale*?"

"I've been chasing the Barrielos Luna organization for a long time," Gamboa said. "If you don't back off and let me walk out of here, you're going to ruin more than five years' worth of work."

"Sure. Let you walk. Good story." Silvio rolled his hand in a *let's-have-it* gesture.

Gamboa touched his swollen eye as if to assess the damage. "We set up El Acólito and the whole Santa Muerte thing because we knew he was a believer. It got me inside the organization."

"Supplying girls," Emilia interjected.

"Not at first." Gamboa's one eye met Emilia's glare. "At first it was just the Santa Muerte worshiper thing, trying to lure him out into the open."

"Explain the girls." Emilia swiveled the *Las Perdidas* binder towards him again. "Because until you tell me where they are, you're just selling one big fat lie."

"The Santa Muerte act wasn't enough to get Barriclos Luna out in the open." Gamboa's finger gingerly moved from eye to lip, which was bleeding again. "But we found out he's got a strange fixation about Santa Muerte approving the women he beds. So the operation expanded."

"Into trafficking women."

"It was a way to get to him."

"This is how *federales* operate?

"Why you?" Silvio interjected.

"I got recruited," Gamboa said. "They created this whole bad boy reputation, how I was so ambitious that I wrecked my shot to be a movie star. Rafa Gamboa disappeared."

"Why?" Emilia pressed. "You had an acting career. You were on the way to something big."

"Undercover is the biggest acting gig there is." Gamboa picked up the ice pack again and held it to his swollen eye.

He was either making it all up or a maddeningly sociopath. Emilia felt rage press against her heart again. "You sold women to Diego Barrielos Luna and raped a few along the way," she said. "Is that how your so-called *federale* operation went?"

"That so-called *federale* operation put the Barrel Bomber in jail," Gamboa said with real warmth. "We trapped Barrielos Luna and nobody in his organization suspected that El Acólito was involved. All that work and he escapes from custody in some fuckup extradition operation and we have to start all over again. But the El Acólito show is done. After Acapulco it got too hot. So we're starting over."

Silvio shook his head. "In Acapulco? Lots of people could recognize you in Acapulco."

"Barrielos Luna is around here," Gamboa said. "He's obsessed with some woman here in Acapulco. Named Emilia. The movie ends with them running off together."

Emilia didn't move.

Gamboa slowly peeled the ice pack away from his eye.

"Emilia," he said, savoring the name. "Supposedly she looks just like Barrielos Luna's first wife, Victoria. Alejandra Messi is going to play both."

Emilia's mouth was too dry to respond.

"Emilia," Gamboa said again. "That's you, isn't it? She's a cop, too. You're the woman he's after."

There was no way Emilia was going to tell this *pendejo* the whole story. "What's in that script is pure fantasy" she retorted.

Her stomach was a cold slurry of disbelief and uncertainty. Gamboa was either the most fluid and facile liar she'd ever met, or he had the most dangerous job in Mexico and one that could destroy her life.

Had he known she was the woman Barrielos Luna was obsessed with? Is that why he got in her taxi? Is that why he kept calling her? Was he acting for Barrielos Luna to trap her? Was the Pablo Arrocha story just an extraordinarily clever cover?

"An operation to catch Barrielos Luna by making a crap movie about his life." Silvio blustered through the tension thickening the air. "This all sounds like bullshit to me. You got any way to prove it besides a script anybody could have written and stuck Barrielos Luna's name on it?"

Gamboa toyed with the ice pack. "From El Acólito days, we knew he wanted a biopic of his life and was writing a script. So we set up Copa Multimedia, put out the word that his favorite actor Rafa Gamboa was available, and he took the bait. Script was delivered by courier."

"You got any proof?" Silvio asked.

Emilia's thoughts continued to whirl with unanswered questions and impossible scenarios. A notorious film about Barrielos Luna might win Rafa Gamboa back his film career but wouldn't keep him from being arrested for El Acólito's crimes.

As a *federale*, however, he was virtually untouchable.

"We know he's got a hacienda in the rough country outside Iguala," Gamboa said. "A couple hundred *sicarios*. If we go in, it'll be a bloodbath. Just like before, we have to lure him out."

The cell phone tucked into Silvio's shirt pocket chirped. He fished it out and walked out of the room.

Emilia found her voice. "I think you're lying," she said to Gamboa. "I think you've been lying for so long you don't know what the truth is anymore."

"If I were you, I'd be damn happy that the *federales* had a plan to take him down," Gamboa said. He tried to smile with the half of his mouth that still worked. A spot of blood leaked out of the corner. "Maybe you'll tell me how it happened and maybe you won't. But being the object of Diego Barrielos Luna's obsession has to be a little scary."

Emilia shoved the *Las Perdidas* binder at him again. "Lila Jimenez Lata. What happened to her? And the other girls?"

"Lila's with Barrielos Luna." Gamboa flipped through the pages as if the binder was a magazine about celebrity hijinks. He tapped pictures at random. "Her, too. Her. Her. This one. Her, too."

By the time he identified nearly 20 women, all young and the most recent additions to the binder, Emilia was drenched in sweat.

"If this biopic operation happens, you'll find all of them." Gamboa closed the binder.

"Shut down the *narcotaxi* operation," Emilia said. "Prove your *federale* story."

"Impossible," Gamboa said, pressing his thumb to his mouth to staunch the blood. "It's the back door into the Barrielos Luna organization. It's part of the strategy. We need it to stay active."

"So you say," Emilia parroted his words back to him.

Gamboa flicked a finger at the door to the kitchen. "What's his name again?"

"Lieutenant Silvio," Emilia said, wary of the shift in conversation.

"Got a first name?"

"Franco."

"What do you call him when you're alone?"

It was an unsettling question. "*Jefe*," Emilia said. "He'll sign all the forms when we bring you in."

"He's your boss?"

"Current boss. Former partner."

"Does he know how you met Barrielos Luna?"

"Yes."

"Are you going to tell me?"

"No."

"Yet, I'm the only thing standing between you and

Barrielos Luna," Gamboa reminded her.

She was negotiating with the devil. Emilia could almost smell the brimstone.

"Get Gabi out of there," she bargained. "To show good faith."

"Who?"

"Gabi. The girl from La Tumba who's tangled up in Barrielos Luna's distribution operation with the *sitio*. The one whose backside you admired."

Gamboa held up his hand. A trickle of blood ran into the cleft between thumb and forefinger.

"I can do that," he said. "But I have one condition."

Emilia knew she'd regret asking but her mouth had a mind of its own. "What?"

"I want to meet my mother."

CHAPTER 38

Emilia's thoughts were miles away the next day, in Silvio's house in El Roble, as she went through the motions of being a reliable *sitio* driver. Over and over, as she hauled fares to beach clubs and office buildings, she picked apart every word, every gesture, from yesterday's conversation with Gamboa at Silvio's house.

Instead of sun slanting off traffic and the jumble of colorful buildings along Acapulco's palm-lined streets, Emilia saw Gamboa's face across the table. Swollen and bruised, yet skillfully parrying her words with a fantastic story about being a *federale*.

If Gamboa was telling the truth, the *federales* had never had any intention of catching El Acólito. He was one of their own. It made sense, given that for almost a year, the *federales* had been actively looking for the notorious El Acólito with no result. Despite the lack of progress, other law enforcement agencies were discouraged from assisting in the hunt. *Lanes in the road*, they always said. *Possible compromise of a federal investigation.*

They probably paid off the owner of that electronics store in Veracruz and dozens of others since the El Acólito operation ended. The *federales* simply created a new identity and a way to take down Barrielos Luna on the presumption that if Gamboa did it once, he could do it again.

But if that movie was released, she would be outed as the

Emilia character. Would her role in the extradition convoy be scrutinized? Would she be accused of helping Barrielos Luna escape? Was the movie a clever ruse by Barrielos Luna to grab her attention?

There were no answers, just more questions. Her thoughts were a spinning hall of mirrors reflecting endless images of danger and paranoia back at her.

As she drove, tuning out the chatter of her fares and the rumble of rubber on hot tarmac, Emilia berated herself for letting control of the conversation with Gamboa slip away. She should have manipulated him into an admission of guilt.

Yes, I did it. I gave you drugs and when you were comatose I raped you. Left my DNA in you for the doctors to find. I did it. I own it.

"Didn't you hear me?" The loud voice burst through Emilia's thoughts like a bowling ball scattering pins.

"I'm sorry," Emilia said hastily. "What did you say, señor?"

"You missed the turn," the man said furiously from the back seat."

Fuck, fuck. "I'm so sorry, señor." Emilia hit the turn signal. "I'll go around."

Except that she couldn't, not really. They were in the north end of the city, on the busy Avenida Lazaro Cardenas and there weren't many places to turn. For the next 20 minutes, as the couple in the back seat fumed, Emilia fought busy midday traffic and beat her way back to the correct address.

Finally, Emilia stomped on the brake and pulled to the curb. The man thrust some peso bills over the seat and the couple scrambled out of the taxi. The door slammed hard enough to send a tremor through the vehicle.

No *propina*. They'd paid exactly the amount shown on the meter.

She stuffed the money into the lockbag and headed for the *sitio*. Even with the air conditioning on full blast, the interior of the taxi was warm, thanks to the bright sunshine. To avoid having to pay the Maxitunel fee, she looped around on the old highway. Every month there were more billboards flanking the rutted road, advertising everything from cheap flights to Guadalajara to Cemex construction materials. Nescafe, Herdez, and Jumex urged her to buy coffee, canned vegetables, and apricot juice. The Patrón billboard didn't bother with words, just a huge bottle of tequila. Drinkers got the message.

The biggest billboard, placed strategically where the highway widened as it headed for the Colonia Garita neighborhood, was the happy visage of mayor Carlota Montoya Perez. Big eyes, white teeth, and dark hair floated by the side of the highway, the face of Acapulco's patronizing guardian angel. *Our mayor Carlota Montoya Perez. Smiling Acapulco!*

City elections were coming up. Emilia didn't know any other candidate for mayor besides Carlota, who was seeking a second term. The point of Carlota's campaign slogan, however, was baffling. Was she smiling on behalf of the city? Were the people of Acapulco smiling because she was mayor? Or was Carlota trying to convince voters that Acapulco was a fucking happy place to be? Happy that lying criminals ran around with a gun tucked into their belts, making fake movies?

Emilia's thoughts fell into the same sucking whirlpool as before. Why didn't Gamboa admit that he'd raped her?

She missed her exit.

"*Madre de Dios*," Emilia exclaimed, furious with her inability to focus. Stuck in the right lane, she had no choice but to continue southwest on the clogged highway as it became Avenida Adolfo Cortines. She waited to get off until she could turn south on Solidaridad, instead of trying to wend her way through tangled side street, but it meant she'd have to backtrack to get to the *sitio* again.

A sign for the El Atún Azul restaurant hung over the street. A line of taxis with the blue Viva Taxis logo on their doors was parked alongside the restaurant. A man approached the first taxi in line.

Emilia slowed, sure that her eyes were fooling her. Don Cisco would never ride in a Viva Taxis taxi. But no, it was him, not a hair out of place. He got into the Viva Taxis car and it pulled away from the curb, passed in front of the restaurant and headed north on Solidaridad.

Emilia pulled a U-turn and closed in on the Viva Taxis vehicle up ahead. She kept two cars between them, hoping that neither the Viva Taxis driver nor Don Cisco spotted the logo on her own vehicle.

The other taxi worked its way west, merged onto the wide Baja California boulevard, and puttered along in the right lane. Emilia matched its speed.

Baja California curved around the sports stadium and traffic slowed. Emilia rode the brake. The messy interchange with Avenida Constituyentes and Avenida Ejido came up faster than she expected. Emilia lost sight of the other vehicle. Had it turned on Constituyentes or Ejido?

Emilia gambled on Ejido, which rimmed the southern border of Colonia Progreso. She drove as fast as she dared, trying to see around every corner and soon spotted the other taxi parked on Calle Rio Bravo, just past a Circle K convenience store on the corner of Ejido and Rio Bravo. Emilia passed the store and found a parking spot in the lot of a nearby strip mall.

She jumped out of the taxi and trotted to the Circle K. From a vantage point in the shade of the convenience store, she watched Don Cisco get out of the taxi in front of a whitewashed residential wall. Once the taxi puttered away, he hitched the strap of his backpack higher on his shoulder and began walking toward the Circle K store.

Emilia backtracked to the strip mall and took a sudden interest in the colorful posters plastered across the window of a tour service offering all the same things as the one in the Hotel Torre Ventura.

Acapulco is for Lovers! Water sports! Scuba diving! Personalized tours!

Don Cisco went into the Circle K. The store's parking lot

was a succession of near accidents as traffic streamed by on Ejido, perpetually snarled by a bus stop on the opposite side of Calle Rio Bravo. As Emilia watched from her vantage point, a black sedan with tinted windows pulled into the Circle K lot. Don Cisco came out of the store, hustled over to the passenger side, and got in. Emilia felt a little thrill in her bones. Los Mozos had made contact.

The sedan backed out of the parking space and angled toward the exit. Emilia zoomed in on the rear and snapped a picture of the *placas* with her cell phone. The car was a BMW with extra tinting on the windows. A classic cartel ride.

She sprinted to the taxi and swung into traffic. Luck was with her as she drove onto Ejido. The BMW was several cars ahead, waiting for the light to change at the next intersection.

Emilia kept the sedan in sight as it headed east on a heading that would take it to the huge Parque Papagayo. Always keeping several cars between them, Emilia followed the BMW as it continued around the lip of the bay, turned north on Avenida Ruben Figeroa, and looped through residential streets to the northern flank of Colonia Progreso, having made almost a complete circle.

The BMW slowed as it approached the battleship-colored walls of a property that occupied an entire corner block. Emilia pulled over, parked, and rolled down her window to consider the familiar location. She watched the black sedan slip around the corner and heard the metallic squeal as a gate reluctantly opened.

She locked the taxi and hurried across the street. The gray walls looked exactly the same as the day she drove Gamboa to the place. The sides pocked with crumbling stucco, the tops studded with broken glass.

There weren't any security cameras. Or at least, none that Emilia could see. Perhaps Los Mozos relied on surveillance detection tricks like long meandering drives instead.

A grinding squeal heralded movement at the gate. Emilia pressed herself into a scrubby bush as the BMW drove out and headed away. She caught a glimpse of more gray stucco beyond a wide drive before the gate reversed itself and closed with a resounding clang.

Emilia waited until the BMW disappeared before approaching the recessed entrance. Four ancient intercom speakers waited to be conquered by rust. Two were accompanied by scratched brass nameplates. Dark patches and empty screw holes showed where the others had fallen off. Neither surviving nameplate bore a name, just an empty slot.

She pushed the button on the nearest intercom. It gave a sticky click, but no buzz of electricity or crackle of static. No voice asked what she wanted. She pushed on the gate but it held fast.

Despite the curving blue sky and warm sunshine on her shoulders, Emilia felt a cold hand glide up the back of her neck. The silent gray walls held the same feeling of haunted desolation as the hotel where Ernesto was held captive by Barrielos Luna's kidnappers.

A sandwich board in front of a small grocery store announced the day's specials. Fruit. Cooking oil. Lottery tickets. The glass door was cracked and held together with duct tape. A window was boarded up with plywood and plastered over with a poster for pay-as-you-go Amigo cell phone cards. Further down the street, spools of chain and twine were stacked in front of a hardware store while the door to a dry cleaner's was propped open with a plastic chair. Moist air curled out of the opening and evaporated in the afternoon sun.

Inside, the store was smaller than her walk-in closet in the Palacio Réal penthouse, with metal shelves running along three sides. A small counter was wedged between the door next to a cooler with a dozen bottles of cola and sports drinks. A rack of magazines and comic books hung crookedly above the counter, weighed down on one side by a wire clothes hanger bent into a circle. Dust lay thick on the cellophane packages of marshmallows and *tamarindo* candy clothespinned to the wire.

Emilia found a bottle of water and a bag of chips and took them to the counter. A teenager sat behind the cash register, engrossed in his cell phone. A slender plastic cord ran from his ears to the phone, as if he was a robot plugged into a tiny power source. Emilia had to wave to get his attention.

He rang up her purchases with one hand, eyes constantly

drifting to the phone.

"Do you know who lives in the big gray place on the corner?" Emilia asked as he handed her the change.

"What?" The kid pulled one earbud away from his head.

Emilia repeated the question.

The kid shrugged and stuffed the earbud back in place.

"Know anybody who might know?" Emilia persisted.

The kid sighed, grabbed a metal pole resting against the plywood covering the window. The pole had a hook at the end, useful for retrieving items from upper shelves. He rapped the curved metal against the ceiling. "*Abuela*," he bawled, tilting his head up. "Question!"

There was movement overhead and an answering rap.

"She's coming," the kid said. He propped the pole back against the wood.

"Thanks," Emilia said but he was already engrossed in the cell phone.

A door slammed above, causing dust to sift off the candy and fall on the counter. A minute later a tiny woman in a plain black dress came into the store.

The kid waved a hand in Emilia's general direction without looking up. "Got a question, *ahuela*."

The grandmother squinted at Emilia. "What kind of question?"

"Do you know who lives in the big gray place on the corner?"

"You mean the Casa de Plata?"

House of Silver. Maybe in better days. "Yes."

"Why?"

Emilia dipped her head shyly and hoped she was guessing correctly that the place was an apartment building and not a suite of offices. "I think my uncle used to live there."

The old woman took a step toward Emilia. "Are you Arturo's boy?"

"Girl, *abuela*," the kid behind the counter bellowed, still working his phone.

"She's wearing a tie," the old woman complained. She wrinkled her nose at Emilia. "Are you one of those girls who thinks she's a boy?"

Emilia resisted a grin. "No, just a *taxista*. I was driving past and remembered going to visit family there when I was little."

"Well, nobody lives there now." The woman sniffed. "Been closed up for years."

"Are you sure?"

"Wasn't I here when the boiler blew up?" The old woman shook her head. "Killed Señora Gonzalez and her baby. The water pump was destroyed. No plumbing. Everybody had to move out."

"When did that happen?"

"Maybe seven or eight years ago." The old woman flopped her hand at the quiet street outside the store. "The city did it, you know. Can't keep the water pressure constant in this neighborhood. High. Low. Who knows? Nothing ever gets fixed."

"If nobody lives there," Emilia interrupted, sensing the

woman was warming up for a high quality rant to a new audience. "Who owns it?"

The old woman spread her hands in defeat. "The ghosts."

CHAPTER 39

The following day was busy but unremarkable. Don Cisco kept to his usual schedule, giving no indication that he'd hopped in his rival's fish-smelling taxi or been threatened by Los Mozos. None of the other drivers even mentioned that the dispatcher took a longer break for *la cena* yesterday. Emilia tried to ask the dispatcher a question or two but Don Cisco shooed her away as the Tin Tan moustache furrowed in annoyance.

At the end of her shift, she drove to the top of Avenida Farallón del Obispo to the huge Mega Soriana supermarket. The long parking lot gave the illusion of being cantilevered over a rolling landscape of green hills and white houses. If the entrance to the supermarket lot wasn't gated and guarded by a private security service, it would have been thronged as a romantic overlook.

Emilia couldn't recall the last time she'd shopped in a chain grocery store. The kitchen in the Palacio Réal penthouse was always stocked with whatever she and Kurt wanted, courtesy of the hotel restaurant. Shopping with her mother Sophia invariably meant a neighborhood market and a string bag for tomatoes and onions.

She passed under the huge heart logo, grabbed a red cart, and proceeded to be overwhelmed by the sheer size of the place. Banners advertised *Rebajas!* discounts above pyramids of paper towels, cooking oil, and boxed juice. The produce section was a neatly manicured forest of choices. Papayas and avocados were heaped in bins as big as the taxi. Emilia wheeled her cart over to a brightly lit row of chilled lettuce, carrots, and *nopales*. Cool water misted her hand as she reached for some romaine. Emilia wiped her palm on her pants and decided she didn't want salad.

The store had its own bakery, a *panadería* with every variety of *pan dulce* displayed in baskets for shoppers to pick and choose. Emilia's mouth watered at the sight of yeasty *bigotes* dusted with sugar, flaky *orejas* as big as her hand, and buttery *mantecada* pastries wrapped in red paper. She went to the bakery counter to get a round aluminum tray and a pair of tongs.

Lieutenant Campos was at the counter, getting a tray for himself. "Ester," he said, not at all surprised to see her. "You might not remember me. I'm Vicente, a friend of your late husband's."

It took Emilia a beat to catch up, but after that it was easy to play along. "Yes, of course," she said, with a sideways smile. "How nice to see you again."

"My wife sent me for *bolillo* rolls," Campos said, as if sharing an important secret. "But I love the sweet breads."

He carried his tray and tongs to the aisle lined with pastries and used his tongs to grab two *bigotes*. They landed on his tray in a shower of sugar.

"The location tracking feature on my BlackBerry appears to be working," Emilia said.

"Yes, it is," Campos said. He stopped next to a basket

piled with crusty rolls called *bolillos.* "I wanted to tell you in person that we brought in the Taxis Coco dispatcher yesterday. He looked through the mug shot books. Didn't recognize anyone."

Again, it took Emilia a beat to process what he said. "You mean Donoso Garay?" she asked. "You brought him in yesterday?"

If her voice was strained, Campos didn't notice as he transferred more *bolillo* rolls to his tray. "Yes, yesterday. Tried to be helpful, but he's a dead end."

Emilia turned to the other side of the aisle and used her tongs to select two big *orejas,* glistening with caramelized sugar crystals. "That's too bad," she said.

"Anything you need to tell me?" Campos asked.

The tongs clanged against the edge of the metal tray but Emilia caught herself before she dropped them. Campos was a man of many talents, but he wasn't a mind reader. There wasn't any way he knew about Gamboa.

She dredged up something from ancient history. "I'm still working the rumor about the contract out on the Los Mozos enforcers."

"Good, good." Campos added another *bolillo* to his collection of breads. "I'm sorry that this assignment is the gift that keeps on giving. You must be missing friends and family."

"I'm okay." Emilia scrutinized the baskets to avoid coming face-to-face with Campos. "Have you talked to Lieutenant Silvio lately?"

"No," Campos said. He kept with her as Emilia drifted down the aisle, tongs at the ready. "Do I need to? Has the champ been giving you grief?"

"In the chief's office, you two seem locked in a death struggle or something." Emilia took her time choosing a paper-wrapped *mantecada*. The calories in one of the cupcake-sized pastries was the equivalent of a week's worth of healthy dinners at the Palacio Réal.

Campos chuckled. "Don't worry about Lieutenant Silvio. I can manage him."

"Of course." Emilia summoned a dry laugh.

At the bakery counter, the clerk transferred the selections from each tray into white waxed paper bags and stuck on a label for the cashier to scan. Campos accepted his bag and gave Emilia a conspiratorial smile. "Until next time, señora," he said for the clerk's benefit. "I hope we run into each other again some time."

"Yes," Emilia said. Her own bag was much smaller. "Perhaps we will."

Campos walked out of the *panadería* area and headed for the cashiers at the front of the store.

The novelty of the supermarket was gone. Leery of running into the lieutenant again, Emilia loitered in the deli section where she could see the line of cashiers. She waited until Campos exited before finishing her own shopping.

Her stomach was queasy from the encounter. A late dinner of pastry and beer didn't help. Emilia sat on the front porch in the dark, flicking crumbs into the foliage and wondering why Lieutenant Campos had lied to her.

☼

"Tell me again why you called me instead of Campos," Silvio said.

Emilia didn't take her eyes off the small electronic device he'd tossed in her lap and its ever-changing digital readout as it sniffed the air to find the right frequency. "Because you know the tech people," she said.

"I got better things to do besides fetch and carry for you. Or run your private prison." Silvio proceeded to rap out a rhythm on the steering wheel.

"Like what?" Emilia wasn't really listening as she stared at the flashing digits.

"I should be at the gym," Silvio said. "Or having coffee with Mercedes."

Emilia grimaced. Like the studio photo, morning coffee implied romantic activity she didn't want to think about. "What's Gamboa doing?" she asked, changing the subject.

"Our prisoner is a strange fucker," Silvio observed. "Seems mostly worried about his face. Don't think he's got any interest in going out in public until he's pretty again. Watches a lot of movies."

"What about Macias and Sandor?"

"They're sitting on him."

"He's going to poison their minds."

"They're all right." Silvio glanced at the digital readout.

"You decide about letting him meet your mother yet?"

The digital numbers froze and the device emitted a squeal. "Got it," Emilia said. She pressed the button next to the readout.

The corrugated metal gate in front of Silvio's unmarked sedan shuddered and slowly rolled to the right, groaning all the way.

It was 6:00 am. Colonia Progreso was still under wraps. The street was empty except for the usual line of parked cars.

As soon as the gate was fully open, Silvio drove through. Emilia hit the button again and the gate rumbled closed behind them. Silvio cut the engine and hopped out. He went to the gate and inspected a battery pack nestled under the eaves of the overhang. "Somebody's rigged up a temporary remote control," he announced.

Emilia stared across a withered lawn to a long gray stucco building that once upon a time was a showpiece of Mexican mid-century architecture. Two lines of balconies fronted by waist-high walls ran across the front, bisected by a double height main entrance with massive wooden doors. Bands of swirling mosaic edged the bottom of the balcony wall while a smaller design encircled the roofline like eyeliner under a frill of clay roof tiles. The windows above the balcony walls were tall and thin and broken.

Streaks of rust from the steel frames etched stripes down stucco decorated with black curds of mold. Random canine teeth of glass glinted in the window frames.

Even more sadly, swaths of the tile mosaic were missing,

leaving behind knobs of mortar and chipped cement block. Bits that still clung to the building twinkled silver and blue in the morning sun.

"What did you say this place was called?" Silvio kicked at a chunk of rubble near the wide stairs leading to the main entrance. Emilia joined him, stopping to peer at the fountain in the middle of the courtyard. A bronze sailing ship poised over a stone basin as big as an armchair. There was no water to be seen. The basin was lined with bird droppings and parched scum.

"Casa de Plata," Emilia said. "It was an apartment building."

The paved lot next to the building could easily accommodate six or seven cars. It was empty. No one came out to challenge them.

Silvio shaded his eyes and squinted at the roofline. "I remember pictures of this place," he said. "In school. The decoration supposedly tells the story of Spain's *flota de plata*. You know, the treasure ships hauling Mexican silver to Spain."

Emilia gazed upwards. Silvio was right. Odds and ends of Spanish galleons sailed around the building on blue waves that disintegrated into gray cement. Created from stone and glass and skill, Spain's flotilla was no match for years of neglect and indifference.

Emilia picked up a piece of blue glass with a ridge of cement stuck to it. "What's your next career? Historian or architect?"

"Funny, Cruz." Silvio pushed on the bronze sail of the fountain's ship. It spun like a weathervane. "It's a famous building. Or used to be. Let's check it out."

The door was a massive carved affair. Silvio jiggled the handle. It turned. The hinges creaked and the door allowed a wedge of sunlight to illuminate a dust-drenched foyer.

Emilia propped the door open with a chunk of cement before taking in the scene before her. Directly across from the doorway, a massive stairway rose from the terrazzo floor and divided halfway as it climbed to the second floor. The iron banister was made out of open circles of wrought iron in a style that Emilia thought of as mid-century modern meets traditional craftsmanship. Stuffing leaked out of two leather upholstered divans that filled the center of the foyer. An enormous sputnik-style brass chandelier laced with cobwebs was still an awe-inspiring showpiece.

"Stop." Silvio held up a hand to prevent Emilia from walking into the foyer.

She saw why. The dusty floor showed two sets of footprints. They were perfect, a forensic technician's dream. Two men, walking side by side, had circled the lobby. The prints were less clear near the apartment doors on each side of the space, where they must have stopped to talk. More footprints led to the stairs.

"Looks like Don Cisco and his buddy are the only people who have been here lately," Silvio observed. "Two sets of footprints. They toured the place."

"I have a bad feeling about this," Emilia said. A musty,

moldy stink clogged her throat. "Don Cisco already pays Los Mozos through a bank account. Why pay a rival taxi service to take him to a strange neighborhood? Then he jumps in a second car to come here? To some old crumbling apartment building? Why not come direct? Why not come in one of his own taxis?"

"You know the answers," Silvio said with a snort.

"To throw off surveillance." Emilia knelt to examine the footprints more closely. A skittering, scratching noise made her flinch. Hopefully, it was nothing more than a gecko foraging for mosquitos.

Silvio squatted next to her. "Maybe they brought him here to beat a little more money out of him?"

"Whatever happened here, he was fine yesterday."

"Maybe they just wanted to shake him up a little."

"This isn't the pattern," Emilia said. "Every other time, Los Mozos threatened Don Cisco at his home. If they really wanted to scare him, they'd come to the *sitio* and make a scene in front of customers and the drivers."

They both stood up. "You think something else is going on?" Silvio asked. "Connected to the *narcotaxi* operation?"

"I don't know," Emilia admitted. "I'm stuck on the fact that Gamboa came here, too."

"When?"

"He looked at a bunch of houses for sale."

"So he was here to buy the place." Silvio squinted at the chandelier. "Maybe your buddy Don Cisco wants to do the same thing."

"Kind of a peculiar coincidence," Emilia said. "Hundreds of properties for sale in Acapulco and these two look at the same one within a week?"

Silvio shrugged, the powerful shoulders rolling like twin avalanches. "You check with the realtor? Maybe it's a bargain price or they're doing a shitload of advertising right now."

"Maybe," Emilia said, loath to believe in coincidences.

"Had enough?" Silvio asked, as the skittering noise drew closer.

They closed the massive door behind them. Emilia turned her face up, greedy for the warmth of the sun after the musty chill of the deserted property.

Silvio spun the bronze ship poised above the empty fountain. It squealed in rhythm with the revolutions. "With a little help, this place could really be a showplace."

"Sure. All you'd need is a crew of specialty workers for about five years." Emilia put her sunglasses on. "Speaking of help, why would Lieutenant Campos lie to me?"

"Lie?" Silvio frowned. "About what? Do I need to pull you out of that fucking taxi?"

"No, listen," Emilia said in exasperation. "Last night he casually bumped into me at the Mega Soriana. Wanted to tell me that Don Cisco had been in his office the day before to look at mug shots. Didn't identify anyone as the Los Mozos thugs who came to his house. Campos called Don Cisco a dead end."

Silvio's frown melted into understanding as he watched

the bronze ship twirl in the morning sun. "You mean that Campos claimed Don Cisco was in his office the same day that you saw the *cabrón* riding around making sure he wasn't tailed so he could end up here?"

"Exactly."

"Maybe Campos had him in the office afterwards?"

Emilia shook her head. "When I got back to the *sitio*, Don Cisco was already there. Stayed for the rest of the day. He never went anywhere else unless Campos saw him at midnight."

"This Don Cisco got a twin brother?"

"Funny." Emilia grabbed the sun-warmed bronze sail and the metallic keening stopped. "Why would Campos lie to me about it? Not only lie, but track me down to lie to my face?"

"He wanted to see your reaction." Silvio picked up a shiny bit of blue glass. "What did you say?"

"I didn't tell him that I knew he was lying, if that's what you're asking."

"Nothing else?"

"We made small talk, bought bread, and went our separate ways."

"How did he find you at the Mega Soriana?"

"He can track me using the BlackBerry with the *maldita* alert function I'll never use again." The BlackBerry was now on the ping pong table in the safe house. It could stay there until the assignment was over.

Knowing Lieutenant Campos had her back was one thing. Knowing that he was birddogging her was another.

"Has he done that before?" Silvio asked.

"No. He always just called before."

"He really wanted to see your reaction." Silvio emphasized the last word.

"Why?"

Silvio took out his keys. "Maybe he's testing you. See if you're right for Financial Crimes."

Emilia gave voice to the question nagging at the back of her mind. "Do you think he's taking a kickback from Don Cisco and the *narcotaxi* operation?"

Silvio didn't meet her eyes but made a production of putting on his sunglasses. "Just do me a favor, Cruz," he said. "Step careful around that *pendejo*."

Emilia kicked aside chips of rubble as they went to Silvio's car. She thought about the way Campos always leaned forward to catch every pearl of wisdom she spoke. How many times he praised her detective skills. Shared details about his family the same as a friend.

He was grooming her. If she hadn't caught him lying to her, Emilia would have continued to suck it up like a thirsty plant.

The best outcome was that Silvio was right about a pending job offer. Campos needed to fill the empty offices next to Jorge and Bruno. Campos probably recruited everyone he deemed potentially useful to his career.

The more likely answer was that he was a dirty cop building his empire with kickbacks from Don Cisco's *narcotaxi* operation. It was hard to justify another reason for lying about Don Cisco's whereabouts.

A buzz emanated from inside Silvio's jacket as Emilia reset the frequency finder to reopen the gate.

"*Rayos*," Silvio muttered. He took out his cell phone and jabbed at the screen before clapping it to his ear. It was a brief call, ending with "Pick him up. I'm on the way."

"Problem?" Emilia asked.

"Got a name for Señor BMW," Silvio said. "If he's connected to Los Mozos, you get a medal."

CHAPTER 40

The owner of the BMW was named Hector Infante Sel. He'd been surprisingly easy to trace.

Infante Sel ran a real estate investment company with an office near Playa Caleta. By 2:00 pm he was in an interrogation room sitting across the table from Silvio and Campos. In his mid-forties with a thatch of prematurely silver hair, a long thin aristocratic face, and a cream linen *guayabera* shirt, Infante Sel was the very image of a successful Mexican businessman.

Or a narcotrafficker's bag man.

Emilia stood in the viewing corridor outside the new interrogation suite, where she could watch the interview through the one-way mirror and listen to the audio. Campos had popped in unannounced and greeted her with pleasant surprise in Silvio's office. Simply curious if there was a connection between Infante Sel and Los Mozos, he claimed.

Campos was relaxed as she recounted Don Cisco's strange journey through the city only to end up in an abandoned apartment building called Casa de Plata. At no time did Campos give any indication that she was exposing his lie but simply nodded and accompanied Silvio into the interrogation room. If he noticed that Emilia never met his eye, he gave no indication.

Of course, she'd said nothing about Rafa Gamboa and his house shopping stop at Casa de Plata.

Watching the three men from the seclusion of the viewing corridor on the other side of the one-way mirror, Emilia was struck by how relaxed Infante Sel was. No fiddly hand motions, sniffling or throat clearing. Nor did he seem intimidated by Silvio, as were so many who had the bad luck to face the former boxer in a confined space.

The difference between the two lieutenants was striking. Silvio in jeans and a white button down shirt, the sleeves rolled back to reveal forearms knotted with muscle. The crewcut, perpetual scowl, and big handgun in a belt holster completed the menacing picture.

In contrast, Campos wore yet another colorful polo shirt, making him appear ready for a drink on the beach.

"Señor," Silvio began. "Thank you for cooperating with our officers. We're investigating a crime and someone you know may be tangentially involved. You are not the subject of our investigation."

"Happy to help any way I can," Infante Sel replied. He crossed his legs and folded his hands on his stomach.

His posture reminded Emilia of guests relaxing in the Pasodoble Bar. All he needed to complete the picture was a cigar and a glass of Kurt's top-shelf brandy.

With Campos immobile beside him, Silvio went through Infante Sel's name, address, and the car he drove. The BMW was a good car for business, according to Infante Sel. People were impressed by European brands, which is why his company was called Oxford Properties.

"We invest in distressed properties," Infante Sel said.

"We buy single residences and small apartment buildings, renovate them, and sell for a profit."

"Distressed properties," Silvio repeated. "Abandoned? Falling down?"

A muscle jumped in Campos's cheek.

"Distressed, but within reason," Infante Sel said. "We don't take on the impossible nor do we have to. Acapulco is full of bargains."

"Is this a profitable business, señor?"

"Extremely." Infante Sel smiled, amused that he had to answer such an obvious question. "I guarantee my investors a twenty-five percent profit."

Silvio scribbled something on a notepad in front of him. "Señor Infante, do you know a man named Francisco Donoso Garay?"

"Of course," Infante Sel answered without hesitation. "He's an investor. In fact I showed him a possible investment property yesterday. The historic Casa de Plata. Four apartments. Beautiful architecture."

"Señor Donoso Garay is interested in buying that property?" Campos spoke for the first time.

"Not by himself, mind you," Infante Sel said. "As a member of our investment group."

"So your company, ah, Oxford Properties, could possibly buy Casa de Plata as an investment?"

"It's exactly the type of property we specialize in."

Campos leaned forward. "Has Señor Donoso Garay ever mentioned any financial difficulty he might be experiencing that would prevent him from continuing to invest in your real estate activities?"

"No."

Campos sat back and pushed on his glasses with a forefinger. His mouth compressed into a thin smile of triumph.

Silvio made another note on his pad before looking up at Infante Sel. "Señor, what can you tell us about a gang called Los Mozos?"

Infante Sel straightened in his seat. "A gang?"

"Yes." Silvio looked steadily at the other man. "Los Mozos. They extort protection money from small businesses like Señor Donoso Garay's *sitio* taxi service."

"I've never heard of them," Infante Sel said. "Is this a warning that they're coming for my business?"

"No, no, señor," Campos interjected. "We have no information that Los Mozos is targeting your business. But if they do, please get in touch with the police immediately."

"Of course."

Without looking at Silvio, Campos stood and opened the door. "We won't keep you any longer, señor. Let me arrange a car to take you back to your office."

Silvio disappeared inside his office without saying a word to anyone. Emilia figured that he and Campos had argued but neither invited her to watch the next round.

She traded a few barbs with the handful of detectives in the squadroom before filling her old Maná mug with coffee and settling in front of the computer on her bare desk to do a little research on Oxford Properties.

It wasn't that she didn't believe Infante Sel, but something was missing from his story.

Oxford Properties had a nice website, listing an address near Playa Caleta and an online form to fill out for more information. The home page lauded its 25% return on investment. Blog posts were all about investing in real estate and the Acapulco property market. The tone was professionally robotic.

The website led to a couple of social media profiles that all linked back to either the website, other real estate blogs, or Mexico vacation sites for tourists. Nothing controversial. Strictly business.

Emilia kept searching, using every online search trick that she knew, and eventually dug herself into an English-language forum for *norteamericano* real estate brokers. Oxford was briefly mentioned in a discussion thread.

AustinSells: Anybody heard of Oxford Properties in Acapulco? Prop investors.

RightWay: House flippers.

AustinSells: Cheap market there.

RightWay: Requires 1M to invest. Dollars.

MaryMcC: Up front. Mex invstrs only.

AustinSells: TKS.

Emilia headed for Silvio's office and plunked herself down in one of the chairs fronting the desk but got up again when Silvio gestured for her to close the door.

"Guess what I found out?" she said impatiently.

"I'm not your personal prison warden?"

Emilia waved away the remark. "Guess how much it costs to invest with Oxford Properties?"

"Something tells me I'm not going to like this," Silvio said.

"A million." Emilia paused. "Dollars."

After a hasty fast food meal at her desk, Emilia expanded the Los Mozos timeline begun in the windowless office in Financial Crimes. It started with Los Mozos threatening Don Cisco into paying extortion money. At the end of the timeline, Don Cisco was rich enough to invest a million dollars in real estate, presumably thanks to his *narcotaxi* operation.

She padded the middle with the note from the glove compartment, with a question mark instead of a date. Added the bit from Montez's snitch El Gatito about a godfather, with a question mark for when that relationship started. That *pendejo* Bino hadn't given her anything to add, just verification that the park vendors were frightened.

It was a scanty timeline. Few facts. Lots of rumors.

Emilia needed the names of Los Mozos gang members and where they congregated. What streets did the gang claim? What cartels did they run errands for? What was the gang's exact relationship to Don Cisco's *narcotaxi* operation and the La Tumba bar? What about the Banamex Bank account? Who withdrew from it?

Another question mark hovered over Chavito's surmise about the untimely end for two Los Mozos enforcers as ordered by the godfather. Even if they were among the numerous homicides in Acapulco since Arrocha's murder, surely the phantom gang was bigger than two enforcers.

So where the hell were they?

CHAPTER 41

It was situation normal at the *sitio* the following day. Don Cisco hummed over his notebook at the dispatch booth. Ricardo smoked and glowered. Lobo said his wife decided to paint the baby's room white. Juan Miguel chattered about the next basketball practice and provoked general sympathy when he mentioned that Pablo's widow, Maria, was slated for surgery to put a pin in the broken arm that refused to heal.

Emilia got to Silvio's house long after 10:00 pm, tired, sweaty, and not at all sure she knew where her life, much less the investigation, was going.

There wasn't much in Silvio's spare bedroom besides a bed, a dresser, and a man who sucked all the oxygen from the air. Macias and Sandor were in the hall behind her, playing cards.

"What do you know about a man named Hector Infante Sel?" Emilia asked.

"Hector Infante Sel." Gamboa rolled the name around in his mouth. "Infante Sel. I don't know the name."

"What about Francisco Donoso Garay?" she asked, leaning on the wall.

Gamboa shoved himself into a sitting position on the bed. His face was still mottled with bruises but he was relaxed in sweatpants and a white tee. There was a paperback book next to him.

"Why should I know either name, Baby?" Gamboa asked.

"They're both interested in Casa de Plata," Emilia said, ignoring his overly familiar tone. "Just like you."

"Smart buyers," Gamboa said. "It's a distressed property for sale at a bargain price."

"Sure," Emilia said. His answer was too simple, too easy. Too wrong. She just didn't know why.

"Have you thought about my deal?" Gamboa asked. "I get the girl out. You bring the mother to meet me."

"It's only a deal if I buy your shit story about being a *federale*."

"You're not a very good detective, are you?" Still seated, Gamboa yawned and reached over his head with both arms, revealing the lean musculature Emilia remembered from the Santa Muerte rally. The seemingly innocent stretch was meant to intimidate.

"You don't know anything about me," she said evenly.

"Your oversized jailer believes me," Gamboa said. "So do his two goons. You should listen to them, Baby."

"You can call me Detective Cruz, *pendejo*."

Emilia found Silvio in his office off the kitchen, reading a copy of *El Sol de Acapulco* with its trademark red masthead. *Ella aumentó el turismo!* shouted the self-congratulatory headline. No doubt the story about Carlota boosting tourism, complete with fictional facts, was planted in the newspaper by Carlota's re-election campaign.

"He called Macias and Sandor your goons," Emilia said and plunked herself into a chair.

"Did you ask him about Infante Sel and the Casa de Plata?"

"Said he had no idea."

"You believe him?"

"I don't believe a word that comes out of his mouth."

"Yeah," Silvio said and folded the newspaper. "About that."

Something in his tone made Emilia catch her breath. "About what?"

"We need to let him go make his movie for Barrielos Luna."

"*Madre de Dios*, Franco," she exclaimed. "I told you he was going to poison your mind. A screenplay and some phone calls are not enough to prove he's a *federale*."

"What other explanation is there, Cruz?" Silvio asked quietly.

"This movie is a stunt," Emilia ranted. "I don't know what the real story is, but being a *federale* isn't it."

"Yeah, well." Silvio looked everywhere but at Emilia. "They need Alejandra Messi's stand-in again."

Emilia's jaw dropped. "Are you serious? No."

"They need you for one day, Cruz," Silvio said. "Same deal as before. Pretend to be Alejandra Messi. Walk around Sinfonia del Mar. Easy stuff."

"That's not the point." Emilia could barely keep herself from shouting. The thickheaded idiot in front of her had fallen for Gamboa's fairy tale. "Alejandra Messi is not coming to Acapulco to be in Gamboa's fake movie. If she was, it would be all over the news. This is all a giant con job, the same way El Acólito made people believe in Santa Muerte."

"Listen." Silvio shifted uncomfortably in his chair. "From what Gamboa says, you were pretty good at it."

Silvio's attempt to flatter was pathetic. "I was terrible."

"Look, do it, get it over with. Then we'll bring in this Don Cisco character. Sweat him a little and find out how he got enough money to buy crap real estate."

"Campos doesn't want to touch him."

"Well, I do." Silvio aimlessly shoved the newspaper around the table. "There could be a connection between Los Mozos, the *sitio*, and that building. Maybe Gamboa's part of it, maybe he's not."

Emilia drew the paper towards her. *Ella aumentó el turismo!*

"So do we have a plan?" Silvio asked.

More mirrors and more mirrors, all reflecting a funhouse full of crudely fitting puzzle pieces. "Gamboa's feeding us a total line of shit."

"Come on, Cruz. His story adds up. He never got arrested because the *federales* are protecting their operation. The notes from Los Mozos to Arrocha support him."

"He's a rapist and human trafficker and a murderer," Emilia said stubbornly.

"Yeah, and the *federales* don't care as long as he nets

Barrielos Luna," Silvio said. "It's why they've protected him all this time."

Emilia spun out of her seat and walked to the door, shaking her head as she went.

"Think about it, Cruz." Silvio's voice hit her between the shoulder blades like a well-aimed stone. "We know for a fact that Barrielos Luna is lurking around, sniffing after you. From my optic, Gamboa is your best bet to catch him before Barrielos Luna takes another shot at you."

"He's using you to convince me to let him meet my mother," Emilia said without turning around.

"He'll get the girl out," Silvio said. "This Gabi."

Emilia pressed a hand to her forehead. She probably had a fever. "He'll say anything."

"If the movie draws out Barrielos Luna, we'll get the others."

"If they're alive," Emilia said bitterly.

"What other chance do we have?" Silvio asked. "I got nothing on any of those women. If I did, they wouldn't be in your fucking binder."

Emilia whirled around. "Gamboa's playing you, Franco. He's a liar. He plays everybody."

"What if you're wrong?" Silvio pressed. "What if Gamboa's telling the truth and he's your best shot at taking down Barrielos Luna? The *cabrón* who nearly killed Ernesto and sent your mother over the edge. You've survived him twice. How many more chances do you think you'll get?"

Emilia swallowed hard. "What if *you're* wrong? What if

he's a *federale* but crooked? What if he's Barrielos Luna's partner?"

"If I'm wrong," Silvio said. "I'll hunt Gamboa down and kill him myself."

Emilia locked eyes with him. Silvio was absolutely serious. The silence between them stretched to the breaking point.

"Okay," she said.

CHAPTER 42

Emilia parked the taxi in the same corner of the parking lot above the Sinfonia del Mar, far from the Buick and Cadillac. As she approached the cluster of trailers, she saw Gamboa introduce Silvio, Macias, and Sandor to the film crew as his bodyguards. No one joked or asked why Gamboa needed heightened security.

Since Emilia made her debut as Alejandra Messi's stand-in, the movie set had swelled in terms of equipment and crew. More than a dozen people wearing identification tags swirled around waving clipboards or plugging in equipment or adjusting huge reflective sails to redirect the afternoon sunlight.

Bob seemed genuinely glad to see Emilia. "We've got a quick scene to shoot, down on the stage."

Lora was there and again took charge of Emilia's transformation into Alejandra Messi, this time in a long-sleeved black dress shot through with silver threads. Once she'd wriggled it on over the push-up bra and stomach-controlling, soul-destroying girdle, Emilia hardly recognized the woman in the mirror.

Once again, her hair flowed over her shoulders like a silk waterfall. Her eyes were bigger, thanks to false eyelashes and skillfully applied dark shadow. Her lips and nails were red and her cheeks sparkled with a dusting of something she couldn't wait to wash off.

Lora carried her heels and a makeup bag as Emilia proceeded down the steep stone steps of the amphitheater. She was conscious of Silvio's eyes on her as she approached the stage.

A narrow track ran across the famous mosaic in the center of the stage. A camera mounted on some sort of trolley waited at one end, surrounded by Bob and the rest of the film crew.

Gamboa met her there and kept up the pretense that she was Ester, the *taxista*.

Stage makeup artfully concealed the fading bruises on his face. He was in character as Diego again with manufactured cheekbones and coal black hair with matching eyebrows. This time she saw the resemblance to Diego Barrielos Luna. Wearing a white guayabera shirt and tan trousers, Gamboa was a dead ringer for the drug lord, albeit 30 years ago.

"All right." Gamboa rubbed his hands together. "We're going to shoot a quite simple scene. I'm Diego and you're Victoria. You know about Victoria, right?"

"Sure."

"All you have to do is walk with me across the stage," Gamboa said impatiently. "I'll do the talking. The camera will follow along the track behind us. You just walk straight ahead. Easy, right?"

"No," Emilia said with absolute uncertainty.

"We've cut the scene so you only have one line," Gamboa went on. "I finish by saying, 'Every woman wants me but I have chosen you, Victoria." That's your cue to say, 'I can't do this, Diego.'"

He looked at her expectantly.

"Tell me again why Alejandra Messi isn't shooting this scene with you?" Emilia asked.

"Because we only have one day of her time and she's shooting all the Emilia scenes. Unless you want to do that?"

They glared at each other. The situation was so absurd Emilia wondered if she was hallucinating. Maybe if she held her breath, the crazy bubble of last few weeks would burst with the pop of a champagne cork and she'd wake up in the penthouse in the Palacio Réal next to Kurt.

Madre de Dios, how was she ever going to tell Kurt any of this?

Silvio clumped over to their folding chairs, expressionless behind a pair of sunglasses. "Ready?" he asked.

"Almost," Gamboa replied. "Running through our lines."

He hopped off the chair and indicated a spot near the camera trolley. "We start here and walk while I talk. Blah, blah, the big line. 'Every woman wants me but I have chosen you, Victoria.'"

"I can't do this, Diego," Emilia said.

"Then I say, 'Don't say that.' That's your cue to walk away toward that marker." Gamboa pointed to the bottom row of benches where someone had placed a board marked with a red X on the first seat. "Don't rush, just walk away, head held high, and sit down. The marker won't be there when the camera is rolling. It's just there now so you know where to go."

"That's all I have to do?" Emilia estimated the distance to the marker. No more than three meters to the spot on the first tier of the amphitheater.

"See. Easy. Let's practice again," Gamboa said. "Every woman wants me but I have chosen you, Victoria."

"I can't do this, Diego," Emilia said.

"Don't say that."

Emilia walked toward the marker.

"Perfect!" Gamboa applauded. "This morning you were a taxi driver, this afternoon you're a movie star."

He was such a good actor that she could believe the tire iron incident and imprisonment at Silvio's house never happened.

They practiced the lines a few more times, until Gamboa was satisfied that she would say it on cue. Emilia alternately repeated the line and inwardly cursed herself for being a weakling, an *estupida*.

Bob and the camera were ready with the camera on its stand, ready to move along the track as they walked ahead of it. Gamboa stood on Emilia's right, between her and the water. On her left, a big reflective screen obscured her view of the upward sweep of the amphitheater.

Someone called out the scene number. The clapperboard snapped.

"Action," Bob yelled.

Gamboa turned to Emilia and smiled. They strolled along the dolly track, the camera capturing his profile but not hers.

"Victoria, you must know how I feel," Gamboa began. He didn't touch Emilia or make big gestures yet radiated energy as if an electric charge flowed through his veins. "You are my prize. My woman. You will always be my woman."

Emilia barely paid attention, her senses trained on a member of the camera crew who kept pace with them, holding a long metal pole over their heads. A microphone dangled at the end of the pole, bobbing in and out of Emilia's peripheral vision. No one had said anything about a metal pole swaying above her head. Despite the size of the amphitheater, claustrophobia seized Emilia by the throat.

"No one can touch me, I'm too strong," Gamboa declared. "You will watch me do great things."

She was hemmed in by Gamboa on one side, the silver shade on the other, and the metal pole with its microphone pointed at her head like the point of a sword.

"Cut," Bob yelled.

Gamboa halted. "What's the matter?"

"She looked at the grip," Bob said.

"Nobody said there was going to be anything overhead," Emilia exclaimed nervously. The equipment was barely a meter above them.

"It's just the microphone," Bob said. "Just keep looking straight ahead. I guarantee it won't fall on you."

Emilia adjusted her dress, trying to suck in enough air to get through this nightmare, and went back to the starting spot.

The clapperboard slammed together.

Bob called, "Action."

Emilia and Gamboa began to cross the stage a second time.

"Victoria, you must know how I feel," Gamboa started again. "You are my prize. My woman. You will always be my woman. No one can touch me, I'm too strong. You will watch me do great things."

Emilia paused, finally paying full attention to his lines. "Wait, is this supposed to be a marriage proposal?"

"Cut," Bob yelled.

"Yes," Gamboa said. "I told you. Diego wants to be with her forever, but Victoria isn't sure."

"That's not the way a man proposes," Emilia said. Diego's lines were braying and idiotic.

"And just what, in your experience, should a man say?" Gamboa reached out.

Emilia drew back before he could touch her. An image of Kurt sinking to one knee in the twilight, the setting sun turning his yellow hair to fire, competed with . . . *this*.

"Never mind," she said.

"Let's stick to the script, okay?" Bob barked.

Emilia scurried back to the starting point, hastened by a few mental kicks and the knowledge that her fellow detectives were watching her lose her mind. What difference did it make to her if the movie was crap? As Lora powdered her nose and sprayed her hair, Emilia vowed to get it right the next time so she could go back to the safe house. Get drunk and curse Silvio.

The third take went better. They were nearly to the end of the camera track when he delivered his final, idiotic line. "Every woman wants me, but I have chosen you, Victoria."

"Ican'tdothisDiego," Emilia said.

"Cut," Bob yelled.

"Nervous, Baby?" Gamboa said under his breath.

Emilia walked back to the starting mark as fast as her stilettos permitted. She wouldn't make the same mistake again.

"Action!" Bob yelled.

They strolled along. Emilia had to concentrate to avoid rolling her hands into fists.

"Every woman wants me," Gamboa ended his monologue. "But I have chosen you, Victoria."

Emilia took a deep breath. "I. Can't. Do. This. Diego."

"Cut," Bob yelled.

They did the scene again. And again. And again.

After the next take, Gamboa conferred with Bob.

"She's solid wood," Emilia heard Bob complain in English. "Having her say a line is a bridge too far. We've got the B-roll. It will have to be enough."

"Look, she'll be fine." Gamboa argued.

Bob shook his head. "We're losing the light."

Lora appeared and sprayed something on Emilia's hair, making it impossible to hear the rest of the conversation.

Gamboa took his place next to Emilia. "Okay, shall we try this again?"

"Look, I told you I'm not an actress," Emilia said.

"Bob's a selfish bastard," Gamboa said as if it was a private joke. "Ignore him. Multiple takes are completely normal. There's enough time for one more take."

Emilia heard the resignation in Bob's voice as he called, "Action."

Once more, Emilia fought against feeling trapped as she strolled next to Gamboa.

"Victoria, you must know how I feel," Gamboa said. "You are my prize. My woman. You will always be my woman. No one can touch me, I'm too strong. You will watch me do great things. Every woman wants me, but I have chosen you, Victoria."

Before Emilia could say her line, Gamboa seized her upper arms, pulled her to him and kissed her hard, bruising her lips against his.

Emilia arched under the heavy pressure of his mouth on hers, the vise-like grip of his hands on her arms, the weight of him bending her backwards. Rage and revulsion boiled up and she tore herself out of Gamboa's grasp. Slapped him as hard as she could, the crack of her palm against his cheek loud and penetrating.

"No!" she cried. "I can't do this."

Gamboa reared back, a hand to his reddened face. "Don't say that, Victoria."

Emilia walked away fast as the high heels and skinny dress would allow, nearly blinded by fury and a powder keg heartrate. A stone bench brought her up short and she didn't care if it was the right seat or not. She dropped onto it and stared stiffly at the ocean lapping against the horizon. The sun was beginning to set, sending a collage of tangerine and pink streaks across the sky.

A breeze whipped her hair around her shoulders. A tear etched down her cheek as Emilia fought for control. She didn't wipe it away but sat with her fists clenched in her lap. *Estupida, estupida.*

"Cut!" Bob yelled.

"Good?" Gamboa called.

"That's a wrap," Bob replied. "Great job, Ester!"

Emilia was still shaking as she left Lora in the wardrobe and makeup trailer. Macias and Sandor met her before she could head for the taxi.

"Silvio wants to talk," Macias said.

"Silvio can go to hell," Emilia muttered under her breath.

Sandor gave her a soft golf clap.

"I couldn't tell you apart from Alejandra Messi," he said as they descended the steps to the stage. "Have you seen *Diamond Run* yet?"

"Twist ending," Emilia said shortly. "Alejandra Messi is an Interpol agent. He's the jewel thief."

"What?" Macias was aghast.

Emilia pushed past the two detectives and took the stone steps through the amphitheater faster than was safe. Behind her, the two detectives argued about the movie and if it was worth seeing now.

"Ester, you did a wonderful job." Gamboa said, for the benefit of the film crew. He was still in costume with Silvio by his elbow.

Bob waited nearby with a clipboard, consulting with one of his people. Other members of the film crew milled around, congratulating themselves on wrapping up a great day of filming. Quiet laughter over certain scenes. Mumbles about where to eat later.

"Alejandra Messi will be on set tomorrow," Gamboa said. "Please come and bring your mother."

The invitation was a broadside she should have expected but didn't. Emilia glared at Silvio. He didn't react.

Gamboa went on, gesturing at the glorious sunset casting a glow over Sinfonia del Mar. "I'm sure your mother is a huge fan of Alejandra Messi. I mean, is there any woman in Mexico who isn't?"

He'd orchestrated the conversation to be in the middle of the film crew's end-of-day wrap activities so she'd feel pressured by the crowd. Emilia never hated a person more.

"I have to work," she said.

"We'll make sure your mother meets Alejandra Messi tomorrow," Gamboa went on, ignoring her feeble excuse. "She can watch a scene being filmed and get an autograph. She'd like that, wouldn't she, Ester?"

"I'm sure she would," Silvio said. "We'll make sure she comes, won't we, Ester?"

CHAPTER 43

Silvio stopped at a red light. He cut his eyes to Emilia as she fidgeted in the passenger seat.

"Alejandra Messi!" Sophia gushed. "Wouldn't that be amazing? I've never met a movie star before."

Emilia twisted over the center console to talk to her mother and Ernesto riding in the back seat of Silvio's car. "Mama, it's not certain that she'll be there. Don't get your hopes up."

Sophia reached forward and patted Emilia's hand. "Alejandra Messi is very famous, Emilia. Make sure you wear your best manners."

Emilia managed a feeble smile. "Look, Mama. There's another thing. Most of the movie people are from *El Norte*. They mix up Mexican names. If they call me Ester, don't say anything, okay?"

"That must be how they say Emilia in English," Ernesto said.

Sophia beamed at her husband. "Of course."

"Did you hear what I said, Mama?" Emilia asked sharply. "Don't correct them."

The light changed. Silvio accelerated, heading west toward the Sinfonia del Mar. "Calm down," he said out of the corner of his mouth.

"I'm going to kill you," Emilia mouthed at him. She slapped on her sunglasses and tried to convince herself that this would all be over soon.

"Alejandra Messi has a dog," Sophia announced. "I read about it in a magazine. Do you think she'll bring it?"

"A dog would be too excited with all the movie people," Ernesto said. "It would get nervous and bite someone."

Silvio gave a raspy chuckle. "I'll bet if she brings her dog, she has someone who takes care of it."

Emilia stared past the traffic and concentrated on not punching the *pendejo* behind the wheel. She knew that she lied too easily. Kept things from Kurt now and then. But she'd never done anything as devious and unforgiveable as this.

Sophia had been walking on air ever since Emilia told her that Silvio had invited them to come to a movie set where he was in charge of security. Sophia had donned her best dress for the occasion, pink polyester with a gathered neckline and a flounce at the knee, which she wore with low heeled brown sandals. It was the same outfit she wore to First Communions and Easter Sunday. Next to her, his cane propped between his knees, Ernesto sported a starched white *guayabera* shirt and dark trousers with the sharpest crease Sophia's iron could produce. His hair was slicked back with gel.

They got to Sinfonia del Mar far too fast. Silvio swung into the parking lot. As they all got out of the car, Sophia and Ernesto gawked at the movie trailers and the rumbling generators with their legions of cables snaking into the amphitheater. The vintage vehicles were still in the lot by the bougainvillea but overshadowed by two limousines and a late model van.

A new awning created a shaded patio stretching between the two largest trailers. A number of director's chairs were there. A woman with sleek dark hair sat in one, her hand extended to a manicurist, while Gamboa stood next to her. He was already in costume as Diego.

"Come on." Silvio herded them all toward the awning.

Emilia's feet dragged. Each step brought her closer to a terrible deception.

Gamboa intercepted them before they reached the awning. "Franco," he said. "Ester."

Silvio introduced him to Sophia and Ernesto as Manolo Bernal, an actor and movie producer. Sophia's eyes slid over him with no flicker of recognition and fixated on the woman sitting under the awning.

"Is that Alejandra Messi?" Sophia asked. "Did she bring her dog?"

"I'll introduce you to Alejandra after we film this scene," Gamboa said.

One of the production assistants escorted them down the stone steps of the amphitheater. They descended slowly, Silvio helping Ernesto. The assistant got them situated a few rows from the stage and provided them with bottles of water and umbrellas to block the sun.

The edge of the stage had been transformed into a seaside café, bounded by a white awning overhead and huge reflective silver sheets on the sides. The distinctive Sinfonia del Mar mosaic was hidden by a sheet of checkered linoleum. The tables and chairs were reminiscent of a French bistro featured in one of Kurt's hospitality magazines. Half a dozen extras in clothing straight out of a 30-year-old disco milled around, along with two waiters in dark pants and long white aprons.

Two cameras, each with a serious-looking crew brandishing badges and clipboards, were stationed on either side of the fake restaurant. Emilia saw Bob deep in conversation with one of the cameramen. He moved to the other side and peered in the viewfinder.

Gamboa, resplendent in a white suit like Pablo Escobar entering a dance competition, escorted the dark-haired woman through the amphitheater to a table. She sank onto the wood and wire chair with a swirl of red satin and flash of upper thigh. A harried-looking woman sprang up out of nowhere and began to fuss with the halter neckline of the actress's dress. Another minion aimed a can of hair spray.

Emilia tried not to stare. It was impossible, but the woman was Alejandra Messi. An entourage orbited around her including the hair and makeup team, a personal assistant juggling multiple cell phones, and a bunch of bodyguards each nearly as big as Silvio.

Sophia could hardly contain herself, squirming with excitement on the stone bench next to Emilia. "That's Alejandra Messi," she whispered over and over.

The extras filled in the empty seats in the restaurant. Tables were set with prop food. Alejandra Messi's minions scooted out of the way.

A production assistant pumped the clapperboard.

Bob yelled, "Action."

It was a first date scene that obviously proceeded the abortive proposal that Emilia and Gamboa had filmed. As the ill-fated Victoria, Alejandra Messi flirted, pouted, and charmed Diego while at the same time emoting a doe-eyed concern that he was a dangerous man. Most of Gamboa's dialogue was the Mexican-patriot-simple-seller-of-oranges stuff of his previous dramatic monologue.

The scene took six takes before Bob was happy. Each time the director yelled, "Cut," Alejandra Messi's personal assistant whipped out a cell phone and placed it in the actress's hand.

In contrast, Gamboa did nothing. He stayed immobile in the little café chair and watched Sophia until the action started up again.

"Where's the press?" Emilia muttered to Silvio during a break. "How could Alejandra Messi be here and absolutely nobody knows?"

"The *federales* have a long arm, Cruz," Silvio replied.

"He's playing us," Emilia warned. "That's not really Alejandra Messi."

"I wonder where her dog is," Sophia said.

When the scene wrapped, all the extras applauded. The production assistant brought the four visitors to the stage to meet Alejandra Messi.

The actress repeated all of their names during the

introduction, making Sophia swoon with joy that the most famous actress in the world had actually uttered her name. The actress had the cool handshake of someone who usually had people to do that. But she thawed slightly when Sophia asked about her dog.

"Astro," Alejandra answered. "He's at home."

She signed a sheaf of glossy photographs for them before her assistant said it was time to change.

"Isn't she wonderful?" Sophia stared open-mouthed as the actress disappeared inside the wardrobe trailer.

"Terrific," Emilia said. "We should go now."

"There's no need to rush." Gamboa ushered them away from the set as technicians moved the scenery and repositioned the reflective screens. "Sophia, what did you think? You're the exact audience this film is trying to reach. Your opinion matters."

A vague frown spread across Sophia's face. "What's the name of the movie?"

"It's called *A Misunderstood Life*," Gamboa said.

"Why is it misunderstood?"

"Señor Bernal's character Diego is a dangerous man who pretends not to be," Emilia rushed to explain. "Just like Señor Bernal himself."

Sophia blinked at Gamboa. Her chin dimpled, prelude to tears of confusion.

"We have to go," Emilia insisted.

"Sophia, just a minute," Gamboa said. "I have a souvenir for you."

"She can't accept it," Emilia said immediately.

Gamboa held out a gold bracelet bedazzled with black crystals. "Alejandra wore this in the scene we just shot."

Sophia let Gamboa fasten the clasp around her wrist. "Something to remember us by," he said.

"Thank you." Sophia raised her eyes from the bracelet and shuffled backwards, nearly tripping Ernesto.

"You're far too young to be Emilia's mother," Gamboa said, dropping the name game. He crowded Emilia out of the way, his head inclined toward Sophia. "Do you have any other children?"

"We have to go," Emilia announced loudly. She felt Ernesto's eyes on her.

"I had a son," Sophia murmured.

"I am getting tired," Ernesto said, his voice barely audible.

"Really, Sophia?" Gamboa smirked like a professional con man about to lay down five aces. "A son?"

Sophia touched the bracelet with a tentative finger. "He's dead now."

The smile froze on Gamboa's face.

"He's been dead for a long time." Sophia held out her arm so Ernesto could admire the bracelet but he took her hand instead.

"My condolences," Gamboa said.

He gave Emilia a strange little bow as if to acknowledge her triumph. His eyes burned with anger.

The ride back to her mother's house was silent, as if they

were all exhausted by the encounter.

Someday, Emilia would explain to Ernesto and ask for his forgiveness. But that day wasn't today.

Halfway home, Sophia realized that her watch was gone.

CHAPTER 44

Don Cisco sat alone in the interrogation room, taking deep shaky breaths. Outside in the viewing corridor, Emilia watched as the normally calm and organized *sitio* owner dabbed a handkerchief against his sweaty forehead. His hand shook.

She passed the bag of chips to Silvio. He put down his can of cola to grab a handful.

"He looks scared enough to pee himself," Silvio observed.

Emilia glanced at the clock above the audio feed speaker. "He's been in there by himself for nearly an hour."

Silvio dusted chip dust off his hands, drained the can of cola, and grabbed up a hefty file folder containing the transcript of Campos's interview with Don Cisco and photos of the two notes attributed to Los Mozos: the claim of responsibility left with Pablo Arrocha's body and the one Emilia found in the glove compartment. Eighteen photographs of the men murdered in Acapulco since Pablo Arrocha's murder rounded out the collection. Half of the homicides had names; the rest were unidentified bodies sitting on a double decker in the morgue.

If the rumors Emilia had gathered were true, any one of those dead men could be the one who killed Arrocha, victim of revenge from the still unknown *sitio* godfather. Maybe Don Cisco would put his finger on two faces as the men from

Los Mozos who'd snared him into paying protection money into that Banamex Bank account. If so, one was likely to be the shooter.

Emilia stayed in the viewing corridor as Silvio went around the corner, knocked on the door to the interrogation room, and smacked it open without waiting for an answer.

Don Cisco stood up.

"Señor Donoso Garay?" Silvio tossed his file on the table. "Lieutenant Franco Silvio. This is in connection to the murder of Pablo Arrocha, one of your *sitio* drivers."

"I already spoke to a Lieutenant Campos," Don Cisco said.

Silvio made a noncommittal noise and sat down. He blew out his breath noisily and opened the file. Studied the text. Frowned. Licked a finger and flipped a few pages, apparently looking for something specific.

Don Cisco blinked uncertainly, the moustache twitching like nervous caterpillars, and slowly sank into his chair.

"Now," Silvio barked. "First question. Was this Pablo Arrocha involved in drugs?"

"No, no, never," Don Cisco said. "A very honest man. A family man."

"Regular clients?" Silvio asked. "People who specifically asked him to drive them?"

"No, not that I recall."

"In Acapulco, most murders are drug related. If he was driving people who transported drugs, for example."

"He . . . no, no, nothing like that." Don Cisco blinked

repeatedly.

"Let's talk about Los Mozos," Silvio said switching topics. Emilia knew he'd eventually circle back to the *narcotaxi* concept like a fisherman. Throw out a line, reel it back in, over and over, until the fish took the bait without knowing it.

Prompted by Silvio, Don Cisco relayed the same story that he told Campos. Members of Los Mozos threatened him at his home. Paid the requested amount with regular bank deposits. Acceded to a second request when they threatened to kill the first driver in line. He paid the additional amount, but they kept their promise.

"Acapulco is a hard place to be a businessman," Silvio said. "But the police can't be everywhere."

Don Cisco bobbed his head. To Emilia's surprise, he didn't rant about thieving villains or the difficulty of being a businessman in Acapulco.

"Take me through the day Arrocha was killed." Silvio made a show of consulting the file. "What time did you arrive at the *sitio* that morning?"

Emilia found the half-eaten bag of chips as Don Cisco recounted the small details of the day, all of which she already knew. Halfway through the dispatcher's recitation of an ordinary day, Silvio closed the file.

"Señor, I've been remiss," Silvio declared. "May I offer you a cafecita?"

"Coffee," Don Cisco replied gratefully. "How kind of you."

Two cups of coffee from the squadroom and the interview became almost jovial; just two men of a similar age talking about life and death in Acapulco.

"Diversify," Silvio said, leaning back. "I hear that's the best thing a businessman can do today. Diversify."

"Diversify," Don Cisco echoed.

"I've heard of this outfit called Oxford Properties. Buys real estate, fixes up old places, and sells them for a fortune." Silvio swirled the coffee in his cup. "Are you in with them?"

"Well, yes." Don Cisco put down his half-drunk cup of coffee.

Emilia took note of the man's uneasiness.

Silvio gave a nod of encouragement. "That's Hector Infante Sel's company, isn't it? He mentioned you were in with him."

"Yes." Don Cisco swallowed nervously. "I've invested a little."

"I hear the minimum to invest with his company is a million dollars."

Don Cisco opened his mouth. Nothing came out. He lowered his head and stared into the coffee cup.

Silvio opened the file folder again, his actions deliberately slow and relaxed. "A million dollars. Not pesos. Despite your problems with Los Mozos, the *sitio* must be a very profitable enterprise."

"Yes," Don Cisco said, his voice barely audible.

"Some taxi *sitios* are asked to transport things that aren't legal." Silvio's tone was still friendly. "Perhaps you know you shouldn't, but the pressure to cooperate is significant."

The Tin Tan moustache tightened over Don Cisco's upper lip.

"We've heard that the Barrielos Luna organization uses taxis to distribute cocaine to its mules throughout the city," Silvio said, more aggressively this time. "Is Los Mozos connected?"

Don Cisco shook his head. "No."

Out in the viewing corridor, Emilia crumpled the empty chip bag and threw it in the trash.

"Did you know that your *sitio* is the only business they've targeted?" Silvio pressed. "The police have hunted high and low and we can't find anyone else that Los Mozos likes as much as Taxis Coco. We think it's because you're transporting drugs."

"No, no," Don Cisco protested. "I run a respectable business. Ask anyone."

Silvio regarded the other man with a baleful eye. "Isn't that why the gang is demanding protection money? Isn't that what really got Pablo Arrocha killed?"

Don Cisco shrank back, the moustache arrow-straight over taut lips. "No, that's not true."

"What about this note?" Silvio laid the photo of the taunt from the taxi's glove compartment in front of the other man. "Did Los Mozos leave this for you?"

Don Cisco touched the photo as if it might bite him. "Teach me a lesson?" he murmured. "No, no, I don't know what this is."

"Written by the same person." Silvio put the claim of responsibility next to the first photo so Don Cisco could compare.

"I . . . I saw this one." Don Cisco indicated the note found with Arrocha. "But that's all."

Silvio slid the coffee cups to the side and took out the remaining photographs. Standing by the table, he arranged them on a grid. "Please look at the pictures carefully and tell me if any of these men are the ones who came to your home to demand protection money from the *sitio*."

"Are they all dead?" Don Cisco asked.

"These men have been killed since the attack on your driver," Silvio explained "It's possible that one or more of them are from Los Mozos and were killed in retaliation." He paused. "Look them over. Take your time."

"Because of Los Mozos?" Don Cisco asked. "They're dead because of Los Mozos?"

His voice was so low it barely registered out in the viewing corridor.

"It's possible," Silvio said again. "Are any of them the men who threatened you at your home?"

Don Cisco half rose from his chair, body tensed for flight. Then he fell back into his seat, put his hands over his face, and burst into raw, guttural sobs.

Silvio sat and waited.

Emilia got a bad feeling in the pit of her stomach. Had Don Cisco taken it upon himself to kill Arrocha's killer?

Don Cisco's shoulders shook with great gusts of sorrow.

"Señor?" Silvio's voice was unusually gentle. "Señor, is there something you want to tell me?"

"Los Mozos." Don Cisco took a shuddery breath but didn't drop his hands. "It's fake. I made it all up. There's no such gang."

Emilia was sure the tinny audio had fooled her.

"Could you repeat that?" Silvio's face looked as incredulous as Emilia felt.

"I made it up," Don Cisco sobbed. "All of it."

Silvio didn't move a muscle. "But if you made it up, who killed Pablo Arrocha?"

"I don't know." Don Cisco wept harder. "I'm so afraid."

CHAPTER 45

Emilia's carefully considered timeline collapsed into a pile of unsubstantiated rumor and tough talk calculated to squeeze cash out of a detective stupid enough to say she was feeling generous.

"It was for her." Don Cisco's chest rose and fell with deep breaths as he struggled to compose himself. "For my wife. So she wouldn't leave me. She wanted things we couldn't afford."

"Go on." Silvio's expression was as hard as flint.

"She . . . she wasn't happy and she took up with another man. So I thought I could make her happy with nicer clothes. Furniture. A better school for the children."

Emilia forced herself to stay in the viewing corridor when every muscle screamed to run into the interrogation room and shake him until the details fell out and assembled into the truth.

"I made up everything about Los Mozos." Don Cisco spoke haltingly, prodded by Silvio's blank-faced menace. "Everyone believed me. The drivers. The people along the street. The vendors in the park. They even prayed for us, that Los Mozos would just take our money and leave us alone. To drive in peace."

It was easy to convince the drivers. They were a close-knit bunch, decent men who all rose to his aid after hearing the story of Los Mozos coming to Don Cisco's home.

Don Cisco showed his wife the extra money and they spent a little before discovering Oxford Properties. Using shady business tips from a YouTube video, he set up a shell company and used it for the Banamex Bank account linked to his account with Oxford Properties. The scheme worked beautifully. His investments with Oxford Properties paid off and Don Cisco's wife stayed faithful as he plied her with a new television, designer clothes, and a better school for the children.

"What about the threat to shoot the first driver in line?" Silvio asked.

"It worked." Don Cisco spoke to the table, still gridded with portraits of the dead. "The drivers were frightened all over again and they paid more."

"And you took the money so you could do more real estate investing."

"Yes."

Silvio's face twisted in disgust. "What about after Pablo Arrocha died?"

"They paid even more." Don Cisco's voice was barely a whisper.

"Did you kill Pablo Arrocha, too?" Silvio said. "Blame it on Los Mozos?"

Don Cisco's eyes opened wide. "I didn't kill him, I swear it wasn't me. I was standing right there when he was shot. I'd never kill someone. I never wanted anyone to die. It was just so I could invest, that's all. I just wanted to invest. Be a man of property. Make my wife happy."

At this point, Silvio stared directly at the mirror. Emilia knew exactly what he was thinking. They had to call Campos. This belonged in the Financial Crimes basket.

When Silvio pressed him about Arrocha's murder, Don Cisco erupted with another wave of weeping, his Tin Tan moustache dripping with tears. Don Cisco had assumed that someone had a grudge against Arrocha, although he had no idea who that could be, until he saw the claim of responsibility from Los Mozos.

It sent Don Cisco into a full-blown panic attack. Who else knew about Los Mozos and would use it to kill Arrocha? The fictional Los Mozos had been around for months. Dozens of people knew about the gang's demands for protection money, but only Don Cisco stood to gain by Arrocha's death because it meant the drivers paid more.

Silvio collected the pictures of the dead. Don Cisco began to sob all over again.

Every third streetlight was out in Colonia Progreso, which wasn't a bad ratio for Acapulco these days. Emilia drove around the corner and found the niche protecting the gates set into the pocked gray walls. As she approached the rusted old intercoms, her headlights reduced to small yellow circles against dark metal. Still sticky on one end from melted peppermint candy, she pointed the remote control from the taxi's glove compartment at the gate and clicked the button. With a long, slow clanging release, the gate trundled to the side and the headlights turned into twin beams stretching past the empty fountain to illuminate the once-majestic architecture.

Emilia drove in. Another click and the remote control closed the gates behind the taxi's rear bumper. She cut the engine.

Sitting in the inky silence, she strained to hear sounds of life. Footsteps, rustling, a cough, low voices. But Casa de Plata was a mausoleum. Moonlight glinted off the remnants of the tile mosaic.

Emilia knew the place was riddled with secrets. The remote control just proved it.

She'd left the police station desperately trying to process Don Cisco's claims that Los Mozos was a fabrication. To her disgust, she knew the dispatcher's story gave credence to Gamboa's claim that Arrocha was a *federale* snitch. Did someone use the Los Mozos legend as a cover to kill Arrocha and protect the *narcotaxi* operation? Was it Barrielos Luna, the presumed godfather?

Silvio had pressed Don Cisco about connections to Barrielos Luna, but the dispatcher insisted, between shuddery breaths, that he didn't know anything about the fugitive drug kingpin. Silvio didn't take it further. Emilia knew the lieutenant was mindful of Gamboa's insistence that the *federales* needed to keep the *narcotaxi* operation going as the back door into the Barrielos Luna organization.

Casa de Plata was the one thing everyone had in common.

As Emilia just proved to herself, Arrocha had a remote control for the gate in his taxi and must have been there before. Gamboa saw the place during his house shopping trip. Don Cisco came with Infante Sel, after moves designed to shake off surveillance.

Emilia switched on the big flashlight she brought from the safe house and made her way to the massive front door. It was still unlocked.

The foyer was totally creepy. The split staircase rose silently like a giant with outstretched arms. Emilia shivered as a draft rolled across the back of her neck. She swept the beam of the flashlight across the terrazzo floor. The dust appeared to glitter.

When she was here with Silvio, two pairs of footprints were clear to see. Now the dust was scuffed and disturbed by more activity.

Tracks led to the apartment door on the far left side of the lobby. It was unlocked but the footprints ended a few steps into the apartment. Emilia swung the flashlight around. The apartment was empty. No furniture or rugs. Buckled vertical blinds covered the windows.

She retraced her steps and followed the tracks up the staircase. Her cross trainers squeaked softly on the stairs. Once upon a time this was a magnificent place to live. Four luxury apartments in secluded splendor.

The trail of footsteps ended at the top of the stairway in front of two doors. Emilia tried both knobs. One was locked. The other swung inward into a dark abyss.

Although not as big as the one in the penthouse at the Palacio Réal, this place was designed for parties, with wood paneled walls, built-in armoires, and a sunken spot under a skylight meant for an indoor jungle. Windows were covered with shades and tattered curtains.

Emilia forced herself to keep on when every instinct told her to leave. A draft played against her skin. Dust motes danced in the beam of the flashlight.

Two tall cabinets flanked a built-in bar complete with mirrored backsplash, drawers for storage underneath, and glass shelves for liquor bottles above. Emilia imagined posh cocktail parties when Casa de Plata was a glamorous address and everyone thought Acapulco's heyday would last forever.

Once again, the flashlight revealed footprints. Two pairs crossed the room in an arc from the door to the bar and back again. She walked to the bar, conscious of the darkness in a way she hadn't been downstairs. Dust lay thick everywhere. No one had touched the open shelves or the sheet of glass protecting the wooden top in years.

Yet the footsteps ended there, as if they were made by ghosts summoned by the old *abuela* in the store down the street.

Emilia played the light over the brass drawer pulls. They were all caked with dust, the same as everything else.

Yet, one had a clean smudge, just wide enough for two fingers. She put a forefinger on the spot and tugged.

The drawer slid out silently to reveal a slender leather wallet, the kind that opened like a book and fit in the breast pocket of a man's suit coat.

It contained five crisp 100-dollar bills.

A scratch cut the silence from beyond the comfort of the flashlight. Emilia gave a start. She held her breath and the broken building rewarded her with more scratching, louder and closer than before.

Gecko. Rat. Ghosts.

The scratching came closer. Emilia threw the wallet back in the drawer, slammed it shut, and sprinted for the door. Her heart pounded as she raced down the stairs, the flashlight's beam bobbing across the foyer as she went. Emilia backed the taxi out so fast that she hit the curb on the opposite side of the street. The remote control closed the gate and she hightailed it out of the neighborhood.

CHAPTER 46

"Gamboa wants to talk to you." Silvio's voice nearly fried Emilia's cell phone.

She blinked sleepily at the chandelier; the metal buffed to a pleasant shine by thin morning light. "What's his problem?"

"Yeah, well, he can explain when you get here."

"Sure, listening to his bullshit was just what I wanted to do today." Emilia scooted into a sitting position against the pillow. "Hey, I went over to Casa de Plata last night. A remote control in Arrocha's taxi opened the gate."

"Casa de Plata?"

"Yes, and get this. There's a big wad of cash in an upstairs apartment."

"Did you take it?"

"No." Irritation at Silvio's utter obtuseness wiped away the last vestiges of sleep. "The point is who's leaving cash in an abandoned building that Arrocha, Gamboa, Don Cisco and Infante Sel have all visited?"

"So you think Gamboa's story about Arrocha being a *federale* informant is true," Silvio said smugly, zeroing in on the wrong thing yet again.

"What if he's the one who killed Arrocha?" Emilia snapped back. "Maybe Arrocha double-crossed him."

"How would that work?"

"Arrocha tells Gamboa about Los Mozos because he

thinks it's true and protection money is eating all his income as a driver. In fact that could be what pushed him to talk to Gamboa in the first place." Emilia scooted herself higher on the pillows as the scenario built. "They used Casa de Plata as a drop zone. The money was payment to Arrocha. Maybe he threatened to blackmail Gamboa, out him as a *federale* unless Gamboa paid him more. Gamboa decided he was a problem and hired somebody to kill him."

"So Gamboa is the killer now?"

"He hired somebody. He wasn't the shooter. Too tall, too broad."

Silvio blew out his breath. The silence grew.

"Well?" Emilia pressed.

"It's a far-fetched theory," Silvio said. "What about crying Don Cisco and Infante Sel? How do they fit in?"

"Give me a minute," Emilia muttered.

"Bring coffee," Silvio said.

"Make your own fucking coffee." But she was talking to a dead connection.

An hour later, when she confronted Gamboa at Silvio's house, the *pendejo* denied knowing anything about Casa de Plata beyond it being a possible real estate purchase for Copa Multimedia. He never met Arrocha there. He didn't know anything about a remote control in Arrocha's taxi or money left in an abandoned apartment. He already answered questions about Infante Sel, who was a total stranger.

"Casa de Plata is for sale." Gamboa was dressed for the movie set in the tan suit retrieved from Hotel Dominga. "It's too big for what I need as a cover for Copa Multimedia, but somebody will snatch it up. You think it could be used for dead drops? With real estate agents tramping through it at random times? You have no idea how the real world works, Baby."

Silvio watched them argue, then informed Gamboa that Los Mozos was a fake. Somebody who knew about the gang killed Arrocha. Given the number of people in that category, it wasn't exactly an actionable lead.

Gamboa flinched in genuine shock. He asked all the questions Emilia expected. She let Silvio handle the answers.

"I'm late for the shoot," Gamboa said, as the conversation wound down with no good resolution to the riddle of Arrocha's murder. He checked his watch.

Silvio jangled his car keys. "Sure, let's go."

Gamboa turned to Silvio and hung his head. "Look, uh, would it be all right if I ride with Emilia? I need a moment to, well, talk. I guess I owe my sister an apology."

"That okay with you, Cruz?" Silvio asked.

"Sure." *An apology?* Emilia was almost too stunned to speak.

Gamboa climbed into the front seat. "I'll even pay extra for the privilege of sitting in front," he said.

Emilia merely nodded. He was going to apologize. He was going to admit what he'd done.

The sky was a cloudless cobalt as she started the taxi and headed out of El Roble. It was going to be a gorgeous day. The day the chains fell away.

"So, what did you want to say to me?" Emilia asked.

"You put her up to it, didn't you?" Gamboa said in a conversational tone. He slipped on the aviator sunglasses. "Our mother. You told her who I was. You made her say in front of everyone that her son was dead."

"I was as surprised as anybody when she said that," Emilia said, blindsided.

"You put her up to it," Gamboa accused her.

"I didn't tell Mama anything," Emilia protested. Sophia's reaction had clearly bruised him. "Mama just . . . says things. Sometimes they make sense, sometimes they don't."

"She's simpleminded, isn't she?" Anger sparked off Gamboa.

"Sometimes," Emilia said reluctantly. She slowed the car as they approached an intersection. "You took her watch. I want it back."

Gamboa slammed a hand against the dashboard and the glove compartment rattled. "She knew who I was, didn't she?"

"I don't know, but that wasn't part of the deal," Emilia warned. It dawned on her that the *cabrón* wasn't going to apologize. He only said that to lure her into a conversation about Sophia.

"Yes, yes, I know what we agreed to," Gamboa said mockingly. "You're such a dutiful cop, Emilia. Saving girls like the angel of virtue. Yet when it comes to murder, your only lead is fake."

"Somebody killed him," Emilia said. "Wouldn't it be

interesting if it comes out that you knew who all along?"

"How could a fake gang kill my informant?" Gamboa demanded. The mocking tone was gone. "Pablo's dead. Somebody shot him."

"*Oye*, that's brilliant." Emilia forced a laugh. "Maybe you're a *federale* after all."

Gamboa glanced around. "Pull in here. I need to think. I need coffee."

Emilia swung the taxi into the small parking lot in front of an OXXO convenience store. "Listen," she said. "We had a deal. You got to meet my mother. Now it's your turn. Get Gabi out of the *narcotaxi* business."

"What do you do when you're not at work, Detective Emilia Cruz?" Gamboa shocked her with the abrupt change of subject. He cracked open the taxi door but made no move to get out. "Make wind chimes out of shells to stretch your puny police salary? Wish you really were Alejandra Messi? No, I bet you clean the church with the other spinsters."

A man walked past and glanced at the dented taxi but continued into the store.

"Go get your fucking coffee," Emilia said.

"Do you have any friends?" Gamboa's tone mocked her. "Or are you too busy proving you can do the job as well as the boys?"

Emilia turned on him. "What do you want from me?"

"I want to get to know my little sister," Gamboa said. His eyes glittered with malice. "Come on, tell me about your friends. What about Kurt?"

Emilia stopped breathing.

"Kurt." Gamboa rolled the name around on his tongue. "That's a German name, isn't it?"

Every muscle in Emilia's body clenched tight.

"That's what you said while I was fucking you so hard you almost split in two. Just that one word." Gamboa's voice became a cloying falsetto. "Kurt. *Kurt.*"

"You fucking *pendejo*." Emilia's vision blurred red with fury.

The passenger door slammed shut, rocking the taxi. Gamboa trotted into the store.

Emilia squeezed her eyes shut and sucked air to keep from sobbing like Don Cisco.

Thanks to the date rape drug, El Acólito's assault had been a blank, but now a film played in her head. Gamboa rutted like a pig as she lay naked and unresisting under him. Her own voice was the soundtrack. *Kurt. Kurt.*

She wanted Gamboa to admit what he did.

But not like this.

Emilia opened her eyes. The door to the glove compartment hung open. The remote control for the gate at Casa de Plata was gone.

"*Madre de Dios*," she breathed.

Gamboa had confessed to the rape, in the most hurtful way imaginable, so that she would do exactly what she did. Dissolve into tears of humiliation and anger. Be too distraught to pay attention to him.

Emilia launched herself out of the car and ran into the

store, practically mowing down the line of customers waiting at the bulletproof glass shielding the cashier. She ran through the aisles, tears streaming down her face, knowing Gamboa wasn't there.

She left the store with her heart hammering, leaped into the taxi, peeled out of the lot, and roared east with her head on a swivel looking for that tan suit. He could have hailed an unlicensed taxi but maybe he was still walking. At the end of the street she had to turn right or left. She picked right because it was in the general direction of Sinfonia del Mar. Emilia vented her frustration on the poky midtown traffic, shouting at cars and clueless tourists meandering through the crosswalk.

A block ahead, a tall figure in a tan suit strode along the sidewalk, scattering morning commuters on their way to work. It was Gamboa. Emilia tried to pass slow moving cars by swinging left into the other lane but was met by an oncoming minivan.

As she swerved back into her own lane in time to avoid a head-on collision, Emilia recognized the distinctive profile of Infante Sel's black BMW up ahead. It pulled to the curb. Gamboa got in.

A minibus cut in front of Emilia and her windshield filled with the view of a belching exhaust pipe and a big ad for Herdez brand *pico de gallo*. People jostled to get on and off. Emilia pounded her steering wheel in a frenzy. When the vehicle finally continued on its way, the BMW was on the far side of the intersection and gaining speed.

Emilia stamped on the clutch and rocketed through first and second gears on her way to third. She was going to force the sedan off the road, drag Gamboa out by his hair and let him have it. She tried to find third gear but the *maldita* shift lever got that loose feel of a spoon in a tub of molasses again. Engine howling, the taxi's speed bled off as Emilia struggled with the transmission. The taxi jolted through the intersection and—.

A truck slammed into the passenger side of the taxi. With an ear-splitting bang, the airbag ballooned into Emilia's face and the world whirled around her. The windows erupted in a hailstorm of glass. Emilia was deafened by tearing metal as the truck plowed the taxi across the pavement.

The carcass of the taxi finally detached from the front bumper of the SUV like a bone dropped from a tired dog's mouth. The deflated airbag draped over Emilia's lap, glittering with bits of glass. Ribbons of metal that were once the yellow front fender trembled in the door frame.

Blinking green numerals showed that the taxi meter had survived. Gamboa owed her 370 pesos.

Emilia unfastened her seat belt. Scrambling out of the wreck, she left a trail of glittering glass pebbles and smears of blood on the white paint.

What was left of the taxi sagged on two tires. Emilia blinked uncomprehendingly at the litter of metal, glass, and rubber strewn across the intersection.

Her legs gave way and she slid to the pavement, her back against the still intact front yellow fender.

"She's drunk," a voice said from far away.

"A girl. In a taxi. Maybe she stole it."

"Señora? Are you all right?"

The voices grew fainter. Emilia put her head on her knees and thought about Kurt.

CHAPTER 47

Emilia lay on the hospital bed in the emergency room of Santa Lucia hospital and stared at the striped curtain promising flimsy privacy. Apart from a few cuts, she was more angry than hurt.

The curtain fluttered, but instead of the nurse, Lieutenant Campos appeared, briefcase in one hand, the other adjusting his glasses.

"Hello, Ester," he said with a conspiratorial smile.

Emilia found the control for the bed and raised it to see him better. "I expected the nurse."

"She'll be busy for a bit," Campos said. Wearing yet another perky polo and khaki pants, the lieutenant sat on the plastic stool at the side of the bed, laid his briefcase across his knees, and beamed at Emilia. "How do you feel?"

"Foolish."

He kept smiling, obviously not taking the comment the way she intended. "Yes, well, I expect we're out of the taxi business."

Emilia nodded.

"My driver will take you back to the house when the hospital releases you," he said. "Stay a few more days to give us time to close things on our end. When you get back to the office, have a courier bring the BlackBerry and the house keys back to Señora Mendez. Your service weapon has been transferred to Lieutenant Silvio."

Emilia nodded again.

"You wrap things up with Donoso Garay when you feel up to it," Campos went on. "Señora Mendez called, said she was your mother and that you were in an accident. Didn't want anyone in the *sitio* to get worried, start poking around."

"Of course not," Emilia murmured.

Campos took off his glasses and pinched the bridge of his nose. "Lieutenant Silvio told me that Donoso Garay confessed to him. I thought we were dealing with a street gang but Los Mozos is a made-up thing. Quite the surprise, wouldn't you say?"

"Here's another shocker," Emilia said with manufactured breathlessness. "You're all in this together. You, that real estate mogul Hector Infante Sel, and a has-been *telenovela* star named Rafa Gamboa. Either getting a cut from the *narcotaxi* operation that Taxis Coco is running or you're trying to take down whoever's behind it."

"Nicely done," Campos said. "By the way, my finances are open for your inspection at any time."

"You're still a *federale*, aren't you?" Emilia groped for another piece of the puzzle. "Financial Crimes is a cover operation."

"Let's keep that secret," Campos said, one happy conspirator to another.

"You need to work on your lies, *teniente*," Emilia said. "You never brought in Don Cisco for questioning or to look at mug shots. He met Infante Sel that day. Nobody named Enrique works in your office, either. That name must be a code you and Señora Mendez use that means *make this go away*."

"Well," Campos said, clearly taken aback. "You are a clever girl."

"While I'm being so fucking clever, tell Señora Mendez that her English is really quite good. Too bad there's so much static on the line."

Campos took off his glasses, tapped the temple on a thumbnail, and gave an abashed chuckle. "Yes, we were quite surprised that Manolo Bernal's driver called that number."

"Tell me about Rafa Gamboa," Emilia said. "Also known as El Acólito, the rapist, murderer, and human trafficker. Currently a fugitive. Or perhaps we are talking about Manolo Bernal, the filmmaker? Or Omar Rodriguez Reyes? I forget what he does."

Campos put on his glasses and fixed Emilia with a stern stare. "Your brother is one of our most successful deep cover officers. We're both dedicated to erasing the scourge of Diego Barrielos Luna, a man who kills his enemies and dissolves them in vats of acid. But I shouldn't have to tell you that."

Your brother. Two words that revealed a big, ugly truth.

Emilia knew that the files connecting her to El Acólito, proven by DNA after the rape, were sealed. Access was limited to Silvio, Chief of Police Salazar, and a select few *federales* involved in the hunt for El Acólito.

She crossed her arms. "So Gamboa really is a *federale.*

What are you? Friend? Protector? His puppet master?"

"His control officer," Campos said.

"Really? Does that mean you're also Señor Hathaway?"

"Not anymore, for obvious reasons."

"For how long?"

"The last three years," Campos said.

"Three years." Emilia felt as if she'd been hit with a sack of wet sand. "You ran him as El Acólito? He trafficked girls!"

"El Acólito was a very successful operation," Campos countered. "We nabbed Barrielos Luna and put him in jail."

"You let him traffic girls and made sure no one caught him afterwards."

Instead of matching Emilia's spiraling anger, Campos oozed sympathy. "I'm sorry for the way you got involved. It never should have happened."

"Do you know how many women are missing because of him?"

"Think of it as their contribution to law enforcement," Campos offered.

"Contribution to law enforcement?" Emilia sputtered. "Bet you wouldn't be so cavalier if Barrielos Luna liked 16-year-old boys who wear glasses."

Campos gave her a weary smile. "If it's any consolation, I think you delivered retribution and more with, ah, what was it? A tire iron?"

Emilia glared at him.

"Gamboa's been under deep cover for too long," Campos

said. "The El Acólito operation involved too many chances. He's an adrenaline junkie without a moral compass. This has to be his last operation."

"I wasn't in that fucking taxi to catch Pablo Arrocha's murderer, was I?" Emilia wanted to slap the fake regret out of Campos. "I was there because you knew Gamboa would sniff around to find out what happened to his snitch. Sitting in Number 17, the long-lost sister he didn't know he had, waiting to help him find his fucking moral compass."

"You were really there to find out about that gang," Campos said. "The rest of it was an added bonus. Two birds, one stone."

"A useful stone as long as I didn't stick my nose into the *sitio's narcotaxi* gig, that is," Emilia accused him. "You were protecting Don Cisco and any whiff of the *narcotaxi* operation."

"It's a complicated situation," Campos said, still gratingly agreeable.

"What about Infante Sel?" Emilia asked. "How does he fit in? Gamboa's helper?"

Campos sighed. "His business facilitates various operations. You don't need to know anything more than that."

"Tell that to the *sitio* drivers. Don Cisco faked Los Mozos to steal from them so he could invest in Oxford Properties."

"An unforeseen development."

Emilia pointed at Campos. "Infante Sel is your recruiter. He finds you snitches. First Arrocha, now Don Cisco who'll do it because he's in debt to Oxford Properties."

Campos pointed at her in turn, but it was more congratulations than accusation. "Donoso Garay's greed is a useful lever. The *sitio* isn't a major distribution link for the Barrielos Luna organization, but we need that toehold."

"If Don Cisco is your new snitch, tell him to pick up his money at Casa de Plata," Emilia said. "Upstairs apartment. Second drawer under the bar."

"You're even better than I thought," Campos said with grudging admiration.

"Arrocha left the remote control for the gate in his taxi. Gamboa took it." Emilia paused. "Did Infante Sel use the real estate scam on Pablo Arrocha, too?"

Campos shook his head. "Let's just say that every man has an exploitable weakness."

Emilia took a deep breath and let it out slowly. The emergency ward hummed on the other side of the curtain; low, calm voices, the rub of gurney wheels against linoleum, doors opening and closing with pneumatic whooshes.

"Did Barrielos Luna order a hit on Pablo Arrocha for talking to the *federales*?" Emilia asked quietly.

Campos nodded. "Given Don Cisco's confession, that appears to be the only answer to Arrocha's murder."

"Do you really think Barrielos Luna is going to fall for this movie?"

"If you're worried about being outed as the Emilia character," Campos said. "Don't be. It's never going to hit theaters."

"What about Alejandra Messi?"

"She's doing a favor for her country." Campos opened his briefcase and took out a thick envelope. "Your last fare forgot to pay."

Gamboa wanted to salve his conscience with cash, the tried and true grease that kept the wheels of Mexico rolling.

"I don't want it," Emilia said.

"Let the man pay his debts," Campos said. He tossed the envelope on the blanket covering Emilia's knee, closed his briefcase, and stood. "I forgot to ask. How's your mother?"

"She's fine," Emilia said, unable to hide the hostility in her voice. "She has Alejandra Messi's bracelet."

CHAPTER 48

"Wait here," Emilia said as the taxi came to a stop in the parking lot of Sinfonia del Mar.

"You gonna be long?" The driver of the unlicensed taxi stank of cigarette smoke. His dirty shirt was mostly unbuttoned, showing off a doughy chest and a silver cross.

"As long as it takes," Emilia said. "I'll make it worth your while."

She climbed out of the cramped VW bug. Like hundreds of unlicensed taxis of the same model, the passenger seat was gone, allowing more people to cram onto the bench in back.

Sinfonia del Mar had gone back to nature. The parking lot was nearly empty except for a few cars and a minibus sporting the loud logo of a tour company. The film people with their cameras and clapperboards had disappeared.

The movie trailers were gone. The vintage Buick and Cadillac were gone.

A candy wrapper scudded across the pavement, scratched Emilia's bare ankle, and continued on its way. The bougainvillea was in full bloom, no longer hidden by vintage vehicles. The bins below the mayor's smiling face were empty. The movie people had even taken their *norteamericano* trash.

Or perhaps they had never been there. Maybe she hallucinated the last few weeks.

Emilia walked across the lot, needing to find some proof that Gamboa, Bob, and the film crew had once existed. She was a bewildered magician unable to conjure the spell a second time.

Even if she could summon Gamboa, did she really want to? He was never going to admit anything. Never going to strike a deal and keep it. He was a hunter. An animal sent to trap another animal, aided and abetted by the worst animal of all. Not a creature with fangs and claws, but a predator hiding inside a friendly shell of a man with a briefcase full of secrets.

Champ.

Emilia slowly descended the stone steps. Most of the benches were empty. It was hours until sunset and the Sinfonia was a hard place to sit for long. The height and horizon made for vertigo and the ocean view didn't come with wifi.

A couple was half-hidden on a bench at the top edge, no doubt hoping for some privacy. Emilia heard the clink of bottles. Drunk sex at the Sinfonia was a rite of passage. More girls got pregnant there than in a bedroom.

A tour group lolled on a bench in the center section while a guide with a red flag on a pole chattered away at them in English. Emilia caught a few words as she passed on her way to the stage.

First, she pretended to be Ester. Then Alejandra Messi, and then the ill-fated Victoria.

Now she was just herself again. A cop. A detective in a

city slowly disintegrating under the weight of distrust, dirty money, and illicit drugs.

Juggling identities and moral decisions for what? Save the city? Save Mexico?

Save themselves.

She sat on the same bench where Bob had filmed her tears after Gamboa kissed her. The tourists and their chirpy guide perched above her.

Far below, the Pacific was both restless and endless. Campos and Gamboa believed they'd bought her silence. Emilia had a sudden urge to throw the envelope full of cash into the ocean and watch the waves lick it away.

Yet, the two *federales* and their dual-pronged operation were her best chance of taking down Barrielos Luna and removing the threat to her family.

Gamboa, Campos, Infante Sel, Don Cisco. Even Silvio. Nobody was who they appeared to be. Everyone hid their true selves under layers of deceit. False identities and hidden agendas. Everyone was a fake.

Almost everyone.

She walked to the wall rimming the stage. The warm sun felt good on her shoulders. Kurt was on the other side of the turquoise ocean. If Emilia jumped in, she could swim straight to Hong Kong.

She had a mental picture of herself in her sundress, churning across the Pacific like a motorboat, passing boats and sharks. It was such a ludicrous thought that a healing peal of laughter escaped her throat.

The taxi was still parked in the shade.

Emilia got in and hoisted her shoulder bag onto the seat. "Do you know where the Cinépolis is?" she asked. "Near the Diana monument."

"Sure," the driver said as the VW engine started to chug. "Everybody wants to see *Diamond Run* there."

"That's the one," Emilia said. "Drop me off there. I'll walk the rest of the way."

CHAPTER 49

It was just 6:00 am. The sunlight was thin and cool as Emilia pushed open the door to the seedy gym on the outskirts of El Roble. The moist smell of sweaty bodies and moldy canvas filled her nostrils. Leather thudded against leather. Chains jangled as a heavy bag was pounded. Someone slapped a speed bag with a rocketing rhythm.

The gym was a well-known incubator for young boxers hoping to be the next Canelo or Julio César Chávez. Most of the interior was taken up by a regulation size boxing ring. A plywood case held trophies and championship belts going back 30 years.

Two men in the ring sparred with oversized gloves. Both faces shone with sweat under padded helmets held together with silver duct tape.

His face as wrinkled as a raisin, the owner of the gym gave Emilia a grunt of recognition.

She slipped him 200 pesos. "I'm next with the champ."

The money disappeared into a pocket. "You bring your own mouthpiece?"

"I've got one."

"No shower," he warned, as always when she dropped in.

"No shower," Emilia echoed. She was hardly stupid enough to take off her clothes in the all-male boxing gym.

The owner went off to collect a pile of sweat-soaked towels. Emilia dropped her sports bag by the grimy window, took out her worn leather gloves, and faced down the other heavy bag. At any other time of the day, five wannabe Golden Gloves champions would be taking turns on the bag, but right now she had it all to herself.

Emilia swayed from side to side and rolled her shoulders before pummeling the bag with a combination of right and left jabs. She skipped backwards to deliver a roundhouse kick, the top of her foot connecting hard enough to set the bag swinging on its chain. Close again, weaving from side to side, now hunched low, now stretching up for a surprise blow against her imaginary opponent's face. *Jab, jab, jab.*

The bag swung and jumped as Emilia vented herself on it, feeling her blood pump and muscles shout as the chain suspending the bag squealed in protest. Above her, the two men in the ring moved around each other, fast and powerful. Heavy feet scraped across the canvas. He was working with a former champ, but the trainer kept up a steady stream of growled instructions as blows landed on training mitts. *Don't slip so far. Roll under the hook. Where's your weight? Speed it up.*

Emilia hit the bag with another combination but stopped when the owner appeared with a padded practice helmet. With her mouthguard in place, she stuffed her hair into the helmet and fastened the Velcro under her chin. He stretched the ropes and Emilia climbed into the ring.

The trainer backed away when he saw her and swung himself out of the ring.

Silvio looked confused.

Emilia danced forwards and backwards, getting the feel of the springy canvas beneath her feet. When Silvio didn't react, she tapped her head with her gloved hands, signaling *Come on, come on* to the former heavyweight champ.

He hung over the ropes to pantomime at the owner, one arm flung out toward Emilia. The big lieutenant clearly communicated *What the hell*? Emilia came at him from behind to deliver a solid body blow.

Silvio sidestepped at the last second but Emilia's glove grazed his ribcage. She hopped away but got in another dig as Silvio launched himself off the ropes. His body compressed into a formidable boxer's crouch, and he returned Emilia's challenge with his left hand with the right held mockingly behind his back. It was nearly impossible to hear anything with the helmet on besides her own breathing but Emilia thought she heard the owner give a cackle.

She rocked on the balls of her feet, watching Silvio, both gloves up to protect her core and face. His blow came fast and high. The leather of his gloves had been sweated through so many times it smelled of old cheese. Emilia slipped underneath and unleashed a combination against his upper body to no effect beside jarring her all the way to her molars.

Emilia had either hit Silvio or a cement truck.

She felt his glove score the side of her helmet and knew he was holding back. Emilia landed a pathetic blow on his shoulder before skipping backwards toward the ropes. Silvio followed and drove his glove into her midsection. Emilia folded in two as the breath whistled out of her.

Astonishingly, nothing came up.

She gulped air and renewed her stance as they circled each other again. The pain radiated away, replaced by a surge of adrenaline. Silvio grinned, his lips drawn back to expose his mouthguard. Emilia flashed her own pink plastic mouth protector.

He lied to you. The pendejo lied to you.

The thought refueled her. Emilia tapped her head again. *Come on, come on.* Silvio planted himself in the middle of the canvas, but his movements were less sharp than before. Emilia reckoned he'd been in the ring long enough to be running low.

Out of the corner of her eye, Emilia saw that all other activity in the gym had stopped. The men pounding the heavy bag and slapping the speed bag had coalesced into a knot near the ring. Along with the trainer, they were there to watch some *chica* pound on Franco Silvio, known by all to be the most successful fighter ever to come out of that gym. His glory days were past but he was still formidable.

She closed in on Silvio again, braced to absorb another punch. His reach was longer than hers and she parried a flurry of jabs but felt the blows on her arms and shoulder as she wove around him, trying to position herself for the proper angle. Silvio radiated condescending amusement, indicating that she had no one to blame but herself for her predicament.

The next second, Emilia threw away the rules of boxing and snapped out a brutal roundhouse kick. Her cross trainer caught Silvio square in the side of the padded helmet.

The kick from her hip came with ten times the power Emilia could pack into a punch. Silvio swayed for a moment, then landed on his ass like a tree cut by a lumberjack.

The gym erupted into hoots of laughter that permeated the thick padding of Emilia's helmet, as did shouts of "Cheat! Cheat!"

Before Silvio could scramble to his feet, Emilia had one glove off. She spat her mouthguard into her hand.

"You lied to me," she shouted at Silvio.

The laughter from the floor tapered into confused mutterings.

Still on the canvas, Silvio spat out his own mouthguard. "What the hell are you talking about, Cruz?"

"You knew Gamboa was a *federale* the whole time, didn't you?" Emilia accused. "All that shit about killing him if he was lying. You knew and you helped him and you played me."

"What are you talking about?" Silvio pulled off his gloves.

"Gamboa really is a *federale*." Emilia stood over him, surprised that he seemed so clueless. Silvio was smart and menacing but he wasn't an actor. "Campos, too."

"Hey!" The owner of the gym shouted at them. "My canvas isn't for love talk."

Silvio got to his feet. "Keep your shorts on," he yelled back.

They gathered up their equipment and climbed through

the ropes. Silvio took some ribbing with good grace before steering Emilia into the corner by the dusty trophy case, grabbing two towels from a laundry trolley along the way.

"Okay," Silvio said. "Tell me again. Who's a fucking *federale*?"

Emilia dropped onto a worn wooden bench under the trophies.

"Campos, Gamboa, and Infante Sel. Campos is Gamboa's so-called control officer," she said. "His story is true. They're really targeting Barrielos Luna with this idiot movie and the *narcotaxi* operation."

"Where'd you hear this?" Silvio hit the bench beside her. It wobbled under his weight.

"From Campos himself." She recounted the conversation in the hospital as she waited to be released. "Gave me a parting gift from Gamboa, too."

"How much?"

"Enough," she said. "But it doesn't make up for the fact that Campos deliberately got me into the *sitio* knowing Gamboa would come sniffing around to find out what happened to his informant. I was bait, sitting in the dead man's car."

"And you beat the fuck out of him with a tire iron." Silvio gave a bark of laughter. "Campos gave his boy more than he bargained for with you, Cruz."

"Yeah, well, now Gamboa's gone. The movie set. The trailers and the cameras."

"I know," Silvio said. "He called. Told me he wouldn't

be back."

"Why didn't you tell me?"

"I thought you were in the hospital."

Emilia glared at him.

"What about the Arrocha investigation?" Silvio asked.

"It's done."

"Because Los Mozos is a fake?"

"Or because I smashed up the taxi yesterday."

"Bottom line, Cruz," Silvio said. "You cost Campos a shitload of money for an investigation that handed him his own snitch's made up gang and beat the crap out of his best boy. Excellent job."

"Well," Emilia considered. "When you put it that way, it was a fucking excellent job."

The tempo of the gym had gone up a notch since Emilia walked in, making the conversation difficult. Staccato beats against bags and training mitts competed with jangling chains and the scratch and scrape of footwork on the canvas floor of the ring. Sweat and testosterone thickened the air.

Silvio rubbed his jaw where the ruddy imprint of the helmet strap was still plain to see. "You've got a hell of a kick there, Cruz."

Emilia tried to feel bad but didn't. "And don't you forget it, *pendejo*."

He laughed. "You need a ride someplace?"

"Yeah, thanks." Emilia stood up. "Gotta pack up."

He dropped her off in front of the safe house.

"I've been giving it some thought." Emilia unfastened her

seat belt. "I guess it's okay if you want to go out with Mercedes."

Silvio tipped his sunglasses down to scowl at her. "I didn't know I needed your permission."

Emilia waggled a finger at him. "Well, now you do."

She got out, leaving the velvet pouch containing Isabel's ring on the seat.

CHAPTER 50

Emelia wheeled her suitcase into the penthouse and shut the door. Kurt's big roller bag stood in the hall.

"Em?" Kurt stepped out of their bedroom, still in his favorite traveling jeans, loafers, and a navy sweatshirt.

Emilia launched herself down the hall. Kurt caught her in a bear hug. Emilia sank her mouth onto his. "I missed you," Emilia gasped when they came up for air. "You would not believe how much."

They made love on the bed, swiftly and seriously, then clung to each other under a hot, pulsing shower.

It was nearly 10:00 pm by the time they had dinner on the balcony as the dark ocean lapped at the shore far below, its soft rhythms competing with music from the Pasodoble Bar. The sky over Puerto Marques wore stars like diamonds, something the night above the safe house never did.

Kurt opened a bottle of wine as he told her about Hong Kong. The hotel had reopened, but protesters were constantly in the streets, many wearing surgical masks. Rumors abounded as to what Beijing was up to, including poisoning the protesters and reshuffling city officials to find the right mix of politicians acceptable to citizens who would also enforce Beijing's crackdown on democracy. The newspapers owned by Beijing were seeded with news stories to test local reaction. It was as different from Mexico's free-wheeling environment as he could imagine.

"How many hours have you been awake?" Emilia asked when he lapsed into English.

"I don't want to get jetlag," Kurt said and rubbed his eyes.

He was asleep the instant his head hit the pillow. Emilia left dishes on the room service cart, slipped into one of his tees, and settled under the coverlet next to Kurt. He sighed contentedly in his sleep and unconsciously molded himself around her.

The next thing Emilia knew, she was wide awake and alone. The bedroom door was partially open. She heard bare feet against the tile floor and smelled the aroma of fresh coffee. She checked the time. It was just after 3:00 am.

Kurt came into the bedroom, sipping from a mug. Silhouetted against the moonlight filtering through the linen draperies hiding the French doors, he was the film star Rafa Gamboa would never be. Clad in a tee shirt and boxers, as he was now, or in one of his tailormade suits from London, Kurt was always himself. He never played a role, but was authentic, centered, unafraid.

Emilia sat up against the pillows. "Did you make enough for two?"

"Hey there, beautiful." Kurt sat on the edge of the bed and held out the mug. "I didn't mean to wake you up."

"Jetlag?" Emilia took a sip of coffee. It was the Palacio Réal's signature grind, rich and smooth.

"I almost pinched myself to make sure I wasn't dreaming. I was ready to come home. Long couple of weeks."

His smile warmed her more than the coffee. Emilia

handed back the mug. "I was worried you'd want to move there."

"Are you kidding?" Kurt took a healthy swallow. "No decent tacos or good beaches or beautiful women named Emilia."

"I like the sound of that."

"Speaking of going places," Kurt said. "Why is your suitcase in the hall?"

"I just got home, same as you."

"Where were you?"

"The undercover assignment," Emilia said. "Investigating the murder of that *taxista*."

"All this time?" Kurt paused with the cup halfway to another swallow. "What happened?"

"It didn't really go as planned," Emilia confessed.

"Tell me about it." Kurt reached to turn on the bedside table light.

Emilia put her hand on his arm to stop him.

"Leave the light off," she said.

"Why?"

"It'll be easier to tell you in the dark," Emilia said honestly.

Kurt rested the mug on his knee. "Are we in trouble, Em?"

"Trouble?" Emilia frowned before she realized what he meant. "No, nothing like that. Nothing to do with us." She hesitated. "Not the way you're thinking."

"Okay," Kurt said and waited.

"El Acólito showed up," Emilia said. "I should have arrested him, but I didn't."

She told Kurt everything. Gabi and the *narcotaxi* operation and how Campos protected Don Cisco. Rafa Gamboa getting into the taxi as Manolo Bernal. How she ended up as Alejandra Messi's body double in a movie that was really a trap for Diego Barrielos Luna. Beating Gamboa with the tire iron only to find that both he and Campos were *federale* agents and that the murdered taxi driver was their informant. Introducing Gamboa to Sophia and the surprising reaction.

Kurt sat silently, absorbing it all. At some point, he gave Emilia the mug. The caffeine pushed her on. She wrapped up by telling Kurt how Don Cisco made up Los Mozos as a ruse to pocket his drivers' earnings so he could buy distressed properties; little knowing he was walking into the trap that would coerce him into becoming the next *federale* informant.

The bedroom was silent for a long time. Emilia hung onto the empty mug, hoping she hadn't destroyed everything.

"It's a good thing I was in Hong Kong," Kurt said at length. "If I'd known Gamboa was around, I would have killed the fucker."

He ripped open the French doors and walked onto the balcony.

Emilia let him go, knowing he needed time and space. The act of telling him had freed her at least. Kurt was upset to be sure, but she wasn't hostage to his emotions any more than she was hostage to Gamboa's ruthlessness. She still had a life. She still had choices.

So did Kurt.

When she saw him relax and lean his forearms on top of the balcony wall, Emilia slid out of the bed, dug into her shoulder bag, and squeezed all of her hopes and dreams into one hand. She joined Kurt at the wall to stare at the tireless water below. In the distance, reflectors on the floating dock cast wavering red lines on the surface.

"Are we okay?" Emilia asked.

He turned to face her. "We will be," he said. Anger simmered under the surface but it wasn't directed at her. "I'm not losing you again. But if I ever meet him, I can't guarantee what will happen."

"I can live with that," Emilia said.

"I didn't plan on giving you a choice."

Choice. That word again.

She had a choice. She could choose to wear Gamboa's chains forever or break them with her own two hands. Choose fear and loneliness or the bonds that Kurt offered.

Those bonds would protect and sustain her. They would keep her upright in a storm, let her stand shoulder-to-shoulder with him to face whatever the future held.

Yet, it wasn't her turn to choose.

Emilia gripped the little box so tightly the corners dug into her sweaty palm. Stars twinkled above. The waves below were edged in froth. Their rhythm was the soundtrack of her life.

It was now or never.

"I love you very much, Kurt Rucker," Emilia said and dropped to one knee. Her fingers were stiff as she opened the box to reveal two braided wedding bands nestled on a bed of folded satin.

Mexican silver and American gold. Bound together in timeless love.

"Will you marry me?" she asked.

Kurt slowly sank to his knees in front of Emilia and cupped her face in his hands.

"Emilia Cruz Encinos," he said. "I thought you'd never ask."

CHAPTER 51

Ester Ruiz Garcia had one last thing to do before Emilia could walk away from the sorry investigation into Pablo Arrocha's murder.

A single taxi was parked against the curb. Juan Miguel lounged on the bench in front of the dispatch booth. Don Cisco was at the podium.

"Ester!" Juan Miguel leaped up as she approached. "We received the report of your accident. I did not expect to see you so soon. How are you?"

"I'm fine." Emilia could not resist a smile as he kissed her on both cheeks.

"I will light a candle on Sunday to give thanks to the Virgin for protecting you."

"*Hola*, Don Cisco," Emilia said as the dispatcher gave her a grave nod instead of stooping to his driver's informality.

"It is good to see you so well, Ester," Don Cisco said mournfully. "What is the state of Taxi Number 17?"

"I'm sorry, but it's a total wreck." She dug the lockbag and key out of her shoulder bag and placed them on the podium.

"Perhaps the car was cursed," Don Cisco said. "First poor Pablo. Now this."

"You were very good for business, Ester." Juan Miguel gave her a fatherly smile. "Will you still come to basketball practice?"

Emilia shook her head. "I'm moving to Puerto Marques. It's too far away."

Don Cisco unlocked the money bag. "Driving a taxi is not for women," he declared. He counted the bills from the lockbag, took half and slid it to Emilia. "It's good you came to your senses."

"My share is only 30 percent," Emilia protested.

Don Cisco made a display of recording the amount in his notebook. "Los Mozos is gone now."

"The police finally did their job," Juan Miguel added.

"Well." Emilia hardly knew what to say. Los Mozos had evaporated with a snap of Lieutenant Campos's fingers, yet Don Cisco was in more danger than ever before as a *federale* informant.

"All the drivers are giving something to Pablo's wife." Juan Miguel eyed the bills in front of Emilia. "Maria is out of the hospital after the surgery to mend her arm, but it'll be a long time before she can work."

Emilia counted out 400 pesos. "Give her this, too."

"Why don't you come with me and give it to her yourself?" Juan Miguel asked. "I was just about to head there. All the drivers are celebrating with her."

The street in front of the Arrocha home was lined with Taxis Coco vehicles. The house itself was neat and white, with a stucco wall edged with bricks laid in a herringbone pattern. Felipe met them at the gate and ushered them into a small courtyard full of giggling children. A pink turtle of a piñata shaped was roped to the limb of a blue jacaranda tree. The denim-hued flowers would probably be a carpet on the ground before the piñata released its sweet treasures.

"Tío Juan!" A tiny girl in a ruffled dress threw herself into Juan Miguel's arms. "I knew you'd come."

He swung her into the air, earning shrieks of delight, before bringing her back to earth facing Emilia. "This is our friend Ester."

"I'm Lola Arrocha Heredia." The child pulled on Emilia's hand. "I'm five years old."

"That's a very good age to be," Emilia said. "I like your piñata."

"Abuela let me pick it out." Lola announced importantly.

"Is today a special day?" Emilia asked.

"It's Mami's coming home day," Lola said. "She was in the hospital because she fell down the stairs." She ran off to join the other children.

Emilia straightened. "Tío Juan? You're her uncle?"

"Her great uncle," Juan Miguel said. "Maria's mother is my sister."

The small house was full of people, talking, laughing, and eating. The celebratory mood was palpable, reinforced with a banner strung across the living room wall that proclaimed *Welcome Home Mami!* It was punctuated with big crayon drawings of stick figures in dresses. Bouquets of roses and parrot tulips hid the television and pink streamers of *papel picado* crisscrossed the living room ceiling.

Emilia tried to assess her murder victim's home with a detective's eye. White walls, simple scrubbed pine furniture. No trinkets or artwork or family snapshots.

Not even a photo of Pablo Arrocha. Emilia had expected to see the mandatory memorial to a slain or missing family member, with an oversized photo draped with black crepe and rosary beads, illuminated by a flickering candle.

Juan Miguel introduced Emilia to the families of the other drivers. Emilia met Lobo's pregnant wife, Gennaro's girlfriend from night school, and Juan Miguel's own wife, a take-charge *abuela* who brought the grandchildren. Emilia fielded questions about the accident, the state of the taxi, and who might buy her *sitio* permit.

She was introduced to Pablo Arrocha's widow Maria in the kitchen, setting out plates with one hand. Her left arm was encased in a plaster cast and held to her side with a sling made from a colorful cotton *rebozo* shawl. Her mother Paloma bustled around with enough food to feed the entire state of Guerrero. The table was carpeted with bowls of ceviche, *albondigas de camarón*, chicken doused in a cream sauce, and salads of all kinds. A huge pot of steaming *arroz rojo* competed for space by a platter overflowing with breaded and fried cutlets in the *milanesa* style.

Maria was lovely, with big luminous eyes and chestnut hair falling over one shoulder. The combination wasn't quite enough, however, to distract from a crooked nose and a puckered scar that pulled down one corner of her mouth.

Emilia gave Maria the traditional greeting of a kiss on the cheek and touched the other woman's shoulder in the process. It was like grasping a brittle twig.

"Make her eat, Ester," Paloma said to Emilia in the tone of a woman used to issuing orders. "Maria needs to sit and eat." She thrust two plates of food at Emilia.

Juan Miguel steered them to the living room sofa. Maria walked slowly. The white blouse and blue jeans sagged on her narrow frame like hand-me-downs.

Emilia set the food on the coffee table. Maria lowered herself to the sofa using her good hand for ballast. It was obvious that she was still in pain from her injuries.

"I've been wanting to meet you," Maria said. "You were very brave to buy Pablo's taxi."

"My condolences on the loss of your husband," Emilia said.

"Thank you." Maria picked at her food.

"You must miss Pablo very much." Emilia wondered if Maria knew her husband had been a *federale* informant. If she didn't, would she want to know?

"He didn't like to be around sick people," Maria said.

It was an odd rejoinder and reminded Emilia of a comment on the basketball court. Pablo liked to talk about himself. Gabi called him a *pendejo*, too.

At a loss how to respond, Emilia concentrated on the *milanesa*. The veal practically melted in her mouth.

Juan Miguel bustled up. "The children are impatient for the piñata," he said. "We'll go outside when you're done."

Ricardo shouldered him aside to set two open bottles of beer on the coffee table. "You should have a beer," he said to Maria. "I brought one for you, too, Ester."

Mouth full of *milanesa*, Emilia nodded her thanks.

"Thank you, *mi hermano*," Maria said.

Juan Miguel clapped the younger man on the back and they headed across the room to join a knot of men laughing and telling stories.

"Is Ricardo your brother?" Emilia asked.

"Yes," Maria said. "My twin brother."

A half-chewed bite of *milanesa* nearly fell out of Emilia's mouth.

Maria cut through a fluffy shrimp *albondiga* meatball with the side of her fork, oblivious to Emilia's surprise. "He told me all about you, driving everywhere by yourself, even to bad places. He tried to keep you from going to that terrible bar. La Tumba, I think it's called. He worried about you." Her mouth strained as she smiled. "Tío Juan wanted to play matchmaker."

"I didn't know he was your brother," Emilia admitted. The family resemblance was erased by Maria's thinness.

"All the drivers are my brothers," Maria said. "Ricardo is just the one from the same mother."

Emilia put down her fork. The missing piece of the puzzle was here, in this house, and had been all along.

Pablo Arrocha was a wife beater. Somehow Campos knew it, too, and used it as leverage.

Falling down the stairs. A miscarriage. Broken arm,

broken nose, split lip. Emilia didn't know how long Maria had endured abuse at her husband's hands, but he had caused permanent physical and emotional damage.

This was why there was no altar to Maria's late husband. Did the fresh paint hide bloodstains? Dents and cracks from his brutality?

The message in her glove compartment had been for Arrocha, not for Don Cisco, and it had nothing to do with Los Mozos. Emilia wondered how many other warnings the drivers gave Arrocha before they decided to make good on their threats.

Stop what you are doing. You know what we mean. Do you want us to teach you a LESSON?

As clearly as if she held the plan in her hand, Emilia knew that all the Taxis Coco drivers had conspired to get rid of Pablo Arrocha before he killed his wife. Emilia marveled at the logistical feat the drivers had achieved. They'd managed to make the lineup appear random, but had maneuvered Arrocha into position at the head of the line and ensured that the two men most likely to be blamed for the murder were there to witness it.

Over by the front door, Ricardo and Juan Miguel enjoyed themselves with the other *taxistas*. Uncle and brother, with perfect alibis for the murder of Pablo Arrocha. It was even recorded on the ATM video. Ricardo and Juan Miguel were both at the *sitio* when the killer ran up and shot the driver at the head of the line.

The other drivers were ferrying passengers. They would vouch for each other. Everyone had an alibi.

No wonder Emilia never found out who slashed her tire. The drivers kept each other's secrets.

Acapulco was full of extortions and shakedowns. *Sitios* were a prime target, making the Los Mozos story wholly believable. It wasn't hard for Don Cisco to convince them. The drivers all paid ever-bigger slices of their earnings so the dreaded extortion gang left Don Cisco alone. They were loyal to the dispatcher, never knowing how badly he took advantage. They were all frightened by the gang's threat to kill the first driver in line.

Gota a gota.

The conspiracy used the gift of Los Mozos. The irony of the situation robbed all the flavor from Emilia's plate.

By inventing Los Mozos, Don Cisco had unwittingly helped save Maria. Upping the antc with the fake threat to kill the first driver in line, the greedy dispatcher gave the conspiracy the means to teach Pablo Arrocha his lesson. Emilia wondered who wrote the notes. Who pulled the trigger. Who decided how to react.

Of course, the conspirators never knew that their Los Mozos cover was fake. Even now, the drivers believed a real gang had successfully extorted protection money from the *sitio* and that the police finally did something useful.

"Shall we go outside?" Maria asked.

"Yes," Emilia said, shaking herself out of her daze.

She followed the reed-thin woman outside where all the adults gathered around the tree. The pink piñata swung wildly as the children screamed. Ricardo and Paco appeared to be the designated wranglers of the excited youngsters. Little Lola wiggled with excitement as Ricardo fastened her blindfold and handed her the stick to take her turn.

Emilia couldn't help but size up all the Taxis Coco drivers against the *encapuchado* who'd outrun her. Paco, Lobo, Felipe, Gennaro--they were all the right height. From the basketball court, she knew they each had the speed and stamina to escape a chase through the narrow streets and alleys that taxi drivers knew so well.

She thought fleetingly of telling Campos. Admit that she thought the drivers had conspired to kill Arrocha, using the Los Mozos gang threat as cover, but that she had no idea who actually pulled the trigger. Unless she did, Campos would continue to blame the Barrielos Luna organization for the murder.

All things considered, Emilia could live with that.

Emilia's cell phone buzzed. She edged back inside the house as the children clamored to break the piñata.

She didn't recognize the number of the screen. "*Bueno*?"

"Is this the taxi lady? Esterrrrr."

"Gabi! Where are you?" Emilia darted into the now-empty kitchen to further escape the party noises outside. "Where are you?"

"He said you made a deal," Gabi said.

Emilia held her breath. "Who said that?"

"A hottie. He said his name was Ernesto, Junior."

Emilia didn't realize she staggered until a chair hit her in the knee. She grabbed the edge of the counter to steady herself. "Are you sure that's the name he gave you?"

"He said I can't go back to La Tumba or the *sitio,*" Gabi said. "He said something to somebody and now they don't want me. He gave me some money but said I had to call you. I'm scared, Ester."

"Where are you?"

"In front of some swank hotel."

"Where? A beach place?"

"I'm not sure. There's a neon tree."

The Hotel Torre Ventura. Emilia closed her eyes, the phone tight against her cheek. "I'll be there in 30 minutes," she promised. "Just wait for me in front of that palm tree. Okay?"

"Okay."

Emilia ran outside to find Juan Miguel, her ride back to the *sitio*. From there it would take no more than ten minutes to grab her Suburban from the parking garage at the Cinépolis and race to the Hotel Torre Ventura.

"There you are, Ester." Maria stood next to her mother, cradling her cast and laughing at her daughter's antics. Lola was blindfolded as she swung a long stick at the wildly swinging pink turtle, its treats still hidden inside. Ricardo kept the other children from crowding. The smaller ones hopped up and down in excitement. The adults chattered and clapped for her efforts.

"Don't you love piñatas?" Maria went on. "Ricardo is crazy for them."

"Ever since they were little," her mother added.

Emilia scanned the crowd for Juan Miguel but Maria was still talking.

"Excuse me?" Emilia asked.

"I asked if you have a brother, Ester," Maria said.

Time slowed. Emilia's heartbeat throbbed in her throat.

He said his name was Ernesto, Junior.

"Yes," Emilia said. "I have a brother."

El Fin

You're invited

You're invited to stay up to date with Emilia and the team in the Mystery Ahead newsletter. Get behind-the-scenes details and must-read recommendations every other Sunday.

Subscribe and receive the Detective Emilia Cruz Starter Library with 2 novellas and the Who's Who guide to the series.

Go to carmenamato.net/starter-library.

There are extra goodies ahead, too.
- ✓ A favorite recipe from a meal featured in the book,
- ✓ Glossary of Spanish words, and
- ✓ An excerpt from the next Detective Emilia Cruz novel.

Watermelon salad with Tajin

Ingredients

4 cups watermelon cut into chunks
1 pinch of sea salt
1 teaspoon TAJÍN® seasoning
Juice and grated zest from 1 lime
½ cup crumbled cotija cheese
1 tablespoon minced cilantro
Honey to taste

Mix the first 3 ingredients. Squeeze on the lime juice and top with the lime zest.

Add the crumbled cotija cheese and cilantro. Plate, drizzle with honey, and serve.

Note: does not keep well in the refrigerator. Eat it all in one sitting.

Glossary of Spanish Terms

Abarrotes: snacks

Abuelo/abuela: grandfather/grandmother

Agua de jamaica: cold tea made with dried hibiscus

Amigo: friend, buddy

Barrio: neighborhood

Cabrón: slang meaning dumbass

Campesino: subsistence farmers, country dwellers

Casita: little house

Cédula: identity card

Chica: girl

Comida: the main meal of the day, usually eaten in early afternoon

Conchas: sweet rolls topped with sugar and shaped like a conch shell

Dios mio: my god, an exclamation

El Norte: the United States

Federales: slang for the Policía Federal Preventiva, federal law enforcement agency

Guayabera: men's button-down shirt with a straight hem and multiple pockets

Halcone: word meaning falcon, used to mean a person acting as a lookout

Hombres: men

Jefe: chief, person in charge

Jitomate: tomato

Libro: book

Loco: crazy

Lotéria: lottery

Madre de Dios: Mother of God, used as exclamation

Maldita: damn, damned

Mercado: market

Mujeres: women

Muertos: papier maché skeleton figures used to decorate Day of the Dead altars

Narcomanta: banner bearing a message from a gang or cartel

Norteamericano: North American

Ofrenda: altar

Palapa: traditional Mexican shelter roofed with palm leaves or branches

Papel picado: streamers of tissue paper cut into silhouette designs

Panadería: bakery

Pastelería: pastry shop

Pendejo: asshole, jerk

Permiso: excuse me

Placas: license plates

Primo/prima: male/female cousin

Propina: tip

Privada: enclosed subdivision and/or the gate to the property

Prohibido el paso: "Keep out" warning

Queso fresco: soft cheese common in Mexican recipes
Rayos: exclamation, similar to "oh hell"
Rebozo: large scarf or shawl
Reina: queen
Salsa verde: tart green salsa usually made with tomatillos
Sicario: cartel henchman or assassin
Sitio: fixed location taxi service
Talavera: hand painted pottery from Puebla
Taqueria: taco restaurant
Taxista: taxi driver
Telenovela: television soap opera
Tiendita: little store
Tío/Tía: uncle/aunt
Zocalo: town square

ABOUT THE AUTHOR

Carmen Amato turns lessons from a 30-year career with the Central Intelligence Agency into crime fiction loaded with danger and deception.

Starting with *Cliff Diver*, her award-winning Detective Emilia Cruz mystery series pits the first female police detective in Acapulco against Mexico's drug cartels, government corruption, and social inequality.

The series was awarded the Poison Cup for Outstanding Series from CrimeMasters of America in both 2019 and 2020 and has been optioned for television.

Her Galliano Club historical thriller series was inspired by her grandfather who was a deputy sheriff during Prohibition.

Originally from upstate New York, Carmen was educated there as well as in Virginia and Paris, France, while experiences in Mexico and Central America ignited her writing career.

Every other Sunday, Carmen shares her top secret(s) in the Mystery Ahead newsletter.

Subscribe at carmenamato.net.